Bacon, Beans,
Tobacco 'n' Whiskey

Bacon, Beans,
Tobacco 'n' Whiskey

by Lynn Edwards

WordsWorth

Cody, Wyoming

Published by WordsWorth
1285 Sheridan Avenue, Suite 230
Cody, Wyoming 82414

Library of Congress Catalog Card Number : 98-61670

ISBN 0-9652942-2-6

Printed in the United States of America on acid-free paper.

For Newt

Thanks to Dolores
and to
Marsha Runge, Jon Willette, Marge Cleasby, David Crisp,
Lee Ullom, Robert Lubbers and Jeanne Garritson,
who encouraged me and then kept after me to finish the book.
and to
K.T. Roes for putting the right touch on the book and cover
and to
Don Anderson for help when I needed it most.

Jon,

A word of caution about this book.
Some of Newt's stories might have become a bit exaggerated over the years of telling
and retelling. Historical time, people and events are true just as some of Newt's stories are true. However, some of his stories are only half true and some of his stories
have had the the truth pounded flat. The fun is figuring out which is which.

Two items have passed down to me from Newt: the bean pot that sat on the Cobb's
coal-burning stove at Fort Steele and a rock pick. They are both in the cover pho-
tograph. Newt claimed the pick was owned by Horace Greeley when he came West
to write his newspaper articles. He said the pick has had two new heads and three
new handles since then.

Chapter One
Yellowstone Park - June 1883

Kramer gave a low warning growl. Newt looked up and swore under his breath. "Damnit to hell, where did SHE come from?" From a squatting position next to the campfire he carefully reached into the flames and grabbed a log. Wincing, he slowly straightened to face the black monster. She was huge! And close! Close enough that he could see ticks crawling on her nose and the bristles in her mane standing up. This was real trouble, she was going to tear him apart. The bullet wound hadn't healed and now he was about to get stomped by an angry moose.

The latest trouble started when two men got off the stage in Rapid City, South Dakota and started asking around for Newt Harvey. They quickly learned where The Sarah Saloon was and went there. Newt saw Bates and O'Toole before they saw him and ducked out the back door. For a long time those two had dogged his tracks trying to kill him. Things had been quiet for a few years and now the haggard-looking pair had found him again.

Newt decided it was a good time to go prospecting near Yellowstone Park for a few weeks. The stage got him to Miles City, Montana and then Newt took the Northern Pacific to the end of the line at Livingston, Montana. He took two days gathering an outfit to spend a few weeks at a mountain gold camp he'd heard about. Newt spent his last evening in town in the Red Bull Saloon playing poker and swapping stories. After three lost hands he decided to quit for the evening. As he crossed the street heading for his room at the Rustler House, Newt saw two men talking to a young boy. He heard one ask where they might find Newt Harvey. It was Bates. Keeping his wits about him he lowered his head and kept walking.

The boy pointed at the Red Bull and said, "That's the best place to start looking." Bates glanced at Newt and recognized him. Shouting, "That's him!" he drew his gun and touched off a shot as Newt dove through the swinging doors of the Pare-O-Dice Saloon. Holding the bleeding wound, Newt ran through the saloon and signaled the bartender. As he went through the back door the bartender reached under the bar and pulled out a sawed off shotgun. In the dark alley Newt turned left and kept running. He heard a shot from the saloon and hoped it meant he was going to get away.

Doc Nunn patched the wound in Newt's side, remarking that it was curious how they could hit such a skinny target. As he finished, a deputy came in asking if the Doc could look after two men over at the jail who had made the mistake of stepping in front of a load of birdshot. Doc promised Newt he would delay the men long enough for him to get out of town.

Newt got his horse and mule and took them to the back of the Rustler House. Packed and ready, he led the animals to the back of the jail. Judging from the yelps, Doc Nunn was still picking shot out of their butts. He heard one complaining about being shot but the deputy was not sympathetic.

"Yer lucky to be alive. That bartender keeps one barrel loaded with birdshot and the other one loaded with buckshot. Sometimes he forgets which side is which, so you two could be lying in a pine box about now."

Traveling south toward Yellowstone Park, Newt crisscrossed rivers and high mountain passes along the east side of the park. Wading through streams chilled him to the bone. The ground was frozen in the mornings but by the afternoon thaw, he and the animals were slogging through cold water and mud. When it got bad Kramer would leap up on the mule's back and lick his paws to warm them up. Newt found a spot where hot water ran into a mountain stream. He quickly took off his clothes except his long johns and eased into the warm water to take the chill off. Dashing out, he dressed and moved on. For two days Newt pushed the animals from daylight to dark. On the third day he stopped to rest and have a hot meal. Now he was face to face with an angry moose.

The nearsighted monster pawed the ground and shook her head, looking for a reason to charge. Most times a moose doesn't need a reason to charge. Newt looked around to locate his rifle and tensed, ready to leap. A movement to the right made his heart sink. More trouble. It was a calf moose looking at him in wide-eyed curiosity, while his nose was sorting out the smell of a human. With a soft bleat, the calf trotted toward Newt. All Hell broke loose when that happened.

Knowing the danger of standing between mother and calf, Newt let out a fierce yell, threw the burning log at the charging mother and dove for his rifle. His quick action avoided serious injury, as her hoof missed his head and struck his shoulder instead. The horse and mule broke their tethers and galloped off. Avoiding hooves, Kramer cut across behind the moose and disappeared in the brush.

The calf, thinking it was playtime, whirled and trotted through the camp scattering bedroll and clothing in every direction. Newt heard glass breaking and his heart sank. He knew he had just lost his only supply of whiskey. Mother swung around and paused, smarting over the burnt spots on her nose and the smell of singed hair. She tore up the ground, then charged back through the camp, inflicting damage to the cooking gear and sending the coffeepot clattering out of sight in the brush. Newt tensed, ready for action from behind a lodge pole pine. It wouldn't stop the moose if she decided to charge again, but it would help steady his gun if he had to shoot. The mother took several agitated steps around the camp, then, seemingly satisfied with the damage, she followed her calf into the trees. Kramer dashed from his hiding place, nipping at their heels to make sure mother and calf kept going.

Newt leaned against the pine gulping air for five minutes before he could take a breath without pain. He was sore along all six feet of his body and the wound in his side felt like a forest fire. It was his own fault; he had been careless and could have paid dearly for it.

Grimacing several times, he kicked the smoldering logs back into the fire. For the next hour Newt gathered up scattered equipment and made repairs to the coffeepot. The calf had damaged his hat, the most distinctive part of his outfit. When he left Omaha in '58 his hat had a stiff wide brim and a tall crown with a deep crease in the top. Now, it was well worn; the brim flopped down at a tired angle and the crown wasn't so high anymore. The rich brown color had long ago faded except for the dark sweat stain around the band. Newt considered it to be a good luck charm when prospecting for gold. The plain leather band was adorned with a small Indian spirit bag and a fang from a rattlesnake.

Newt put a pot of beans on the fire and poured a cup of coffee. The steam from his cup looked like a geyser as he leaned back against a tree to relax with Kramer. Kramer was a large black dog with expressive eyes and face. Describing Kramer as a mutt would be high praise. He had tangled with a bear that left scars on his back and along the left side of his head. He was tough, smart, and very loyal to Newt. He was the second dog Newt called Kramer. The first Kramer was a small white terrier that had followed him through Colorado, Wyoming, and Montana. Newt wasn't much on thinking up names so he used the same one for his dogs. Most every horse he called Misty and each of the saloons he owned was named The Sarah for good luck.

Newt cut a hunk of meat from a deer haunch and trimmed most of the hair and dried blood off. He walked to the fire and dropped the meat into the hot greased skillet. This was his first hot meal in three days. After shooting a deer the day before, he had tried cooking the meat by dangling it in a geyser pool. The taste was awful. He offered it to Kramer who refused to touch it. The smell of beans and bacon simmering in the pan made him hungrier than ever. Unable to wait any longer he dove into the beans, relishing the taste and the warmth it brought to his insides. When he finished the beans he speared the meat with a knife and ate right off the blade.

While Kramer cleaned up the scraps, Newt lit a cigar and jotted a few lines in his journal, including a notation of the date. He thought of the Colorado gold camps and his friends Horace and Augusta Tabor. It had been some years since he had been to Oro City. Maybe that was the place to hide from Bates. At that moment he wished he had that bottle of whiskey. Newt banked the fire then gathered wood for the night.

The springtime sun's last moments made an orange and red backdrop to geysers and steam vents near the camp. It was too early in the spring for warmth to stay in the air after the sun started to drop on the horizon. He gingerly put his feet in the cold bedroll and waited for it to warm up. The sun sank lower filling his eyes with the park's beauty at sunset. The fading light deepened the wrinkles and scars put on his face from a lifetime of living and working outdoors. When the fire died down he crawled into the bedroll.

To keep his mind off the cold he thought of Martha and their sons James and Wilbur. He wondered how different his life would have been if he hadn't been afflicted with gold fever. His life seemed to revolve around panning for gold, throwing dirt in a box, and drinking whiskey. Nothing had worked out the way he wanted and prospects for the future looked as bright as it is two hours after midnight. At the age of forty-two he was still wandering in the territories getting into scrapes. This latest encounter with Bates and O'Toole made him realize he wasn't safe in Montana anymore. He could not figure out why those two would still be after him over a shooting in Omaha fifteen years ago. Unless it was the incident in St. Louis when Bates' Ol' Man lost several hundred thousand because of him. One thing for sure he needed to put an end to the hide and seek game they were playing. With a pistol under his hat, a rifle on one side and Kramer on the other, Newt drifted off to sleep.

The cold air forced him up before daylight to start a fire and warm the coffee. The sun was too low for its warmth to reach them by the time Newt packed the mule and saddled Misty. One last gulp of coffee and it was time to go. He swung up in the saddle and helped Kramer up behind. He pointed Misty in an easterly direction figuring it would be a days ride to the Shoshone River. The river flowed to lower elevations where he turned southeast to connect up with the Big Horn River.

Four days later Newt could see the canyon of the Wind River in the distance. Now he was traveling through rolling hills of red and brown soil covered with buffalo grass, sage and rocks. The area was dotted with small stands of timber surrounded by large patches of shrub cedar. By evening they were close enough to see steam and vapor rising from hot water pools on both sides of the river.

Newt worked his way several miles along the river before seeing a spot with good grass and a supply of wood. Best of all there was a hot pool nearby that was not too hot for him to soak in. Knowing he would be staying for a few days he put extra effort into setting up the camp.

That evening he got out his journal to make a few notes. "Boys," he said, talking aloud to the animals. "I'm pretty sure today is the twentieth. That means James turns eighteen in two days. Wonder where he and Wilbur are these days and what they are doing. I sure hope they grew up to be good men and not like that bastard Bates." Finished with writing, he took out a letter and read it as he had every day for the past month.

Newt visited the pool twice a day to take advantage of the healing waters. While soaking in the hot water he spent some time thinking of his problems with Bates and O'Toole, and the police in Omaha. He came up with several solutions and the one he liked best included a visit to California. Belle's letter made him lonesome and as always it ended with an invitation to come to San Francisco. It had been too many years since he had seen them. Sky would be seventeen or eighteen by now.

By the time he was ready to leave, Newt had mapped out a plan to elude his pursuers. He would go south to Fort Steele for a few days and then would take the train to San Francisco to visit Belle and Sky. The trip to Fort Steele would have to include a stop at Fort Caspar for supplies. He packed up and pointed Misty east over the rolling hills, taking a longer route perhaps but one that was better for his animals and his body.

Chapter Two
Near Fort Caspar

Four days of riding through sagebrush, cactus and powder dry land had parched Newt and his animals. When he found a small stream meandering through the dry and barren land he dismounted to check the banks for alkali deposits. Only then did he allow the animals to drink. The first two large gulps of water tasted dry from all the dust in his mouth. He splashed water on his face and neck and then dipped his hat and poured it over his head.

"This should be Caspar Creek so we're not too far from the fort now. We'll take a quick rest and keep going so we can get there before dark. It will be good to get supplies, we're about out of everything."

Newt's habit of talking to his horse Misty and the mule made them less nervous and he enjoyed their company as they never interrupted or argued. Kramer always seemed to understand what he was saying.

Refreshed by a short nap Newt mounted up and they headed southeast. Two hours later they topped the ridge and looked down on the Platte River Bridge. Just beyond lay Fort Caspar. The bridge was important to travelers who wanted to avoid twenty miles of rough trail on the north side of the river. The fort was small as forts go. In its day it served the purpose of protecting the bridge from Indians. Now it was a place to get supplies, rest and learn the latest news. Compared to Custer's fight and the Bozeman uprising a few years back the soldiers stationed here were on light duty.

"It will be nice to have a regular bed and grub and I'll bet you'll like some oats tonight, eh boy. I hope that sutler isn't a Methodist because I'd like to have a bottle of whiskey tonight and more to take with me."

Most sutlers were known for being dishonest and had reputations for gouging travelers. Post traders, called sutlers were given contracts from the government to sell supplies to the soldiers and many of them abused the privilege. This sutler was a large man with arms as large as his legs from blacksmithing. His smile showed three teeth in front, two up and one down. The accommodations were sparse. The only space for Newt was in the barn with his animals along with another traveler. To his surprise and delight the food prepared by the sutler's wife was good and there was plenty of it. The other guest that evening was a young preacher heading for Idaho. Like most traveling preachers his only possessions were his Bible, what he could tie behind his saddle, and the horse he was riding. Brother Hightower tried to keep a pious look that reflected his calling, but his youth and friendly disposition broke through. He was a congenial guest and a good storyteller, matching Newt story for story.

Newt asked, "What denomination do you cling to?"

"Brother Newt, I am a Free Will Baptist, and preach individual interpretation of the Bible."

"I too had a Baptist upbringing, but out here I have not felt its influences to any extent. I bought a bottle to pass the evening. In respect to your calling I would not be offended at your refusal of a drink."

"I believe every man is allowed to exercise his own free will. Pour away." The rest of the evening was spent in exchange of experiences and beliefs that lasted well into the early hours of the new day and well into a second bottle.

The next day they rode west together. Newt pointed out familiar landmarks while telling of his first trip along the Oregon Trail. The two camped on the east side of Independence Rock, a well known landmark along the emigrant trail. After a roasted rabbit dinner supplied by Newt and Kramer, they settled by the fire to talk of personal trials and victories. Newt brought out a bottle, took a swallow and handed it over.

"Reverend, how is it you are going to Idaho? I'd think you could settle 'most anywhere out here and have folks needing your works and prayers."

"I've got a brother at the Salmon, Idaho diggings so my father suggested I come West to do the Lord's work."

"How did you come to be called?"

"My father is a minister, called to serve a church in St. Jo, Missouri. I am the youngest of five boys, the worst behaved of the lot. Last fall the church had a tent revival that attracted people from three counties. On the last night I was sitting in the back row to amuse myself watching the crowd. About halfway through the service there was a call to accept the Lord and something came over me. Next thing I know I'm walking down the isle and up to the front while the crowd was singing and clapping. Preachers were praying and laying their hands on the people's heads. I just got carried up in the moment.

I wanted to do the Lords work, but with no formal education past the sixth grade and no religious training I couldn't take a regular calling. I'll be a greenhorn preacher and have to use what I remember from my father's preaching and the inspiration from the Lord."

"Well, Brother, a preacher in the West needs to know how to fix a wagon, herd livestock, drive a six-mule hitch and patch bullet wounds, as well as preach and save souls. You'll soon get the hang of it and once folks learn you're not against drinkin' they'll listen to you. There's a lot of need for praying out here, though from my experience most prayers go unanswered."

"Newt, my father preached many times on unanswered prayers. He thought God should get help from the person doing the praying. He says that if you pray for a chicken to feed your family, sometimes you might get it. But if you pray for the Lord to send you for a chicken, then you'll always get one."

"I'll remember that."

"I've heard a lot about the mountains of Wyoming and Montana, but so far I haven't seen much except grassland and sagebrush. My brother says we'll be working the mountains around Yellowstone Park."

"Yellowstone Park is the most beautiful area I have ever seen. Miles of timber dotted with the most striking green meadows covered with flowers. Bright colors of yellow, blue and red everywhere. You'll have to see the geysers for yourself. The hot water and steam shooting up into the sky is something I never tire of watching. There's one you'll see that blows its top regular like so the folks have named it Old Faithful. Most of the mud pools are too hot to bathe in, but a good way to take a warm bath is to find a spot where the hot water pours into a stream or lake. That way you come out warm and clean. The smell near some of the hot pools can be something awful. Heard it was the sulfur that does it.

"I made my first trip into the Park from Virginia City, Montana in '65 or maybe '66. We stayed mostly to the north to hunt and fish. Now the Bassett Brothers at Beaver, Canyon Idaho run an outfitting service. They take you to the geyser basin where you can hunt and fish as much as you like. Old timers say the area reminds them of Hell because of the strange-looking land, but I think of it as God's country and I'm thankful to get to play in it. There are lots of strange sights and wonders to see out here."

"What other sights have you seen?"

"Over near the Black Hills there's a huge pillar of rock that looks like a large tree stump rising hundreds of feet in the air. The Indians thought it was a place of evil and most people call it Devil's Tower. I've got a drawing of it in my journal I can show you. It is a wonder how that rock could have been put there. I've been told that somewhere north of Fort Caspar is a rock formation in the shape of a teapot, but I haven't seen it. A few days back I came out of the east side of Yellowstone Park and down the Shoshone River. I saw several rock spires in unusual shapes and one giant boulder looks like an elephant. The land east of there would be good area for building a ranch and grazing livestock. Water and grass are plentiful and I think the winters are mild in the lower parts."

"I remember reading about some of the famous people like Custer and Buffalo Bill Cody. Did you know any of them?"

"I never met Custer. Good thing too because of what happened to him. I met Billy Cody in Colorado Territory in '59 when we got swept up in the Pikes Peak gold rush. I've seen posters promoting Buffalo Bill Cody's Wild West shows. The picture on it looked like the Billy Cody I met in Colorado only now he's got a mustache and goatee.

"I knew Calamity Jane as Martha Jane Canary. She was twelve or thirteen when her family came to Virginia City to live. That was in '65. She was a wild brat of a girl who would fight with the boys and cuss like a man. When Calamity showed up in Deadwood she was a wild brazen woman who could outcuss and outdrink us all. She can do any job a man can do."

"Is it true she and Wild Bill Hickock were married?"

"She claims they were married for a short time and that she bore his daughter. Colorado Charlie said they were never married and I am inclined to believe that. I know she was smitten by Wild Bill's good looks and the notoriety he had. Eastern writers wrote about Calamity and Wild Bill but most of it was a pack of lies just to sell their stories. I was in Deadwood when Wild Bill was killed. I didn't see the shooting though. Calamity sort of went crazy after that, and for a time was drunker and louder than before. There's talk she's tracking for the Army now."

"Do you have a family?"

"I have two sons living in Omaha. James just turned eighteen and Wilbur, who I adopted, is nineteen. I would like to have them out here with me but I doubt it will happen. I got into some trouble with the law back there and I can't return. I've got two men dogging my tracks trying to kill me because of some other trouble I stirred up. They caught up with me a few weeks ago and nearly killed me. I'm sure they're still on my trail."

"I remember one of my father's sermons. It's from the book of Matthew. I have the passage marked, ' . . . do not worry about tomorrow, for tomorrow will bring worries of its own. Today's trouble is enough for today.' Then he would say, 'Turn and stare your problems down. But don't try to stare down more than a day's worth.'"

"I've got troubles to fill more than a day but I'll try that."

"Newt, when did you come out West?

Newt got up, stirred the coals and threw more logs on "I came out in '58, twenty five years ago. I've prospected for gold, ranched and owned saloons. Those early years were the toughest. Lots of hard work and danger from drunken miners, Indians, and mine accidents."

Newt recounted in more detail the events in Omaha that kept him from seeing his family. While they talked, the night air was getting colder, by morning they knew a layer of frost would cover everything.

In the morning, while Newt packed his mule, Brother Hightower walked to the top of Independence Rock for a view of the prairie stretching out for miles. Returning, he stood on a large boulder and delivered several comforting prayers for Newt's safety and a happy issue from his troubles. They mounted up and rode West.

After passing Devil's Gate, Newt pointed toward South Pass.

"There's the way you need to go. That road will take you all the way to Idaho. Brother Hightower, I want to thank you for listening to my tale of woe and for your help."

From his pocket Newt pulled out a pouch and handed it to the preacher. "I have grub-staked many men to find gold. This here is a grubstake for you to help men find their souls. Good luck in Idaho."

"Thank you brother Newt, you will always be in my prayers."

Chapter Three
Devil's Gate to Fort Steele

Newt watched Brother Hightower ride westerly until he was out of sight. Instead of going south Newt urged Misty along the preacher's trail for a mile before he veered to the north. He was searching for a particular spot by weaving back and forth through the sagebrush. He came on the charred remains he was looking for and dismounted. The grave markers were gone and the mounds almost level. It had been fifteen years since he had been across this land. Wind, rain, and snow had erased the scars left by the attacking Sioux. He walked around until he identified the burned wagon he was looking for. Walking a few steps north he knelt and prayed for Molly, Alex and their baby girl, Rebecca Ann. Retrieving a shovel from his outfit he cleared away sagebrush and tumbleweeds. With scraps of wood he made a cross and placed it on the grave. He sat for a long time thinking of them and James and Wilbur.

After leaving the graves at Devil's Gate, Newt pointed Misty south, turning his back on the gold camps and saloons of Montana. Newt sat easy in the saddle and let Misty pick a trail through the sagebrush and boulders while reflecting on the graves and the passages Brother Hightower quoted from the Bible. He wanted to quit worrying about every stranger he met and to stop looking over his shoulder. "Maybe I should stay in one place and face my troubles as Brother Hightower suggested," he thought.

In the late afternoon of the next day he found the bluff described by the sutler at Fort Caspar. It was part of a large mountain chain that stretched north and south. The bluff was on the west side of the mountain and ran intermittently for thirty miles. It took a bit of searching to find the U-shaped ridge of boulders with a stand of quakies at the upper end. In all the miles of barren land and dry washes this was the only spot that had a small spring trickling through it. Newt was thankful the sutler knew of the spot.

It had been a hard day and there was still plenty of work to do. He removed the saddle and the pack tree before picketing Misty and the mule nearby. Kramer watched while Newt laid out a camp and collected wood. With camp in order, he picked up his rifle, intent on finding something for supper. Kramer trotted along to one side, keeping alert for a signal from Newt.

Both heard low growls and barks ahead. Peeking over a rock Newt could see a fox circling a porcupine, with dinner on his mind. From his actions the fox was well aware of the danger. Newt watched the two thrust and parry. The porcupine used his tail of sharp quills to keep the fox away as the fox jumped in and out to avoid the barbs. He knew he had to flip his meal over on its back to attack its soft underbelly. Newt decided that the fox was not going to eat porcupine that day so he stood up and walked toward the pair. The fox took one look and was gone. Wise to the ways of a porcupine, Kramer trotted off to hunt for something less dangerous.

Porcupine flesh is fatty like a bear's, but not as dangerous to come by. While the carcass cooked on a spit Newt fried the liver along with wild onions and his last sweet potato. Newt ate rapidly to keep the food from getting cold. His thoughts were on ways to end his continual running and ducking bullets. He finished the meal with hot coffee and a cigar, while Kramer cleaned up the scraps.

Later, with a full cup of steaming coffee in his hand, Newt stood facing the sunset, watching the grass dance and sway to a breezy tune. He wrestled with his problems until it was dark and the coffee was cold. He stirred the coals and tossed more wood on. Then he sat down to watch the flames flicker at first and then grow stronger and brighter. Hypnotized and warmed by the flames he wrapped up in his bedroll, thinking that he was getting too old to be sleeping out in the night air using his saddle for a pillow and a piece of canvas for a mattress. Looking at the stars for a while he drifted off.

A growl from Kramer alerted him. He strained to hear what Kramer heard. Soon the clicking of horseshoes against rock and the creaking of saddle leather came to him. In one motion Newt rolled out of bed, picked up his carbine and levered in a shell. Moving out of the firelight he stepped behind a rock for cover. As he waited and listened he fingered his pistol to make sure it was loose in the holster and looked for his animals to be sure they were out of the line of fire. When the horses were close enough that he could hear their breathing and see movement, he shouted. "That's far enough."

A man shouted back. "Saw your fire and smelled the coffee, any left?"

"Come on in, but leave your hands where I can see them." Ordinarily, Newt would not be so cautious in accepting strangers to his camp but the wound was still a painful reminder of the events in Livingston.

Two men walked into the firelight so they could be seen. Both were short and slender, dressed for traveling and leading fine horses. Once Newt was satisfied and Kramer gave his wag of approval, he said, "There should be enough coffee for the two of you." He signaled Kramer to watch them. "Put your horses over there with mine. There's a good place to lay out your bedrolls just on the other side of those rocks and if you have anything to cook, you're welcome to the fire."

One man busied with the cooking while the other took care of the horses. They ate quickly with little conversation explaining only that they were from Colorado and had business at Fort Caspar.

Everyone was up and moving at daylight. Before riding off, the strangers had a quick breakfast of jerky and hardtack with Newt's hot coffee to wash it down. With a nod of thanks they rode north along a ridge and then dropped out of sight. Newt climbed the nearby rocks to watch the pair ride off. He watched them for more than an hour until his suspicions were confirmed and he returned to camp.

Once the mule was packed he swung up on Misty and whistled for Kramer. Picking his way slowly around boulders he reached the high sandstone bluff that ran east and south toward the Platte River. It also afforded a view of the plains below. Newt could watch for danger and quickly duck out of sight if the situation called for it. At midmorning he found a pool of water in the rocks. Newt got his water first and then let the animals have their fill from the shallow pool. Waiting for the animals to finish, Newt noticed haze floating up from the valley below. He eased out on the bluff to get a better look. Seven riders worked their way up to the bluff he was on. One man paused for a moment to scan the land ahead and gestured for the others to follow. They were definitely headed his direction. Newt went back to the horses and moved them to a dense growth of cedar brush to wait.

It wasn't long before Newt could see six men in Army uniforms and a civilian tracker. He moved out where he could be seen and waited. The troops stopped and looked him over then approached with caution. The Lieutenant began asking questions. "Have you seen two men in the area?

Newt nodded. "Two short men with good looking horses camped with me last night at the spring near the end of this bluff. They said they were going to Fort Caspar but I doubt it. From what I could see they were headed toward South Pass. What'd they do?"

"They robbed the bank in Rawlins. Part of it was Fort Steele's payroll. They're a bad pair when it comes to robbing banks, but they try not to harm anyone unless they get in the way."

"Kramer passed on them so I figured they was okay. It was the way they kept eyeing their saddlebags that made me suspicious. While saddling up this morning I saw they had a sack marked U.S. Army. I didn't let on like I noticed otherwise I'd be dead now."

"What's your name?"

"Newt, I'm going to visit the Cobbs at the trading post and maybe stay a while."

"I know Kyle and Carrie. Nice folks. I'm Lieutenant West. Thanks for the information. You should make the fort before suppertime tomorrow. Sergeant, move the men out."

Later in the day Newt crossed a ridge and looked at the broad plains that stretched out to the south. On the eastern horizon Newt could see little slivers of blue marking the meandering North Platte River as it flowed near the fort on its way north to Fort Caspar. After making camp, he studied the distant horizon for a landmark he could use the next day to stay on course for the fort. Further south he could see the peaks of the Laramie Range as it made its majestic way into Colorado. His meal that night was hard bread and jerky washed down with water he brought from the last camp. He made several entries in his journal that evening before the fire died down and then crawled in the bedroll.

Shortly after noon the next day Newt could see the long hump of the railway bed running through Fort Steele. After crossing over the rail bed and turning east he paused at the abandoned "Hell on Wheels" town of Benton. As the railroad expanded west the workers were followed by gamblers, women, and merchants, who were bent on taking their wages. The town was made up of tents set up on flooring for easy dismantling and erecting. When the tracks reached the Benton town site, the town was dismantled and loaded on flat cars for the trip. Benton arrived on flat cars with the townspeople riding in and on the train. Overnight, tents and buildings were up and open for business. Women, gambling, and whiskey kept the men continually broke and they were forced to work to make ends meet. Once the tracks reached the next town site the process was repeated leaving Benton as a scar on the land.

Newt studied the few remaining buildings, looking for one that might be suitable for his plans. The sun reflecting off bits of glass and metal sparkled among the discarded wood and iron pieces around the area. One building had lost three walls to decay and the fourth was soon to follow. A lone cabin standing on the west end of the town looked to be in one piece. Newt spent an hour poking around inside and out.

Fort Steele had been built to protect the railroad and the settlers in the area. It was laid out along the railroad right of way with most of the military buildings and parade grounds on the north side of the tracks. On the south side stood the quartermaster warehouse along a siding. The siding allowed the twice a week local trains to stop for loading and unloading, leaving the main line open for the passenger trains. A small station house was built between the main track and the siding for passenger use. The saloon stood next to the quartermaster's office indicating that the commandant was not against liquor. If the command changed and the fort was declared dry, the saloon would be torn down and moved beyond the fort boundary.

East of the warehouse along the tracks stood the civilian houses, livery, and Cobb's trading post. Riding south of the quartermaster warehouse, Newt headed Misty for the rear of the trading post. Kramer dashed into the yard, barking for eight-year-old Lewis Cobb. It had been some time since Newt had visited Kyle Cobb, his wife Carrie, and their son Lewis. They had been friends for many years and now were partners in the trading post. Lewis came out the back door of the house and threw his arms around Kramer, all the while getting his face licked. As Newt led Misty to the barn Kyle came out of the trading post and walked into the barn.

"Carrie had a notion you was about to show up. She's been baking for days."

Newt held a bucket of oats up for Misty. "It's good to be here. About the only place left where I'm safe. How's the business doing?"

"We've had a good year, best yet."

Kramer ran into the barn followed by Lewis. "Dad, supper's ready and Mom says we should wash up."

Kyle lifted the heavy cast iron pot from the oven and put it on top of the stove. He reached for the lid, then thought better of it. Picking up a small towel to remove the lid, he watched the steam roll out. Inside carrots, onions and potatoes covered a large roast. Newt caught the aroma and knew he was in for a grand meal. Carrie moved her husband aside before he could reach in and get a snitch.

"Kyle please go yell at Lewis again, I can't get him to leave Kramer and come to supper." After putting the roast on a large platter she put the potatoes and carrots around the edge. Newt watch as she slowly poured a mixture of flour and water into the brown liquid in the bottom of the pot. While stirring with one hand she reached up to the shelf above the stove and added several spices. Steam from the gravy worked its way around the room and Newt wasn't sure he could wait much longer before they ate. When Carrie removed a towel from fresh baked rolls and sat them on the table he had to set on his hands to keep from taking one.

Over supper Newt recounted his trip from Montana, telling mostly about the moose and Reverend Hightower. His meeting the two robbers pursued by Lieutenant West and his troopers interested Kyle. After Lewis was in bed Newt told them about his encounter with Bates and O'Toole in Livingston and the likelihood that he could be on the run for years. Newt talked about his earlier plans to go to San Francisco and his recent decision to stay in one place and face Bates and O'Toole. Kyle and Carrie were distressed at his resolve to stand and fight but in the end they agreed to his plan if they could enlist the aid of Lieutenant West. Kyle said. "Lieutenant West is a good soldier and friend. If there's any problem with strangers nosing around we can get help from him and his men."

The next day as they rode out to Benton Newt explained an idea for throwing Bates and O'Toole off his trail. They closely inspected the ruins and the cabin. Newt showed Kyle what he wanted done while he made a trip to Cheyenne for supplies. He was not going to change his habit of going to Cheyenne just because of Kyle's concern for his safety.

Chapter Four
Omaha

Named after an Indian tribe, Omaha had started as a fur-trading store, later to become a river ferry station across the Missouri from Council Bluffs. Its early prosperity came from its location in the path of emigrants needing supplies for the journey West. Now, in 1883, it was a major city and supplier of goods all the way to San Francisco. It had the same rough, dirty and dangerous inhabitants as before, only more of them.

Construction had been continuous over the years, with businessmen gambling fortunes to build a secure life for future generations. Frederick Walters had found Omaha to be generous. His Walters' Wholesale Company had grown and prospered with new additions built onto the older and smaller buildings. Thanks to the railroad, sales were ten times what they once were. The Union Pacific moved people, animals, and goods along the same path in days, not months as in the early years.

Wilbur McCall Harvey crossed the street and entered the new section of Walters' Wholesale Company, letting the door bang shut. Though he was of medium height, Wilbur's presence came from a stocky build and serious manner. His smile, while slow in coming, was sincere and warm. He had a round face with dark brown curly hair. As a child his curls had prompted teasing from classmates and led to more than a few fights. As he matured, his wavy hair, piercing blue eyes, and easy ways were an attraction to the ladies and he was pleased with the attention he got. At nineteen he was sought after for his looks and because he was the grandson of Frederick Walters. With the recent passing of grandfather Walters, the estate would soon pass to grandsons James and Wilbur, cousins by birth and brothers by adoption. Wilbur was nearly a year older than James and a full two inches shorter. He had a powerful build that got them out of the fights James got them into. Wilbur's quiet disposition was slow to anger, but once provoked, he would jump into a fight with relish and usually had the better end of it.

He followed the narrow aisle to the stairs leading to the mezzanine office. Each step revealed more of the high stacks of crates, barrels, and boxes addressed to stores and businesses west of Omaha. He paused on the stairs at a point where most all of the warehouse was visible and began playing his favorite game. Wilbur liked to think about the destinations of the shipments below - Tarryall, Colorado; Medicine Bow, Wyoming; Carrine, Utah; Bannack City, Montana. He hoped to see those places someday and explore the land around them.

Today, rather than going up to the office, he let his mind wander back to the years before the railroad had linked Omaha to San Francisco. In those years, Walters' Wholesale relied on freight companies to supply freight wagons pulled by teams of six horses or mules. The wagons were backed up to the dock for loading and then pulled around to the waiting group. When all the wagons were ready the wagon master would signal with a wave of his hat. The boys thrilled at the swisssh . . . then C R A C K from the bullwhips flicking out over the teams. Whistles, shouts, and curses filled the air as the animals lunged in the harnesses. Each wagon, creaking under the weight, started, then rolled slowly out on the trail.

He and James would dash to the roof of the warehouse and climb the ladder up the water tower. From there they could watch thirty or more wagons and teams in motion. They stayed there until the noise of the whips and shouts of the drivers faded away.

Many times they had climbed on one of the extra wagons parked alongside the building. For hours they would fight Indians and outlaws while pretending to drive a wagon to Fort Laramie. When a little older, they managed to hide in one of the wagons, intending to make the trip for real. They weren't discovered for several miles. Two very angry outriders had to put them up behind and bring them back to the warehouse.

Wilbur turned and tread the final steps to the office thinking that although the railroad was the best way of shipping goods now, the sense of adventure was less and it wasn't fun anymore. The office contained desks and cabinets, its floor space cluttered with stacks of catalogues, price lists and samples. Only Wilbur's area was neat and tidy. Over the years he had held almost every position in the company and now he was in charge of the book-keeping and finances of the business. Here he excelled and found he liked controlling the money and dealing with the financial side of their business. Wilbur acknowledged good mornings from the men and settled at his desk.

For the next four hours he tallied and checked the previous day's business and prepared the bank slips. Stewart Prosser, the company manager, looked up at the clock and then at Wilbur. "Wilbur, it's time to head for the lawyers office." Wilbur nodded and continued to add the numbers.

Once satisfied that they were correct he put away the papers and stood up. "I'm ready. The walk will do me good and I want to tell you about a decision James and I have made."

He left the office, following Stewart down the stairs, waiting until they were in the street and headed for the lawyers' office before talking.

"Stewart, as you know Grandpa Walters was successful because he knew his customer's needs and had a ready supply for them. None of us has that ability like he did, but James seems to be better than the rest of us. We have decided that he should take a trip west to drum up business and to look for new opportunities."

"When does he plan on going?"

"After we return from St. Louis."

Stewart said, "James could look for Newt while he's in Colorado and Montana. Your father was here only once but I could tell he was a good man. We all felt bad about Newt's problems with the law and the Bates family."

"Stewart, Grandfather promised us that one day he would tell us what he knew about Father and what happened back then, but he died before he told us much."

"Wilbur, there's one man that should tell you his story and that's Newt."

James Harvey spent that morning inspecting the land around his grandfather's home. It was the only home he and Wilbur had known and they were still living in it. James wore his stiff black hair brushed straight back from a high forehead. As he had grown up his grandfather would point out that James' sharp nose and facial features were like his father's and his smile and light blue eyes must have come from his mother. His height was six feet but his thin body made him look taller. Impulsive to the point of recklessness, James threw his whole being into whatever work or activity he was doing. People often remarked how he could brighten a gathering. At the military academy he earned a reputation for thinking up pranks for the others to pull. When it came to finances he was too generous and he admitted his inability to handle money. He and Wilbur made a good match when it came to running the Walters' Wholesale Company. James could work out problems in the warehouse and the men worked hard for him. His outgoing and friendly nature made it easy for him to gain new customers and sell larger orders. Wilbur was able to control the company's money and kept them out of trouble with the bank.

Every tree and feature of the estate held memories for James. He and Wilbur had spent their boyhood days playing games in the large grounds that surrounded the home and guesthouse. James's thoughts were interrupted by the sounds of a carriage and horses coming up the circular drive. By the time he reached the corner of the house the carriage was stopped in front. George and Irene were standing at the top step along with their houseguest.

George and Irene Lansing had been butler and cook for the Walters family for over twenty-five years and were considered members of the family. George ran the household efficiently and quietly. Irene was outspoken in running the kitchen and the household but she deferred to George in everything else. Irene's other responsibility had been the raising and care of James and Wilbur. To them she was their other mother.

Their houseguest, Charlene Dawson, a second cousin to James on his mother's side was here for the reading of Mr. Walters' will. She operated a freighting company in San Francisco in partnership with the late Mr. Walters. George and Irene waited until James reached them before getting into the carriage. After giving instructions to the driver, James helped Charlene Dawson into the carriage sitting next to her, opposite the Lansings.

George said, "Your grandfather told us that we were provided for. Do you know who else will be there for the reading of his will?"

"No I don't. Grandfather's attorneys have been strangely silent in the matter of his estate."

Irene spoke. "We are happy that you could be here, Mrs. Dawson, and of course you are welcome to stay as long as you like."

"Thank you. I have enjoyed my stay very much. No one has mentioned Newt. Has there been any news of him?"

Irene looked quickly at George then spoke again. "No, we have had no word of his whereabouts or if he is still living. He had a stubborn streak when it came to his mother-in-law and her overbearing ways but he loved Martha and the boys. I'm sure he missed watching them grow up. It was Marie Walters that spoiled everything. I didn't shed a tear when they finally lowered her in the grave, I tell you …."

"Irene!" George was shocked and red faced.

"Now, George, you know very well there wasn't one soul at the funeral that came to grieve. They came to support the family and to make sure she was gone for good! Ask James if that's not so."

"Irene, I'll admit the house was more peaceful after she was gone but you shouldn't speak ill of Mrs. Walters."

James raised his hand and spoke. "Well, Grandfather did smile more and he spent more time at home with us."

George laughed to himself at something he had just remembered. "There were times when it was not so peaceful in the house. The worst was when Martha came home from Colorado and announced she had married your father. It was many days before Mrs.

Walters would come out of her room."

Irene reached out and touched James' hand. "It wasn't so peaceful when your mother decided to adopt Wilbur. Sometime after Newt brought Wilbur back to us, Martha realized that you two were being raised and treated like brothers, so she decided to adopt Wilbur. Mrs. Walters was dead set against that and there were several family discussions that could be heard clear to the front gate. Mrs. Walters knew that if Martha and Newt adopted Wilbur the chances were good that she would take you boys to Montana to live. When Mr. Walters sided with Martha it was bad for a while but everyone else agreed that it was best for you two to grow up as brothers. Mrs. Walters went to St. Louis for the summer and when she returned it was done. Martha surprised us all by going out to Montana herself to see Newt. She returned two months later with the adoption papers changing Wilbur's name from McCall to Harvey. As if that wasn't enough she announced that she was taking you boys to Montana the next spring. But by Christmas, Martha was so sick …."

"Here we are," interrupted George.

The carriage pulled up to a large newly constructed office building and stopped. A large black sign hanging to the right of the door read in gold letters, "Alderson, Beckworth, & Clarke." The driver jumped down and opened the door. James got out first and then helped the others.

As George stepped out Irene said. "Oh, good, here come Wilbur and Mister Prosser."

All three stood on the boardwalk and waited for Wilbur and Stewart to join them.

Chapter Five
Reading the Will

The receptionist ushered the group into a meeting room. The sidewalls were lined floor to ceiling with shelves of large imposing legal volumes and stacks of manuscripts. It had a smell of old dusty books, stale smoke and furniture polish. Portraits of the senior partners hung on the end wall with a small table sitting underneath. One partner, Milton Clarke, had recently died, leaving Charles Alderson and Jim Beckworth as controlling partners. Introductions were made and all sat in the richly upholstered chairs, leaving the far end of the table open for the lawyers.

Stewart Prosser commented to Charlene Dawson, "I remember when you came to Davenport with your freight company. Your gamble in the freighting business made it easier for us to get our goods to Omaha."

Charlene replied. "With Uncle Frederick helping me it was not that much of a gamble, just a lot of hard work."

Conversation died, leaving an imposing silence as the lawyers appeared. Charles Alderson entered carrying a small file, followed by Jim Beckworth and a male secretary carrying a large stack of files and papers. Introductions were made and silence returned while the lawyers got settled. James and Wilbur sat at the opposite end of the table with Stewart between them.

Mr. Alderson started off with the necessary legal explanations and the routine reading of the opening pages. After that came the provisions for loyal employees at the wholesale company.

Next came the bequests to the family. "To my faithful servants George and Irene Lansing I leave the sum of twenty-five thousand dollars and each of you is to receive your present salary for the rest of your lives. In addition you will have the use of the guesthouse for as long as you wish.

"To my niece Charlene Dawson, I grant my interest in the Quinn Freight Company."

A surprised reaction came from her. "Uncle Frederick is very generous. I expected his share of the company would go to James and Wilbur."

Mr. Alderson continued. "Special bequests are as follows. Wilbur McCall Harvey, James Harvey, Mrs. Charlene Dawson, and Newt Harvey are to receive the amount of twenty five thousand dollars each." A stir and slight noises from the people at the table, prompted Mr. Alderson to pause and look up before continuing. "The balance of my estate including the home, its contents, the Walters' Wholesale Company, and all cash and securities are to be held by my attorneys until the following stipulations have been met."

Puzzled looks came on the faces of everyone as Mr. Alderson turned the page and continued.

" Stipulation number one: Over the past eighteen years Newt Harvey was separated from his sons at great sacrifice. James and Wilbur, it is my wish that you take the next year to go west and find your father. If you do not find him or if you learn he is dead then return to Omaha and Mr. Alderson will hand over my estate." Mr. Alderson stopped at the reaction from the three men sitting at the end.

James and Wilbur turned to Stewart at the same time and asked. "Did you know about this?"

"I am just as surprised and dismayed as you. This means I'm not going to have Wilbur to help me with the financial management, and you won't be around to keep the orders moving on time."

"If I may continue?" Interrupted Mr. Alderson. "While James and Wilbur look for Newt my capable and loyal employees will run the business under the supervision of Stewart Prosser."

"I don't like this." James frowned at the lawyer. "We just can't up and leave the business, for Stewart to run alone."

"Why do we both need to go?" Wilbur spoke up.

George Lansing turned to the young men. "Boys, that grandfather of yours knew what he was doing."

Mr. Alderson turned the page. "Stipulation number two. If Newt is found, he is to return to Omaha and claim his twenty-five thousand and my estate is to be divided among my immediate heirs."

Mr. Alderson laid the will down and took papers handed to him by Mr. Beckworth. "These are the papers each of you needs to sign, acknowledging your acceptance of his bequest. Details can be explained by myself or Mr. Beckworth."

Later as the people were leaving the meeting room James took Wilbur aside. "Wilbur, Grandfather sure gave us a big surprise this time. What are we going to do?"

"It would appear grandfather wants us to go find Dad." Wilbur thought of his dream of seeing the West. "I was dismayed at first but now maybe I'm glad for the opportunity to see the country."

James picked up his papers from the table. "On the ride over Irene mentioned we should look for Dad. But I'm not so sure. We don't know him at all. We don't know where he is or where to start looking. Besides, we don't know if he will want to see us."

"James, we don't even know if he's alive."

Chapter Six
An Important Telegram

George entered the front door of the Walters' home reflecting on the latest events. This week had been hectic with the reading of Mr. Walters' will the previous day. Tonight they would celebrate James's and Wilbur's birthdays. Sounds from the kitchen indicated that food preparation was proceeding under the watchful eye of Irene. Everything was going smoothly judging from their light and chatty voices.

George went into the library to make sure the dusting had been done and fresh flowers placed on the mantel. Next came the billiard room. Long ago the table had been moved to the basement so that Mr. Walters had a place for his gentlemen guests to smoke and have a whiskey. Large, comfortable, wingback chairs had replaced the table and a bar was built in front of the cue rack. George made sure that the bar was stocked with everyone's favorite drink.

A knock interrupted George's tour. He walked quietly and unhurried to the front door, looking through the side window before opening it. On the other side of the opened door stood a messenger from the telegraph office. George took the telegram, and began to close the door. Looking up, he noticed the disappointment on the boy's face at coming from town for no tip. George quickly reached in his pocket and handed him ten cents.

The telegram was addressed to James Harvey from Luis Eaton Esquire, Denver, Colorado. George placed it on the side table next to James's mail received earlier.

Charlene Dawson's arrival three days earlier had brought back many pleasant memories of the family's early years in Davenport. George remembered her as a tomboyish girl who knew her own mind and followed it, even to the point of wearing men's clothing when it suited her. George was glad she had worn a dress today so that he would not have the women in the kitchen any more distracted than they were. Other guests expected for dinner included the Walters' Wholesale manager, Stewart Prosser, and the family lawyer, Charles Alderson.

Tonight's party was for James's eighteenth birthday and Wilbur's nineteenth birthday, three weeks past. When James requested that two extra places be set Irene suspected that James and Wilbur had invited lady friends to help them celebrate their birthdays. This morning James had informed George that it was he and Irene who were the two guests. Instead of serving tonight, they were sitting with the family.

The festivities began in the library with Charlene Dawson relating stories of her experiences in San Francisco. When the conversation turned to current events at the warehouse and the previous day's reading of the will, Irene said, "George and I are so grateful for Mr. Walters' generosity to us. It's a blessing to have the guest cottage for our remaining years. When James and Wilbur get back they will have run of the house and we can still be a part of their lives."

"And she will still boss them around," added George.

James said, "I see it's time to move to the dining room. Charlene, I want to hear more about California."

After supper the guests moved to the billiard room for cigars and some of Grandpa's best whiskey. James did the honors at the bar and George passed the drinks around. Irene regaled the group with stories of James' and Wilbur's exploits as youngsters. After several stories she asked to be excused. "I want to make sure all is right in the kitchen for tomorrow. Then I'll retire."

James suggested another round. After drinks were in hand, Wilbur picked up the cigar box and passed it around. To no one's surprise except for Mr. Alderson's, Charlene Dawson took a cigar and lit it with relish.

"These are fine cigars. The ones we get in San Francisco are not as good. I'll have to take a few boxes with me when I leave."

"How is it that you became partners with Mr. Walters?" Charlie Alderson asked.

"Uncle Frederick was having trouble getting dependable freight companies to haul his goods. I was working for the Quinn Freight Company in St. Louis and the owner wanted to sell out. When I asked my father for the money he refused. He laughed at me, saying a woman couldn't run a freight company. After that I was determined to buy the company and show father I could do it. I wrote to my Uncle Frederick about the opportunity. He wrote back that he would put up the money in exchange for priority service in and out of Davenport and Omaha. Father was mad, of course. He told my brothers that it would serve Frederick right if he lost all his money. He never spoke to my uncle again.

It wasn't easy moving the company to Davenport, but it was worth it. Every year we needed more wagons so we started building our own in Council Bluffs. We built a special high-sided wagon that could carry heavy loads. By '57 we were hauling freight west of Omaha, using over a hundred of those wagons. In '58 we got a contract to haul a large shipment of mining equipment to San Francisco. Took almost three months. Boys, your father was traveling in the train with us and for a time he worked for me as a stock tender. Once in San Francisco I found demand for freight hauling was high and we could get higher rates, too. Uncle Frederick had enough wagons for his own needs, so I stayed in San Francisco and established the company. We sent some wagons to Omaha each year until the railroad was finished. Now, there is plenty of work, hauling from the railheads to other cities and the mines. Thanks to Uncle Frederick, I own the company now."

Charlene leaned over and flicked ash from her cigar.

"James, Irene says that you were three before Newt saw you. How did that happen?"

James answered, "We still don't know all the answers. Mother came to Omaha to help Grandfather when he hurt his leg. Dad was to stay in Denver and help Uncle Alex. After he escorted Mother to Fort Laramie Dad nearly lost his life in a blizzard trying to get back to Denver. The next summer he went to Bannack City, Montana. I had just been born and we couldn't join them."

George said, "In those years the mail was slow to arrive and many times letters never arrived at all. The Indian problem was bad and a lot of mail was destroyed. It was better and safer for them to stay where they were until times were better."

Irene interrupted, "The worst problem was right here in this house. Mrs. Walters was reading Martha's mail from Newt and using the information to turn Martha against him. For a time, Martha hesitated to go West and was not encouraging Newt to come to Omaha. The second summer Mr. Walters decided that Newt could help him with their expansion into Wyoming and Montana. He sent a telegram to Bannack City, but got no reply."

George stiffened. "Telegram. James, I just remembered a telegram came for you this morning. In all the excitement I forgot to mention it to you. Did you get it?"

James shook his head, "No, I guess I haven't looked at my mail for a few days. Who is it from?"

"It's from a lawyer in Denver."

James said, "Denver? Well, what do you suppose that's about? I'll look at it tomorrow."

Charlie Alderson turned, "Denver lawyer? Was the name Luis Eaton?"

George thought a moment, "Yes, I think that was the name."

"Luis Eaton is Newt's lawyer and partner. I suggest you read it."

George stepped into the hall and returned with the telegram. "It's from Luis Eaton all right. Here James, open it."

James opened and read the short message. He passed it to Wilbur and then on to the others. The telegram read,

ARRIVING OMAHA, JUNE 23.

IMPORTANT INFORMATION ON YOUR FATHER.

LUIS EATON ESQ.

DENVER COLORADO

Wilbur spoke first, "Twenty-third? That's tomorrow."

Chapter Seven
The Arrival of Eaton

James stood at the corner window of the depot, staring through the crusted dirt and coal dust. He squinted into the western sun, looking up the tracks for the train from Cheyenne then turned around and leaned back to watch the crowd.

The Union Pacific had been carrying people and freight to the West Coast for five years. People of all types and nationalities came through Omaha. The regular fare bought space for a man or woman in the accommodation car. Passengers rode in poorly heated cars sitting on bare wood benches. Many times they had to endure crude and dangerous fellow passengers. When the train stopped for loading, the occupants could purchase food at dirty lunch counters near the stations.

A much higher priced fare provided for luxurious travel in private compartments and porters to attend to every need. Passengers enjoyed meals prepared by experienced eastern chefs and served in elegant style.

James observed farmers with large families being loaded in box cars with their livestock and farm equipment. They had purchased land from the railroad, including the price of transporting their families and equipment. The land, given by the government as a bonus to the railroad companies for building the railroad, was sold at inflated prices to the farmers. In return, they would work to raise crops and stock that would be hauled to market by the railroad, again, at inflated rates.

Stirring from his position, James walked along the windows parallel to the platform. His face and manner gave no hint that a fox was chasing a family of squirrels in his stomach. His anxiety showed, by the short quick puffs on his cigar and the rather violent way he flicked the ashes. He stood for a moment looking at the confusion of porters and travelers trying to match boxes and luggage with the rightful owners. He flicked ashes from the cigar, missing the cuspidor by a wide margin and returned to where Wilbur calmly leaned against the wall.

After another look up the tracks, James moved from the corner and continued his pacing. His thoughts turned to the telegram in his coat pocket. Lawyers! He and Wilbur had spent the past two weeks with lawyers. They were not prepared for the work required to settle Grandfather Walters' large estate. They learned that attorneys could take the simplest handshake transaction and turn it into three days of oratory, all the while using words no one understood. Worse yet, they charged outrageous fees for their services. James had thought they were rid of them and now another lawyer was coming all the way from Denver.

James's' patience was about gone; he and Wilbur had planned to be in St. Louis instead of at the Union Pacific station in Omaha. The only thing holding him now was curiosity about the father he had never known. As a child he had not understood why his father lived in Montana and they lived in Omaha. What was so important about him and Wilbur finding their father now? In the past weeks several people had suggested they look for him. Their grandfather was insisting on it even though he was no longer alive.

All this time, Wilbur stayed in one place, leaning against the wall next to the window. He smoked quietly and deliberately, letting James walk off his agitation over the meeting with the lawyer. He had learned not to talk to James when he was this agitated. Better to let things settle down first and then they could discuss the events of the past two weeks.

First, smoke and steam were visible above the line of buildings and then the locomotive was in sight. James' stomach tightened. James and Wilbur moved closer to the confusion of people and porters getting off the train, looking for a man they did not know. A man stepped out of the crowd and called out. "James Harvey! I'd know you anywhere. You look just like Newt did when he was your age." Conversation was awkward at first but Luis Eaton's smile was genuine and his outgoing nature soon put them at ease.

The three men left the depot and began the short walk to the Omaha Grand Hotel. James walked beside Mr. Eaton and Wilbur followed. From the back, Wilbur observed that Mr. Eaton's build and height were similar to his own. Everything in his appearance and manner reflected the down to earth customs of the West. Luis was definitely not a stuffy, high handed lawyer like the ones they had dealt with in the past few months. From the way he handled himself, Wilbur was sure anyone who called him prissy with have those words stuffed down their throats and maybe elsewhere.

After he registered, Luis asked for thirty minutes to freshen up before getting down to business. Wilbur and James decided that Mr. Eaton was honest and could be trusted. They liked him instantly.

Chapter Eight
Eaton Speaks

Luis Eaton sat in one of the ornate high-backed booths with a whiskey in hand. To his right were two envelopes and a package wrapped in brown paper and tied with rough brown cord. It was evident that the package had been wrapped in this manner for many years. In front of Luis were two more glasses, a whiskey bottle, cigars and matches. The boys spotted Mr. Eaton and hustled across to his booth. They sat across from him with puzzled looks when they saw the envelopes and package. No one spoke while Luis poured drinks. When they lifted the glasses he said, "To Martha and Newt and a special salute to Grandfather Walters."

After a moment, Luis leaned back, sizing the two young men up and asked, "How much do you know about Newt?"

James answered, "We know very little about him. He went West to look for gold and the last we knew he was somewhere in Montana Territory. When I was three he brought Wilbur home and was here for a week and left."

"Do you know what happened on that visit?" Luis asked.

"I was too young to remember anything. When I was ten, grandfather told me that while he was here Dad got into a fight with two men and one was killed. Dad was accused of murder and had to escape to Montana. He was planning to live with us but it never happened. Many years later, another man confessed to the murder and the charges against Dad were dropped. We never heard from him after that. If we were going to hear from him, we would have by now."

"Why did he stay out West after he was cleared?" asked Wilbur.

"Why did mother stay in Omaha?" James echoed.

"I think you should read the letters and open the package to see what information you get. Then I'll tell you as much as I know. What have you two been doing for the past few years?"

James answered, "We've worked at our grandfather's business since we were old enough to walk. He started a wholesale business in Davenport, Iowa and later expanded to Omaha. Grandfather liked to tell the story about how he arrived in Davenport with the clothes he was wearing and carrying all his possessions in a paper bag. In a few short years he had a thriving wholesale clothing, fabric and notions business. When trade from the territories grew he opened a large wholesale company here in Omaha. We started working full time after we finished our schooling at a military academy. Grandfather was working too hard and it wasn't long until he was in poor health. Wilbur and I helped him as much as we could but we were not as talented in making it run right. With the help of friends and his doctor, we finally got him to sell the Davenport business so he could work less. But it was too late."

Wilbur asked, "Why do you want to see us?"

"Mr. Walters instructed me to deliver this package to you, after you both were over eighteen. I believe it contains the answers to some of your questions about your father and what happened to him."

"Did you know grandfather?"

"No. Our dealings were only by letter. It was because I've known Newt since '63 that your grandfather asked me to deliver this to you. I met Newt at Oro City, in Colorado Territory and I have been his lawyer, business partner and friend ever since. Mr. Walters intended for you to look for Newt and thought I would be able to answer questions about him and where he might be."

"What's in there?" James pointed at the package.

"I don't know. This is the way I received it from your grandfather and he gave no hint as to its contents. Boys, I am tired. I will give this to you and say good night. When we meet for breakfast I'll answer as many of your questions as I can."

Chapter Nine
A Pair of Letters

James opened the envelope. Why had grandfather gone to all the trouble and expense for the small package and the envelope? He hoped it would clear away the shadows of his fathers past and fill the emptiness he was beginning to feel. He looked over the letter from their grandfather and began to read it aloud to Wilbur:

> Dear James and Wilbur,
> I received this chest and journal from your father in 1873. He was concerned that you two would never know him, so he asked that I give this to you when you are both grown up. I do not have long to live so I am sending this to Luis Eaton, Newt's lawyer in Denver. He is your father's closest friend and the one most likely to know where he is. Mr. Eaton will deliver this when the time comes. I am sorry that I cannot give this to you personally. I have included the newspaper clipping about the shooting in '67 and the clipping in '73 about Newt being innocent of the murder. We tried to locate your father but we never heard from him.
> I knew he was innocent from the beginning. You will never know the anger I felt when we found out it was that bastard Bates who lied to the police. Your grandmother was blind to that man's faults and could not see what a good man your father was. The cloud hanging over Newt's head prevented him from living with us in Omaha.
> James and Wilbur, I want you to find your father and bring him back.
> Good luck and God Bless. Grandpa Walters.

James picked up the package and held it for a few moments before untying the string. He peeled back the paper exposing a small wooden chest about ten inches long, seven inches wide, and two inches deep. The wooden chest was well made but it had seen rough times. James couldn't tell how old it was but it was stained and scarred, showing the hardships it, and its owner, had endured. James found that only one of the two latches worked as he opened the chest.

On top were clippings of the murder and another of the confession by the real killer. A third clipping described the involvement of Conrad Bates, his arrest and escape. James read it with interest before speaking, "Here's an article about Conrad Bates being mixed up in the killing they blamed on father. Bates was arrested but escaped and was thought to have gone West. I guess the name Bastard Bates is justified."

Wilbur looked over at the chest, "I didn't like the man and neither did Grandfather. He was afraid that if Mother married Conrad he would get hold of the business and ruin it."

James reached in and picked up an envelope. It was addressed to James and Wilbur. He used his knife to cut open the flap and then he carefully removed a letter that was stiff with age. The dried edges tore in places as he smoothed it out. Once it was unfolded he began to read.

Dear James and Wilbur,

When I realized we might never be together, I wrote this journal so you would know more about me. I was lucky compared to others and the fact that I am still alive convinces me that a guardian angel was following me around. I have a lot to . be thankful for.

I want to tell you about my great adventure in the West looking for gold. I followed my dreams and managed to stick to them. I do not regret the way my life has gone except that I did not have your mother at my side and I did not get to watch you two grow up.

Now, you are on your own and whatever dreams you may have, follow them. Don't let anyone or anything stop you.

Good luck and God bless you.

Dad

James looked over at Wilbur, pulled the chest closer and lifted the book out. The journal was wrapped in a piece of soft leather and tied with a leather thong. He untied the thong and took the book out of its leather wrap. As he fingered the book he noticed the cover had stains from sweat or tears and it was scratched and cut in several places. The corners were bent and showed much wear. Lost in his thoughts, James turned the journal over and noticed what looked like blood spots. He wondered if it was his father's blood. He sat quietly for a moment, feeling a thread of the past flicker out and attach itself to him, a thread that was to grow stronger in the coming months. He looked up as Wilbur asked, "Are you going to read it now?"

"Not yet, it will take some time to read and I want to think about all this first." He wrapped the leather around the journal before putting it and the letters in the box and closing the lid.

The next morning James and Wilbur met Luis for breakfast, eager to learn more. After ordering and small talk, they let Luis read the letters. As he handed them back to James he asked, "What questions do you have about Newt?"

"Did he get to fight any Indians?"

Expecting many other questions to be first, Luis was surprised. "Once or twice I think. I remember he saved an Indian's life while prospecting in Colorado in the early years. The young warrior gave him a small beaded spirit bag with a bear claw and tooth in it. Newt wore it around his neck for a while. Later he attached it to his hatband along with a snake fang."

"Mother didn't say much about him. James thinks he had another woman out in Montana."

"Another woman? No, there was no woman in his life except Martha."

While they dug into their steak and eggs, potatoes, gravy and coffee, Luis answered more of their questions about Newt and Martha. After the plates were cleared off and more coffee poured, James continued.

"Mr. Eaton, I'll admit that up until last night we didn't think about our father much. But in the last few days his name has come up several times. Besides Grandfather's request in his will there are other people suggesting Wilbur and I go West to find him. Now you deliver a package with letters and such. Well, we read the letters and stayed up most of the night talking about what we should do. We want to know more about our father and hope to find him or find out what has happened to him."

"What should we do, Mr. Eaton?" Wilbur asked.

"I will be glad to help you find him but first both of you should start calling me Luis. I suggest you boys get outfitted and head for the territories to look for Newt. After you find him you might decide that the West is a good place to live, work and start a family."

Chapter Ten
Newt's Journal

James and Wilbur stood on the platform in the early morning hours waiting for the 7:35. Luis had suggested wearing old clothing to reduce teasing and harassment while traveling in the West. In spite of this, their clothing selections had a noticeable Eastern look. In the early days of their search they would be easily spotted as Easterners. As the weeks rolled by the mud and dust would help them to blend in with the people they met but they still couldn't hide their Eastern accent and mannerisms.

"All aboard!"

Climbing on the train with Mr. Eaton, they began a four-day and three-night trip across Nebraska to Cheyenne, Wyoming. The train was equipped with three coaches, two sleeping cars and a dining car hooked behind several boxcars. Best of all, it had a smoking car at the rear of the train. For the next four days they would smoke, drink, eat, and relax while reading Newt's journal. They would endure many stops and starts for passenger loading and unloading but the three travelers soon got used to the disruptions. They wouldn't know most of the small towns they stopped at, but they would recognize Lincoln, Grand Island, and North Platte.

After settling into their compartment, the men got comfortable and James took the journal out of the chest. He untied the thong and removed the leather wrap. With some anticipation he opened the journal and inspected the first few pages while he gathered his thoughts.

The whistle blew, then the engineer opened the steam and the cars jerked forward. While the train began picking up speed, James turned the page and began reading aloud.

Ohio 1858

Gold was all I talked about and all I thought about, as I grew up in Ohio. I was too late to be a Forty-niner but that was okay. I read story after story of the discoveries in California and Nevada that lured men to pack up and leave home for the gold fields. That's what I dreamed of doing. I wanted the adventure of prospecting in the territories and finding the riches I had read about. I kept maps with the locations of each strike and wrote in the names of the towns and gold camps that sprang up. Even the gold strikes in Australia got my interest. The stories stirred up my mind, boiled my blood, and drove me nearly mad with desire to dig for gold. There had been a few of our neighbors who sold everything they owned, pack up, and head for Oregon Territory. I tried to sign on and go with them.

Instead of looking for gold, I was digging coal for the Union Coal Company and hating the dangerous work. I was discouraged with the prospects of going West and kept telling myself I was trapped. An accident in the mine was all it took to make me pack up and leave home.

I was seventeen, and had been working in the mine for less than a year. Already my face looked like I was thirty. At the end of a shift my body felt like it was fifty. Each day as we waited for the platform to stop at our level I asked myself how Dad could have worked like this for ten years? No wonder he wasn't afraid of death. Anything was better than mining, including farming, and Dad had gone broke doing that too.

Every day was the same. Picking and shoveling coal two hundred feet under ground. Dirty, dangerous work that numbed your mind and eventually killed your body. Our hands and faces were covered with coal dust mixed with dried on sweat so that we blended in with the walls. With goggles off we had a comical appearance. The clean skin gave us a fish-eyed look. One day at the end of a shift we walked to the shaft to wait for the cage to stop at our level. When the cage arrived eight of us stepped on. At the surface a steam engine powered a pulley system to raise and lower the cage. The operator engaged the clutch and our cage was yanked upward. We had not traveled far when the engine lost power and for a moment lost its grip on the cable. The platform dropped five feet and then abruptly stopped. This happened once or twice a day and with a load of eight men we expected it. This time the jolt was too much for the bolts attaching the floor to the cage. The floor tore lose under where George and I were standing. The other side of the cage jammed into the wall of the shaft and stayed there. Yelling and cussing the men grabbed for any wood, steel or cable that was handy. Two men grabbed my clothing before I fell through the opening and lifted me up until I could get a hold. George wasn't so lucky, before anyone could grab him he fell to the bottom of the shaft. When the excitement died down, one of the men yelled that the cage might not be safe for long. We worked our way back down to the level we had been on and stood there in silence, each of us remembering George in our prayers and thanking God for those who were saved. It took six hours to repair the damage and get us to the surface. George had plunged two levels below ours and was dead.

At the time shack, the foreman reminded us that our shift would start again in four hours. As we headed for the gate we could see the mine superintendent through the window grimly figuring up how much the delay would cost the company. I silently watched the pathetic sight of two men carrying George's body past the office. No one took notice.

The men told me later that they saw a look on my face and in my eyes they did not know. My quiet, gentle nature was gone when I reached the office door. I busted into the office. The clerks jumped out of the way when they saw my blazing eyes all bugged out. Now Mr. Hindricks could not have known me, even if I had taken a bath. I told him who I was and asked if he knew George. "No," was the reply.

I said, "You should know about a man when he dies on company time." In a few sentences I explained how George would take the extra shifts or the more dangerous jobs for the extra pay just so his children would have something extra. Well, now there would be nothing extra for them. I talked about George and his family living in a two-room shack that the company had the gall to charge rent for. I asked to have my pay figured and paid then and there. I went back to my rooming house and gave notice I was pulling out in two days.

So, in the spring of 1858, just before I turned 18, I was going West to see if it was a dream or a nightmare. As for being rich, I wasn't worried much. Even if I was to get rich it would all be gone before I was.

Spring 1858

Like many immigrants I had no horse or mule to make the trip easier. I left for California with what I could carry. At first, Mother and then Uncle Frank tried to talk me out of going but I was determined to go West and they finally gave up trying. I spent a week walking to Georgetown, where I could wait for a wagon train that needed a driver or stock tender. Problem was, I was so thin and gaunt, folks didn't believe I could do the work of driving or tending stock.

It was more than a week before a group came through that needed help. A stock tender by the name of Pete had been hurt when the team he was hitching got spooked and made a short run of it. He came back to camp reporting that one of the horses had kicked his hat. Trouble was, his head was in it. I found the leader, Hugh O'Brien, and told him I had been raised on a farm and could handle the stock. He hired me to replace Pete, until he healed.

It took four men to handle the O'Brien's stock and to hitch up the teams. Two of the men in the group were brothers: Jake and Pete Samson. Tom Ahlbright, the youngest of the four, was a jokester. The leader, Ben Morrison, was the oldest and took his responsibilities seriously. A stock-tender's job is one of the hardest and most dangerous jobs in a train. We would take over the stock at the end of the day and herd them to water and a place to graze. Every day we had to deal with spooked animals, runaway teams, and lack of sleep. There were times when we took the stock more than two miles to water, and then two or three miles for a good place to graze. After bedding them down, we stood guard through the night and then brought them back safely to the train by sun-up. We helped hitch the teams and kept the other stock bunched until the train got underway. The ladies would have a cold breakfast laid out for us. Many times we took the food and crawled into the wagons to eat before we fell asleep. Some days sleeping was interrupted by breakdowns and rough roads.

At one small town, a young man driving a wagon full of goods approached us. He was headed for Davenport with his freight and wished the company and protection of our train. The men voted him in and he happily wheeled his wagon in with the others. That night I learned his name was Alex McCall. He was a friendly, good-looking young man with lots of energy. When my chores were done I went over to his wagon to talk. We became friends and during rest stops he let me sleep in his wagon which was a whole lot better than sleeping on the ground. I learned he was a driver for the Walters' Wholesale Company of Davenport, Iowa. He had been working there for some time and was sweet on the owner's' daughter Molly who worked in the office.

The day came when we reached the banks of the Mississippi River and had to wait for our turn to cross on the ferry. I had never seen so much water going by one spot. The power and sound of the water was something I had never been around before. When we got into town, Alex invited me along to help unload his wagon of fabrics and notions. While he and a laborer were getting the items moved to another section of the building, I stayed near the wagon. At one point I was walking back and forth when I came face to face with a very pretty young lady. I noticed nothing about her except her deep blue eyes. I liked her instantly. She asked if I needed help and I all I could get out was, "No." When faced with pretty females I usually was unable to speak more than one or two words together with a lot of "uhhs" in between.

"That's Alex's wagon, isn't it?"

I said. "Yes, it is."

When Alex returned we went up to the office to get paid. The young woman was there at the desk. He introduced her as Molly Walters. They made arrangements to meet that evening while I stood by too embarrassed to move or talk. I noticed that Molly was almost as tall as Alex. They were so robust and full of life. I could tell the two were meant for each other.

On the way back to the O'Brien train, Alex explained that he was going to haul a load of items to the new warehouse in Omaha. If the O'Brien train was leaving in the next two days he would join us again. He also would have a job for me if the other stock tender was now able to work. I said I would check on things and let him know.

Road to Omaha

The next day Alex stopped by to make arrangements with the O'Briens to travel to Omaha. He found me working on the harnesses. I accepted his offer and was glad to be able to travel with him and help take care of his stock. We pulled out the next day with me riding comfortably in the wagon.

As we rolled along, Alex told me more about the Walters family and the wholesale company. The family home was in Omaha but at that time, Molly was living in Davenport and working for her father there. That suited Alex because he and Molly were not under the watchful eye of her overbearing mother. He told me about Molly's older sister, Martha, who worked in the Omaha office. She worked with her father and was helpful to him. When it came to business dealings Martha was stubborn at times but everyone liked her and respected her business judgment.

Their mother was a social climber who liked the social events in St. Louis more than Omaha. She was domineering, demanding and cool to those she did not feel were her equal. She was especially interested in a man by the name of Conrad Bates whom she had chosen for Martha's future husband. Mrs. Walters and her brother Levi Swan had inherited the family fortune and home in St. Louis. She had a snooty attitude that Alex did not like. He worried about Mrs. Walters' devious nature and her uncaring feelings for those around her. If someone crossed her they paid for it.

Mr. Walters was a friendly and successful businessman. Though of slight build, he could load a wagon as easily as his employees. Alex admired his intelligence and ability to anticipate demand for goods and have them ready in the warehouse when needed. At home he was soft-spoken and let Mrs. Walters run the household.

For the next few days Alex would think of some story about the Walters family and talk for hours. He told me about Mr. Walters buying twenty acres at the edge of Omaha and building a large home. He built it to please Mrs. Walters. She wanted to impress the townspeople and her family living in St. Louis. Molly didn't like the house because it was cold and no one lived nearby.

A tinker by the name of A. J. Wright joined us at one town. His wagon was loaded down with tools, merchandise, cloth, notions, and lots of household items. A tinker's wagon was a general store on wheels. A. J. was always welcome because he had news from other towns and was up on all the scandals and bloody events, as well as the latest jokes and stories. He traveled with us for two weeks before I learned his name was

Alphonso Jurrard but no one dared call him that. A. J. stopped at the homesteads along the way to do business. He always caught up to the train after dark. Our journey across Iowa was uneventful, except for one dustup A.J. had.

One evening he came into camp as if the devil himself were after him. A.J. was battered, bleeding and so bug-eyed scared it took thirty minutes and several swigs of whiskey to get the story from him. Seems he made a stop at a homestead and called on a lonely and neglected housewife. She invited him in for coffee and to see his merchandise. One thing led to another and they ended up on the kitchen floor. He said everything was going just fine until her husband rode into the yard. A.J. yelled, "Quick, where's the back door?"

"We don't have a back door," she tells him.

"Well then, just where do you want one?" he asked.

A.J. traveled with us to Omaha. He intended to restock his wagon and return to Davenport, although I'm sure he took a different route back.

Omaha

By the time we reached Council Bluffs on the east side of the Missouri I had been gone from home almost a month. While we waited our turn to ferry across into Omaha, time became my enemy. Homesickness hit me hard when I remembered the scoldings my brother and I got for teasing our sister. I especially remembered the evenings when father would read the Bible to us and the whole family would sing our favorite hymns. After Dad died, the Bible reading fell to me, and I tried to read some each week. This was the first big test of my determination to go West and I wavered for several days before resolving to follow my dream. Later, as the months went by, thinking of home and friends would bolster my sagging spirits. Especially in those first years when I was cold, drunk, hungry and thinking I would never do any better.

After crossing into Omaha, Alex and I headed for the Walters' Wholesale building. It was an older, two story, wooden warehouse with a water tower on top for fire protection. Alex wheeled around to the side door and waved to some of the men. I helped unload the freight while Alex caught up on the local news. I had just handed out the last box when the men started snickering and making remarks. I looked where they pointed to see a large man standing across the street at the corner.

He was dressed as if he was in downtown New York City instead of Omaha, Nebraska. He stepped off the boardwalk, gingerly stepping around the deeper mud holes. As he passed our team he whipped out a white handkerchief and flicked it. A very stupid thing to do around horses. Horsemen will tell you that a team will work hard and pull a wagon through all kinds of weather and will work alongside other teams with whips cracking and drivers cursing. The animals were conditioned for gun shots and lightning, but if some piece of paper or leaf flickers past their eyes, the horses will bolt and run for miles.

That's what happened when the Idiot gentleman flicked the handkerchief. The nearest horse reared, causing the team to bolt, nearly throwing me from the wagon. I dove for the reins as we careened up the street, missing the fool by inches. The wheels hit a large, deep mud hole, splashing him from head to toe with muddy water and grit. When I got the team under control and stopped, I sat for a moment first cussing the man, then laughing until I hurt at the sight of him dripping mud and water. All he saw was me, doubled up in laughter and pointing at him.

Alex dashed up mad as hell because he was responsible for the team and wagon. He yelled at the man that he should have known better than to wave a hanky around a horse. When Alex found out everything was okay, he busted out laughing, too. We turned around and drove back to the loading dock. The men were gathered around and as we pulled in, they gave us a round of applause, which puzzled me a little until Alex explained the men did not like Mr. Conrad Bates. They were happy when he got splashed.

Martha

While Alex and the foreman finished the paperwork, I stayed with the wagon. In a few minutes I was bored and began to wander around a bit. At the stairs leading to offices on the mezzanine I could hear voices coming from an open office door. The door opened wider and a voice asked if she could help me. I turned and looked up and all I remember seeing was a beautiful woman standing there impatiently waiting for me to answer her question. I stammered, "No, I was just waiting for Alex." I was awestruck by her frail beauty and just stood there looking up.

Alex came up behind and got me moving toward the stairs to her office. He was acting strange and I didn't understand what was going on at first. He started telling her about the incident with the team. Alex told her that I had stayed with the runaway wagon at risk to my own safety and took control of the team. He was embellishing the story to the point I was attempting to correct him but he just kept on with his version of the wild ride. He was happy to report that Mr. Bates had escaped injury thanks to me, but alas had been splashed with a little water and so was headed back to his room to freshen up.

All that time I was standing there, frozen to the spot and hoping it would never end. I was bit by love and bit hard. In a short time I had memorized everything about her. I sealed in my memory the way her long black hair wound around on the back of her head and the way she turned her head from Alex to me as he told the story. Most of all I watched her eyes and the way they danced when she laughed.

Alex had command of the moment. He stopped in mid sentence when he noticed the way I was looking at her. Changing his tone of voice, he introduced her to me as Martha Walters, Molly's sister. This was Martha! She held out her hand to shake mine and I don't remember what I said but it must have been okay because she smiled and thanked me for what I had done. She talked to me and asked where I was from and if I was going to stay in Omaha. We talked for a few minutes and I managed to tell her about my going West to look for gold. It was Alex's turn to stand and watch us talk.

Finally, we realized we were still shaking hands and that Alex was getting a great deal of pleasure out of watching us. Red faced and stammering, we tried to continue our conversation but we were so aware of the attraction that was taking place we had to change the subject.

Alex and I went back down the stairs and through the building to the wagon, got aboard and started up the street in silence. A block a way, Alex stopped the team and set the brake. He turned to me and began to whoop it up, slapping me on the back, yelling. "She likes you! You like her! She loves you! You love her!" After that outburst he sat and laughed. I must have sat there with a silly grin on my face because every once in a while he would look at me, point and start laughing again.

While driving back to the O'Brien train he told me more about Martha. The man I had splashed was Conrad Bates from the St. Louis Bates. His family was in banking and finance. His mother and Martha's mother had been planning for those two to get married since they were ten years old. Martha's mother wanted the marriage so that the Walters family would be in a higher social circle in St. Louis society. It was said that Conrad's mother figured it was the only way to get her idiot son married and have grandchildren. Everyone knew that Martha was probably the only woman he would get to marry him. He was not ugly but close enough that it was uncomfortable to look at him for long. He took to wearing the New York fashions but they fit poorly on his large body. As if that wasn't enough, he had an uncontrollable temper that was easily triggered when he was put in embarrassing situations or when someone would poke fun at him. He was mad most of the time. He was known to get into such rages that he shot at people or beat them bloody. Alex said that he had been able to control his temper around Martha but it was only a matter of time before he did something in front of her and would lose her, too. Conrad's father, Ol" Man Bates, was okay about their marriage. He wanted the Walters' Wholesale Company to be a part of his son's financial empire.

Mr. Walters and Molly opposed the marriage because they knew the problems that Martha would have to endure and Mr. Walters did not want someone like Conrad Bates to get his hands on the family business. Alex was happy that Martha had met me and hoped things might change. The only problem was going to be Mrs. Frederick Walters.

Omaha to Fort Laramie

People in Omaha were getting reports of Indians and outlaws raiding the smaller trains as they moved across Nebraska and Wyoming. We were advised to travel in a larger train for protection and mutual help on the trail. It didn't take long for us to find a group of wagons ready to head west. Most of the men were farmers and merchants. There were a few shady characters who had some mighty hot reasons for leaving their hometown and heading west. It was usually a woman, a creditor, or a sheriff.

I saw Alex one more time before we pulled out. He told me he was going to ask Molly to marry him on his next trip to Davenport. He wanted to go west and find a growing town to open a general store. If I found a town that I thought showed promise of growing and prospering I was to send a letter to him in Omaha. We promised to see each other again and I hoped I would see Martha again.

The O'Brien's train decided to keep me on to help with the livestock. The pay was twenty dollars a month and found. I was glad to stay with the O'Briens. Their idea of found was meat in the soup and all the bread we wanted. Some of the men got only a plate of beans and a slice of bread. For meat they had to buy or trade for it. Some had to hunt for birds or small game to get meat.

We pulled in next to the Quinn Freight Company from Davenport, Iowa. The owner was Charlie Shaw and his foreman was Sam Dawson. Their wagons were well-built and the men were experienced in handling the wagons and teams. They had ten freight wagons loaded with mining equipment. It took ninety horses, six dogs, two cook wagons and one dairy cow to complete the outfit. One of the cooks was over seventy years old, which was a miracle, because he ate his own cooking. Sam said he was so mean and cantankerous that the Lord and the Devil were still arguing over who had to take him. The men tolerated him because he made coffee that was black as the Devil, stronger than death, sweet as love and hot as Hell, which was just the way they liked it. They claimed that he could take a year old piece of rawhide and the bleached bones of a steer and serve up a satisfying meal. We could only hope that his skills would not be put to the test.

Another freighter to join our train was Dwight Johnston. He pulled up with seven wagon teams; six wagons were loaded with whiskey and one wagon was loaded with flour. We kept asking what he was going to do with all that flour. The combined train of fifty wagons was imposing in size and difficult to manage. Too many men had too little experience hitching and handling six horses, or four oxen. Each day we had delays and injuries. If the entire train was moving by three hours after sun-up it was considered an exceptional day. This resulted in fights and arguments among the men every morning and evening. The more experienced drivers and freight companies were unhappy with the lack of progress and injuries. On the fourth day a meeting was called and after a heated exchange the men voted to split up into three groups. One group of wagons would be pulled by oxen. The other two would have wagons pulled by mules or horses. That way, members of each group would travel at the same speed.

I was glad the O'Brien group joined with the Quinn and Johnston wagons. These groups had worked together and were all experienced drivers and handlers. Our five stock tenders joined forces with their stock tenders. That made it easier to move our stock to water and grazing areas. Once the animals were in the bedding ground and guards posted, we would start a small fire to boil coffee.

One driver, known as Banjo John, would strum tunes quietly while someone would occasionally sing along. I got to know the Quinn bunch during those talks around the campfire. They talked about Charlie Shaw, the owner, and Sam his partner, and the big bonus they would receive for going all the way to California. We talked about Indian trouble and the danger ahead of us. Each man secretly wondered how he would measure up, if he were forced to fight face to face with an Indian.

After leaving Omaha, the trail got worse. For six weeks we ate more dust than meat. The food was exactly the same each day; beans, sourdough bread, wild game, and coffee. Only when game was scarce and the men had not had meat for several days would they eat beef. Oh, how I longed for my mother's cooking.

Those of us working on the train made our beds by wrapping prairie hay up in a wool blanket. The blankets were a natural haven for lice, making a full night's sleep impossible. Water was precious, so we seldom took baths or did washing. On rest day we "washed" our bedding by laying the blankets over large anthills. While we did repairs and rested, the ants "washed" our bedding by hauling off the lice. We slept well for a night or two until the next batch of eggs hatched.

The further west we traveled the worse conditions got. Frequently we were forced to travel up to five miles from camp to find water and grazing. That put more stress on the animals and the men. At each stop the women and children had to take more time gathering wood for the cooking fires. Sometimes wood was not available and they had to pick up buffalo chips. That was a dangerous chore. There was a chance of tangling with a rattlesnake or Indians. When we reached Grand Island, we stayed to the north bank of the Platte, as the water and grazing was expected to be better.

Two days after getting to Grand Island, Banjo John had a real dust up. His team spooked and took him and the wagon into a steep sided coulee. The wagon broke up and the cargo was pulverized by the impact. We tied ropes to the rear wheels to pull the wagon off him. When Charlie rode up, Banjo John said, "My wagon quit on me."

One horse had to be put out of its misery, three couldn't be worked for weeks and the other two were never seen again. Banjo suffered for three days before he died. Sam said his innards were all busted up. We buried him along the trail like hundreds of other pioneers and marked the grave with a simple cross with the name Banjo John printed on it. I joined the Quinn outfit to take Banjo's place. What I remember mostly about our trip across Nebraska was the dust and the bone weary work that was necessary to keep things moving.

We were camped on the Platte near Chimney Rock when we got news about a gold strike near Pikes Peak in Colorado Territory. Day by day the rumors of gold strikes and speculation of riches fluttered from wagon to wagon like summer butterflies. By the time we got to Scotts Bluff a group of men prepared to leave the train and head for Colorado. I joined them because I wanted to start digging for gold before I was too old to dig. One of the men suggested we leave the train before getting to Fort Laramie. That was voted down because most of the men needed provisions or needed to send mail back east. As we continued toward Fort Laramie those of us going to Colorado formed a company and prepared our gear. That was no effort for me because everything I owned was on my back or stuffed in a fifty-pound flour sack.

Three days later we were camped on the Platte about two miles east of the fort. Some of our break away group rode in to check on mail and to get provisions for the trip south. We got disappointing news. Prospectors on their way back home told about the hard work, bad food, and death along the Cherry Creek diggings. The men were cussing the reporters and the newspapers who had written glowing stories of the riches being found near Pikes Peak. They felt they had been victims of a hoax. Later, as they talked about the Indian trouble along the trail, I could see the gold fever evaporating in the eyes of our group.

The train had been slowing down for a few miles and the porter entered the car.

"Gentlemen, if you wish to stretch your legs we'll be here for 'bout an hour."

James, Wilbur and Luis left the car and strolled along the platform, watching people come and go. It was almost an hour and a half before the conductor signaled for boarding. They decided to continue reading in the comfort of the smoking car. By the time the train was in motion and picking up speed, drinks were poured and Wilbur took over the reading until the porter announced dinner.

Dinner conversation was centered on the two exceptional looking young ladies eating nearby. They were obviously talking about James and Wilbur and giggling over the interest the boys were showing back. Luis thought the boys might lose interest in reading further until Wilbur suggested they return to the smoking car. James reluctantly agreed. Once they were settled James continued reading from the journal.

Pikes Peak or Bust

After hearing the bad news about Cherry Creek, many of the men decided they would continue on to California. Only a small group of us were determined to go to Pikes Peak. Dwight was going, expecting his three remaining wagons of whiskey and one of flour to bring good money at Cherry Creek. I figured I was going to die someday anyway and Colorado would be a shorter trip.

Dwight went over to the sutler's store to do some dealing. Mr. Parker's contract with the U. S. Army to provide goods for the soldiers allowed him a big advantage when it came to dealing with the emigrants. Before we pulled out, he bought a wagonload of whiskey and all of the flour from Dwight. The price included the wagons and horses. The sutler had high expectations of selling all the whiskey and flour. The wagons and horses could easily be sold or traded to the emigrants. He sold rested stock to the emigrants and would buy or trade for their stock that was in poor shape. With good feed and rest for a few weeks they would be ready for sale to the next immigrant train. He had a captive trade and was making the most of their plight.

I collected my meager pay from Sam Dawson and said goodbye to Ben Morrison and the men I had worked with. They all wished us good luck. I still did not have the money to buy a horse or mule but I had enough to get new pants and boots from the sutler's store. I posted a letter to mother about going to Colorado and that I missed her and the family. I signed on with Dwight, to help drive one of his wagons for a flat rate of ten dollars and found. The other driver he hired was Tom Ahlbright from the O'Brien out-fit. I was getting closer to my destination but not in the fashion that I would've liked.

Our small group joined a larger group of prospectors who had arrived from the east and were heading for Cherry Creek. They were going to see for themselves if the sto-ries of the gold strike were the truth or a hoax.

The trail to Pikes Peak was littered with equipment and prospecting supplies thrown out by those returning from the gold strike. I got a gold panning pan and a nearly new rock pick to complete my prospecting outfit. We came upon a group of burned out wagons and stopped to poke around. I found a 50 cal Hawken rifle lying in the brush. Old, but still usable it was untouched by the fire. I bought a small supply of powder and two bullets from one of the men.

At one place, I spotted a small dog hiding under a wagon. I reached in and pulled him out and held the whimpering pup. In a matter of minutes that mutt stuck a claim on me. I don't know which of us was more down and out. I named him Kramer, after my brother. Tom said he was a terrier breed. When he had a bath he was mostly white with brown markings over the ears and left eye, but most of the time he was the color of dirt. His legs were too short to be able to catch much but if he got something cor-nered or in a hole he was quick enough to get it. He was cunning and smarter than most of us. It was his curiosity and lack of fear that got him into trouble. His tail curved over his back like a divining rod. I could tell what was about to happen by watching that tail.

We saw evidence of Indians and suspected a raiding party was following us. Our size was enough to repel most attacks. The danger was being caught out alone or in a small group. I felt a little safer once I was armed.

As we approached the Cherry Creek diggings I could see Pikes Peak looming many miles to the south. It was used as a reference point for the men, even when they were high in the mountains it could still be seen. The miners had established a gold camp called Auraria on the point of land where Cherry Creek and the South Platte River came together. On the east bank the town was called Denver. We decided to go a mile or so west to a camp called Montana City. We heard estimates that the population was near three hundred, but with so many pulling out and many more pulling in, it was hard to tell exactly.

When a camp gets crowded the men want a place to meet, socialize and conduct business. They build a saloon as a way of keeping the more dangerous men off the streets. Montana City at that time had fourteen tents and buildings for business use. Five of them were saloons and six were bars. We speculated about how many dangerous men must be living there. The bars, set up in tents, served whiskey and beer only. The saloons in buildings, offered games of chance and served food along with the liquor.

The camp also had two general stores and a barbershop. The barber offered a bath, shave, and hair cut for a dollar and a half. He would also pull teeth, lance boils, and since no doctor was available he would do what he could to fix up a man after a fight or getting shot. Some of the building owners were adding a second story to rent to doctors and lawyers. If the town was lucky, one of them would soon rent a room to a lady. The area around the town was crowded with tents and makeshift lean-tos.

Dwight said Tom and I could sleep under his wagons until we found accommodations or he moved on. I got a letter off to Mom telling her I was okay and where I was. Next I wrote a letter to Alex to tell him Denver looked like a good town to establish a general store if he was still interested.

Montana City was so busy and crowded that you had to watch not to get run over, robbed, or shot. It is said that there was no law west of Kansas City and some claimed there was no God west of the Missouri. Justice out in the territories depended on the local system. In some towns the procedure was to "give 'em a fair trial and then hang 'em."

When we learned that the saloons were making whiskey out of whatever was available, we pulled the three wagons in a "U" shape. Tom and I laid out planks on empty barrels at the open end to make a bar, while Dwight watered down the whiskey. We started pouring drinks and even with it watered down, the men thought it was the best whiskey they had ever experienced, Dwight watered it down a little more and we kept on selling the stuff.

While selling whiskey for Dwight, I overheard several conversations about where gold was and places where it wasn't. I also learned where camps were located and which ones to avoid. Having arrived in early August, I hoped to get in two months of prospecting before the weather got bad. I bought some bacon and beans and tobacco. I couldn't afford whiskey but got a small amount of coffee instead. I would be able to get game meat with the rifle. All I had for prospecting was the small rock pick and panning pan. After I packed up what little I owned, Dwight said I wasn't even a "single blanket jackass prospector" because I didn't have a jackass.

Kramer and I headed west and south into the foothills, prospecting some of the areas

I had heard about. One day, I met two old prospectors with a mule packed high with provisions. As we passed they took one look at my greenhorn outfit and started laughing. One, looking at Kramer, asked if my burro had shrunk. I could hear their laughter for an hour after they were gone. From then on, when I met a prospector, I hid.

I explored several small streams and dry creek beds that fed into the Platte River. I worked standing in the cold water until my feet were numb and my ankles hurt so bad I had to quit. That was a learning experience. I learned how easy it was to twist an ankle walking in the streambed. I learned that if you leave food lying around, the varmints or the bears will get it and destroy everything else at the same time. More important, I learned that I didn't know spit about prospecting for gold. Kramer learned not to mess with porcupines and skunks. When I pulled out the quills he whined at each tug. The skunk was another matter. I made him sleep downwind. In the night he would crawl up close for warmth until the fumes woke me and I would shove him away. He was a long time getting rid of the smell.

One thing about prospecting, you're either one foot from a million dollars, or a million feet from a dollar. Either way, it's a lot of work and you never know if you quit too soon or should have quit at the first panful. Over the centuries the gold was freed from its rocky home and washed downstream and deposited where the water flow slowed down. For the prospector it is a process of using a pick to loosen the gravel and sand and scooping it into the pan. The pan is lowered into the stream to allow the water to wash over the dirt. Holding the pan with one hand the prospector picks out the larger rocks then swirls the water, washing out the pea size gravel and leaving smaller and smaller grains to be swirled and swirled until there's only the black sand left. Hope starts high with each pan of dirt and ebbs as the gravel dissipates. All hope is gone when no nuggets appear and no color shows in the dark sand.

I had to repeat the process time after time until my legs were numb from the cold water and my back in pain from bending over. When a small flake of color appeared my heart would leap and the pain would go away for a while as I picked up the pace of digging, swirling, and throwing out pebbles. When a small nugget appeared in the pan I would get excited and work the area with quicker strokes and renewed energy.

While I was prospecting the streams, news of the strike at Cherry Creek was spreading east and west. By Christmas over fifty thousand men abandoned their homes and joined the rush to the new El Dorado. It was Pikes Peak or Bust! For the inexperienced men like me it was a bust. I would have to find work to feed me and Kramer that winter and beg for a grubstake come spring.

Bear Attack

One day I had parked my weary body under a tree to have a smoke. Further upstream and on the near hillside, a ruckus began with growling and slashing of underbrush. I checked my Hawken, then Kramer and I slipped across the creek. I worked through a stand of aspens and stood at the edge of the trees, looking for the source of the noise. Kramer was real agitated, growling deep in his throat with his hair standing up along his back from head to tail.

All of a sudden, a young Indian came out of the nearby timber at a full run toward me yelling, "nakohe .... nakohe." Blood was streaming all over him. He was running for his life with the biggest bear I ever hoped to see about to catch up with him. I leaned my rifle against a tree to get a steady shot. The Indian stumbled and went down. The bear was so close and going so fast, he went past him lying on the ground. He whirled around and reared up to locate his prey. It was then I saw an arrow shaft sticking out of his neck. He flicked his paw a time or two trying to brush the shaft away. His back was turned to me and I touched off a shot at his heart. At such close range I wanted a solid hit because I might not have time to reload and shoot again before he got to me.

The sound of bullet hitting flesh was the only indication that I made a hit! He dropped to all fours and took a step or two to the right, sniffing the air for his enemy. Kramer rushed in barking and nipping at the bear's rump, distracting him while I reloaded. He must have caught my scent because he reared up and turned to locate me. He swatted at the arrow shaft again and then at the bullet wound. I was shaking bad, but I got enough control of my breathing to aim and shoot again. Only then did he show any signs of being hit. He slumped, then slowly collapsed right on top of the Indian.

Reloading took a little longer as I was constantly looking up to check on the beast. My hands were shaking so badly I spilled power and had to get more out of the pouch. That caused me to put too much in the barrel. Kramer stood stiff legged and growling a few feet away from the beast. When the gun was ready, I took a deep breath and circled the animal with the barrel pointed at its head. I went around twice to get my wind back and to calm down. I was shaking so bad that if he tried to come after me I would have to press the muzzle of the rifle against his side to keep from missing.

The bear's body had the young buck pinned to the ground. From his groaning I realized the weight of the bear was painful. Holding the rifle with one hand I pressed the muzzle to the bear's chest. I reached out with my free hand and grabbed a bloody arm to pull the Indian away. The bear made a noise and moved so I pulled the trigger. That's when I found out I had definitely put in too much powder. The recoil tore the gun from my grasp, flipping it over my head into the brush behind me. I ran over to the gun and picked it up then ran back, grabbed the Indian around the waist and ran for the trees. I checked over my shoulder several times to see if the bear was following us. I dropped the Indian and reloaded with my last supply of powder. After a moment's rest, I moved downwind before cautiously approaching to make sure the bear was dead. He had flopped over dead with that last blast.

I carried the Indian to a spot near the stream where we could make camp. I washed off the blood to expose horrible looking slashes on his back and deep cuts on his chest. There were other cuts and scratches on his face and hands. While cleaning him up, I guessed he was a young Ute Indian, probably just about to become a warrior. It was lucky he had managed to outrun the bear until I could shoot. When I think about it, if a bear like that was chasing me I would have been able to run a little faster, too.

After I cleaned him up I made camp and laid in firewood. When I skinned out the bear I found that in my haste to shoot the first time I forgot he was standing with his back to me. I had shot him on the wrong side, missing his heart completely. I fed us from the bear meat and I picked chokecherries and blueberries growing along the stream to give us a little variety.

The Indian spent a week fighting infection and fever with me working on him day and night. Several times he became delirious and had screaming nightmares. He would yell out, "seve nakohe - seve nakohe." I held him down to keep him from flopping around and getting hurt. After several minutes he would pass out and lay quietly.

It took a week to stop the nightmares and another week before the fever was completely gone. Several times I tried to talk with my warrior friend but my sign language was limited. When the warrior was well enough to travel I presented the pelt, claws and fangs to him. He was obviously surprised that I would give up such a prize. He took out a small beaded spirit bag and put one of the claws and a fang in it. He made some sort of speech while pointing at me and the sky and the bear's hide. All of a sudden he began to dance around me, chanting and singing, before presenting the bag to me. Abruptly he gathered his things and walked away, not looking back. I attached the small bag to a thong and wore it around my neck for a few years. Later I attached the bag to my hat.

When Kramer and I got back to Montana City, I was surprised to see that Dwight was still at the same location. He was out of whiskey and had sold two of the wagons. He was preparing to head back east for more merchandise to bring to Colorado. He wanted me to make the trip with him but I declined.

Winter 1858-59

I needed to find a place to stay before Dwight pulled out, so I inquired around town about any shelter available. It wasn't long before I located a man who was pulling out. Two beers was all it took to get possession of his small drafty lean-to that had no stove. I used scrap wood to make needed repairs and chinked the walls with mud but it didn't help much. We didn't sleep cold that winter. We laid awake cold. I was a long way from the warmth and love of my home in Ohio. There, I always had plenty of good food, warm blankets, and family to help with the chores.

During the winter of '58-'59 there was a flow of excited argonauts heading to the new El Dorado, using guide books that told of the fabulous riches in Colorado. At the same time, a tide of dangerously mad prospectors with broken spirits and smashed dreams was heading away from Cherry Creek, cussing the authors of those same guidebooks. A man came in the saloon one day and announced he was giving up and returning home. He was with the Lawrence, Kansas party that came into the area that summer to prospect. Like many others, he was broke and had been selling his equipment just to get out of camp. Some men were forced to sell equipment for ten cents on the dollar and when they couldn't sell the items, they would abandon them.

The man could not take his partner with him and he did not want to abandon her. He was looking for someone who would take good care of her. She was a burro with large brown eyes that I named Sarah, my mother's name. Though skinny from a lack of feed, she seemed to be in good health. Matching her brown eyes were several brown patches on her back and feet. I attached a small corral and shelter against the lean-to and spent some of my hard-earned gold for hay and oats. One stretch of cold weather forced Sarah inside with us and that's a week we won't soon forget. I think Sarah was offended by our smell and the cramped space.

I got work at the Bear's Claw Saloon, hauling the whiskey in and empty barrels out. When the owner John Reed learned I knew how to make whiskey he set me to making some. John said there was only four gallons of pure grain alcohol left and it would have to last until the next shipment arrived, which was unpredictable.

My recipe for Brave Maker calls for three gallons of alcohol mixed with six gallons of water. It had the reputation of making a rabbit chase a bear. At the Bear's Claw, I had to ration the alcohol and substitute other ingredients but it was still a tolerable whisky. I started with a six-gallon bucket of spring water and added three twists of tobacco, a bar of soap, and a pound of pepper. The tobacco makes them sick, the soap puts a head on it, and the pepper gives the taste a whiz as it goes down. It is important to use fresh, clean, spring water because water from the diggings tends to give the whisky a bad taste.

I put the bucket over hot coals and tossed in fresh cut sagebrush. I let that simmer until it was the right shade of brown and had a distinct flavor. After cooling, I strained it through a flour sack into a ten-gallon barrel and poured in two gallons of alcohol. I tried to let it age overnight, but when the boys learned that there was a fresh batch of Brave Maker they stood around like thirsty pups until I agreed to set them up. As a rule, if it smelled like gangrene and a deep swig was like flaming kerosene, then it was a fair whiskey. Some claimed a large jolt could stop a watch. Nevada Jones swore that my whiskey cracked his glass eye when he threw a shot down too fast. Whiskey from other saloons got so bad, some of the men accused the bartenders of holding a bottle under a horse and then spitting tobacco juice in for color. Some of those accusations could not have been denied.

When we ran low on raw alcohol I added strychnine. When the strychnine ran out, I got five rattler heads and nailed them inside the barrel before adding the other ingredients. I nailed the heads between the eyes, being careful not to break the venom sac behind the head. That way the venom slowly seeped out through the fangs into the mixture. Aging makes a difference. Sometimes that last gallon had a real buzz to it. In the gold camps it's not murder to sell whiskey to a man if he lives long enough to get out the door. Almost every day men had to be helped out the door to their tents.

My first Christmas in Colorado Territory became a time when I learned to face my misfortunes and make the best of it. In November of '58 Montana City went dry because we ran out of alcohol. The general store was low on supplies and prices were high. I was low on beans and plumb out of bacon and tobacco. I had a few ounces of gold and had lost my job. On many a cold and hungry night, Kramer and I growled ourselves to sleep.

With the prospects of a bleak Christmas and hardly any gold left, I was afraid I might not be alive come spring. I was feeling sorry for myself for getting caught up in the Pikes Peak rush. Most of the men in camp were in the same fix. Tempers got so high it was dangerous to make a sudden move or cough. One man had bullets flying through his tent when his snoring got too loud.

Two days before Christmas a wonderful thing happened. Word came from Auraria that a trader by the name of Wooton had pulled in with wagons full of supplies, food and whiskey. He also had barrels of Taos Lightning and the first drink was on the house. Now I had heard of the mysterious fire water and its reputation that no man lived long enough to become addicted. So naturally, I was in the first group going to Auraria for a taste of Lightning.

Along with our supplies, the men in our group decided to buy a five-gallon barrel of Taos Lightning and a keg of raw alcohol. They gave me the alcohol to make up a special Christmas drink. On the way back to camp, the men and I picked berries. They were long past ripe but I figured they would still give some flavor to the mixture. I mixed the crushed berries in with water and the alcohol.

The men banded together to cook game meat, sage hens, and trout while others prepared applesauce, bread, and pinon nuts. When all was ready, we gathered together for a feast. The men were delighted with my drink and named it Newt's Nectar. After eating we sat around the fire and sang songs and told Christmas stories. The singing, eating and storytelling helped us forget our troubles for a while. Later, the men tapped the keg of Taos and the celebrating continued. Those who stayed away from the awful stuff reported on the exploits of those who had too much.

After the celebrating died down, I had to face my problems. I was in a desperate situation and had to come up with a solution soon. My last few ounces of gold would not be enough to get me through the winter. If I was going to survive, I was going to have to use my talents and take a big gamble.

I went back to Wooton's cabin and spent all my gold on a keg of alcohol and the ingredients to make Red Death Whiskey. I returned to camp and began looking for my five-gallon barrel. Finding the barrel was easy. The hard part was getting the drunken miner to part with it. The fragrance from the barrel was better than the smell in his tent so he was reluctant to part with it until I explained what I was going to do. With the promise of two free drinks, the barrel was mine.

I heated water in a kettle, then poured in a jug of molasses followed with a twist of tobacco. While that was simmering I set to work crushing red peppers and added them to the syrup mix. It would have been better if I'd had more tobacco and peppers but it was all I could buy at the time. I poured the mixture into the barrel with the alcohol and more water. By New Year's Day I'd sold every drop for twenty-five cents a shot, bringing in a profit of over two hundred dollars. Two hundred dollars wasn't a lot but it kept me in bacon, beans and tobacco for the rest of the winter. Sometimes I had beans and bacon minus the bacon and sometimes I had bacon and beans minus the beans, but I managed.

Spring 1859

By March of '59 the whole town was talking about the Gregory strike on North Clear Creek and the Jackson strike on Chicago Creek. A third strike up along Boulder Creek was so good they called it Gold Hill. Those strikes had been made by experienced miners and prospectors, which meant I had a lot to learn about finding gold. The Clear Creek bonanza attracted over two thousand frenzied miners to the area that spring and summer.

Luck was all that mattered. A man could prospect for a month with no leads and the next man could hit a rich outcrop in an hour. The lucky ones got three to fifteen dollars a day out of their sluices. The luckiest were getting fifty to a hundred dollars a day for their work. The unlucky ones and those arriving late to the diggings got work for a dollar a day.

The gold I had from selling the whiskey bought a small grubstake and we headed west into the mountains. When Kramer, Sarah and I got to the Gregory Diggings, I stayed for a few days to check prospects there. The hard work for a dollar a day was not to my liking. We could have spent the summer with thousands of men crowded into the richest few square miles along Clear Creek. But I did not like the prospects of living and working in those conditions. I headed west into higher country, glad to be in the open air, away from the crowded claims. I headed Sarah higher, to the headwaters of the small streams and creeks feeding into Clear Creek. We were not alone in the area but it was not crowded either.

I found small pockets of color and an occasional nugget that would give me renewed hope only to have it play out and leave me discouraged again. I do not know how I could work so hard, for so little. I walked hundreds of miles, had heatstroke during the day and froze at night. I was kicked by my partner, chased by a bear, and dug rock until my hands bled. I fought mosquitoes, dysentery, and loneliness. What makes men do this is beyond my reasoning. People call it gold fever. If that's gold fever, the only cure for me was a shot of whiskey or a shot of lead.

Sarah and Kramer fared better than I. Sarah always seemed to find grass and Kramer fed himself very well on rabbits and squirrels. More that once, I made him share his catch with me. Sometimes the small piece of meat was hardly worth all the growling and biting. By August, I was down to a small chunk of bacon, a handful of beans, and a little flour. When I ran low on tobacco I mixed in Red Willow Bark, making for a vile, stinking smoke that would drive off skunks and bears. Worse yet, I had been out of whiskey for a month.

With supplies near gone, I started down the mountains to spend the winter in Denver. When I got to the gulches that had been crowded in the spring I saw devastation and desolation. The claims had been stripped of surface deposits and abandoned for easier work elsewhere. Charred remains gave evidence of a brush and tree fire that had raged up gulches and beyond. Water was so low, it was restricting the use of sluices and Long Toms.

I stopped at one operating sluice box and talked with the owner. He pointed out several abandoned claims I could work. One in particular he recommended, because the two men who had been on that claim were lazy and careless in working the ore. He gave me directions to a camp where I could file my claim and get supplies. If I was not going to stay, he said there were small groups of men heading for Denver. Some men were so broke and discouraged they were heading back to the states.

On my way to file the claim I stopped for rest and a smoke to kill my hunger pangs. Sarah was quietly grazing and Kramer was looking for food, knowing I didn't have anything worth begging for. I could hear a man walking along my back trail, talking to himself for entertainment. When he got to me I invited him to sit and rest, explaining that I had no food to share. He dropped his bag, sat cross-legged for a minute and then, without a word, leaned back against a tree and went to sleep. He seemed too young to be on his own, but that must have been the case. I guessed him to be thirteen or fourteen.

I finished my smoke, then went over to Sarah to look in the grub bag for any leftover items. All I could find was a small plug of tobacco I had not finished. When I glanced over, the stranger was watching me. I walked over and offered the plug to him. He grabbed it and popped it into his mouth with relish. For several minutes he worked to get the tobacco juices going and then swallowed a few times. I introduced myself and learned his name was Billie Cody. He said he was returning from Wyoming Territory. When he got to Fort Laramie several men in his party had decided to check out the Pikes Peak gold strike and he came along with them. They had arrived at the Gregory diggings with hundreds of other hopefuls, finding only hard work and low wages. I told him I was going to stay for a while and he was welcome to share a claim with me. He said he was not going to throw one more shovel of dirt or clean out one more Long Tom. Instead he was headed back to his family in Kansas.

Kramer trotted up to us with telltale blood on his hair. We quickly threw Billy's bag on Sarah and followed Kramer to the source of the blood. A recently killed deer lay surrounded by three coyotes who were not happy with the idea of sharing. It was evident that they were not starving because they gave up the carcass with only growls and whines. Kramer dove in and I had to shove him off the front quarter, which had the most meat left in one piece. By the time I had the meat cut and trimmed, Billie had a small fire going and the skillet out. I cut off a chunk of tallow and threw it in the pan. When it was hot and smoking, I dropped the steaks in. Afterwards he said that was the first real food he had got his mouth around for almost a week.

The next morning we finished off the meat before going on. By the time we reached the fork in the trail I had decided to stay. The left fork would take Billie to Denver and the right fork led to the camp where I could register my claim. We said our goodbyes and parted.

The camp may have had a name but it was not evident when I walked up the one and only street. I purchased a few meager supplies and asked to file the claim. There were a few snickers and then outright laughter from some of the locals, when they heard where I was making the claim. One of the men asked me where I had been prospecting. When I told him, he allowed that I had fared better than many of the men who had worked in the gulches. Also, I had avoided the spring floods, mountain fever, and a fire that had killed over twenty men. I introduced myself and learned I was talking to a miner by the name of Horace Tabor. He was getting a small amount of gold from his claim but not enough to feed a family. His wife Augusta was doing better by feeding and boarding miners. He invited me over for a meal and a slice of the dried apple pies she was famous for.

Having done my own cooking for so long, I was not prepared for the delicious feast that Augusta Tabor set before me. By the time I paid for the meal and two helpings of the famous apple pie it was dark. I rented a bed and stayed for breakfast and two more helpings of that pie.

Back at the diggings, refreshed and fortified, I took a day to put up a lean-to over the opening of a dugout cave so we could have some kind of shelter. Kramer was not interested in gophering it with me. He'd sleep under the lean-to but refused to crawl into the cave. Many a cold night he growled himself to sleep. I repaired a Long Tom and used it to work the dirt and gravel looking for missed pockets of gold. The Long Tom is larger than a rocker. It allows a man to wash the dirt thoroughly to get more of the gold out. It still takes a lot of shoveling and standing in cold water. In two weeks I was doing well enough to go back to Tabors for more of Augusta's apple pie. Horace told me they were planning to stay the winter and continue their operation in the spring. I was unsure if I wanted to stay the winter. It depended on how easy it would be to get supplies.

During the next three weeks the snows came more frequently and heavier. When I got my poke out and figured my assets, I decided I would have to spend my winter in Denver City and get work there. I packed up and headed over to Tabors for one last pie. When I got there the cabin was empty which surprised me because I thought they had planned to stay for the winter. When I inquired at the store about them, one of the miners said they had pulled out sudden like and he thought they were going to winter in Denver City.

Fall and Winter - 1859

I got to Denver with enough dust and nuggets to get a place to live and have a grub-stake for the next season but I would have to work for food for the three of us. The town was growing faster than a man could think, and yet there were hundreds of men busted and discouraged who had pulled out for other strikes. It was going to be tough for us too if I didn't get enough work to get us through the winter. I set out to find whatever work was available. I found a general store, and I stepped in to inquire about working there. I asked for the owner and was told to see Alex McCall. At first I could not believe my ears but it was him sure enough. After a noisy greeting he led me to the back room and introduced me to Molly.

I told them I was going to stay for the winter and needed to find a place to settle. Alex offered the storage room in the back until I found something. I was grateful for their hospitality. I tied Sarah out back and made a space near the back door for my equipment. I intended to cook there and sleep inside. I wanted to ask about Martha, but I was not ready to hear the expected answer. I was hoping Alex would offer the information first.

Molly invited me to supper that night and I accepted. Leaving Kramer to guard my stuff, I went over to the barbershop to clean up a bit. When I got back I mentioned to Alex I would need a new set of pants and a shirt. He suggested I go next door and get whatever I needed and he would carry me until I got work. He had opened a clothing store next door to his general merchandise store. I found some pants I could afford but was having trouble finding a shirt to suit me. The clerk suggested I go up to the mezzanine to see other selections and get help from the lady up there.

As I turned for the stairs I looked up, and then stopped walking because my mind stopped working. For a few moments all I could do was stand and stare at the angel looking down at me. I'm sure she must have almost laughed out loud at the strange, backward man with a struck dumb look on his face. Somehow I made it up the stairs. Her smile and charm would have melted gold right out of the ground. She melted my heart for the second time and it had never even been singed by anyone else. I asked If she remembered me and of course she did, mentioning the runaway horses.

She told me that Alex and Molly had gotten married in December in Omaha. They had decided to come to Denver and open a general store. Later if the area was still growing they would open a branch of the Walters' Wholesale Company. Still in a state of shock I went over to the store to see if Alex needed any help. He admitted that he deliberately forgot to tell me that Martha was next door. I offered to do the cleaning around the store to pay for my rent. I told Alex I would continue to do the cleaning as long as I got to see Martha.

That evening in their living quarters over the store I had supper with Alex, Molly, and Martha. Alex told Martha that it was the letter from me that set everything in motion for them to marry and come west. Mr. Walters was looking for a new location in the West and my letter came as the tales of the bonanza in Colorado Territory reach the states. Alex said, with a wink, that Molly's mother was not happy about them going to Denver.

Whenever I looked at Martha it was plain to them that she had put a brand on my heart. A pin on her blouse caught my attention and I asked about it. Martha explained that a jewelry maker approached their father about doing special work for him. Mr. Walters invited the man to stay in the cottage behind their home for several months while he made three cameos.

The jeweler carved the likeness of Martha, Molly, and Mrs. Walters in ivory. Then he attached the carvings of Martha and Mrs. Walters to black onyx. On Molly's pin he used a deep blue stone to match her eyes. Martha took her pin off and turned it over explaining that each one had a different inscription in French on the back. Hers was "Lune," the word for moon, because the artist thought her pale skin and quiet personality reminded him of the moon. Molly got her pin out and showed it to me. Her inscription was "Terre" for earth because he thought she was mothering and faithful. She explained that their mother's pin was inscribed with the word "Pierre" for gem.

I had a lot to tell about my trip and the adventures of prospecting. Mostly I talked about the hard work and how discouraging it was to hear others had made big strikes that summer. I had worked just as hard and had barely made wages. In spite of that, it still beat farming and coal mining.

The next day I located my former boss John Reed and asked about work. He said he could use me at his new saloon called Reed's Emporium. It was a saloon and gambling hall with two ladies on the second floor as the main attraction. I was back to making whiskey again, only now with better ingredients. I found the post office and got several letters from home, each begging me to return. They made it harder to stay and stick it out since things weren't going so well.

It took several days of looking before I found a shack to live in. I packed up and moved out of the store that day. I could not afford to rent the cabin by myself but it was easy to find someone to share the expenses. I met a prospector who was as broke as I was.

Sharing the shack suited us both. The shack had no furniture, but it did have a stove. I knew him only as Ned and he never admitted his last name. We built a corral for our animals that wasn't much bigger than the shack. Ned was a small man, but tougher than a cornered wildcat. He slept on the short side and I stretched out with Kramer on the long wall in front of the stove. Ned had been in California and knew about prospecting and placer mining. It was a good partnership. I learned prospecting and mining from him, and he got whiskey from me.

It wasn't long until I heard of a restaurant that was famous for dried apple pies. I found the place and sure enough there was Augusta. She and Horace were living over the store across the street on the money she was making off her pies. After two pieces of pie I walked over to their room to visit Horace and ask about his decision to come to Denver. He said a miner had stopped by for a meal and was telling them that each year avalanches came down on the land where their cabin was and buried everything under thirty feet of snow. Horace packed up Augusta and infant son Maxy and came to Denver for safety.

Alex was anxious for his shipment to arrive from Omaha. There were reports of Indian attacks on the trains coming from Fort Laramie and he was worried about the men's safety. I was not so excited for the train to arrive because Martha would be returning to Omaha with them. I got to see Martha for two weeks before the last shipment arrived.

When the train arrived I was pleased to see that Ben Morrison was the wagon master. He and I and Martha spent an evening catching up on the news. He told about getting the O'Brien outfit to California and later signing on with the Quinn Freighting Company. When the Quinn outfit pulled into San Francisco, after covering almost two thousand miles of trail, they were down to seven wagons, one cook wagon, fourteen men, fifty-three horses and fourteen dogs. I said the increase in dogs was not a mystery. It was because the dogs got by on the cooking better than the men did.

Charlie discovered there was more money to be made hauling supplies and equipment to the mines and decided to stay. Then Sam and Charlie settled down and got married, to each other. That's when they learned that Charlie was really a woman by the name of Charlene Marie Shaw. None of the men had ever suspected that Charlie was a woman, only Sam knew. Charlene knew that the men did not like taking orders from a woman so she had dressed and talked like a man.

Martha quietly spoke up that Charlene was a cousin on her mother's side. When she wanted to buy a freight company it was Martha's father who put up the money. The family had a fit, but she was better at running a business than most men. We sat stunned for a moment before Martha began to laugh. She said that women in her family seemed to have a knack for running businesses.

When Ben and I were alone I asked him about Martha and Conrad Bates. He was not encouraging. While she had ample opportunity, she had passed up marriage and family for helping her father to run his large and growing business. She was definitely a social and businessperson and not a homemaker like Molly. Martha preferred living in the larger cities like Omaha and St. Louis.

I did not know what the future would bring but I was forced to overcome my shyness around her and speak up. I hardly fit in with her group of friends. All I could hope for was that she would agree to come west next year. The evening before she was to leave I brought up the subject of our future together. Of course she wasn't surprised. My feelings for her weren't a surprise to anyone. She admitted she liked me, and hoped to return next summer.

The next day we loaded her belongings and said goodbye. The wagons were not out of sight before I began to miss her. It was a long and lonely winter. I wrote a few times and she wrote twice. I asked Molly put in a word to Martha for me when she wrote. I knew it would take a lot of luck for me to win her over.

"Gentlemen the dining car is open. The chef has prepared oysters for this evening. I suggest you go soon, so you don't miss out."

"Thank you porter."

The men got up, stretched and walked through the cars to the dining car. James sat next to Luis with Wilbur across from them. Luis smiled to himself when he realized they were posting themselves to watch for the young ladies if they should enter the car. The menu featured oysters, trout, potatoes, gravy and vegetables.

After giving their orders to the waiter, Luis thought of a story, "Having oysters reminds me of the time I saw a woman admiring a necklace warn by a large Indian scout. She said 'I suppose that bear's tooth necklace holds the same meaning for you as a pearl necklace does for me.' 'Not quite' he answered, 'Anyone can open an oyster." After an excellent meal, Luis suggest a drink in the smoking car where they could read a while before retiring.

With a drink in hand, Wilbur took over the reading.

Spring - 1860

While Ned and I were passing a whiskey bottle back and forth during the long winter nights, we made plans for the next season of prospecting. Ned was headed northwest toward Boulder Creek. Speculation that South Park had good prospects got to buzzing around Denver during the winter so I was going to check it out. We shook hands and wished each other good luck and went our separate ways. I stopped to get supplies from Alex and let him know where I was going.

As Sarah, Kramer and I wandered over Kenosha Pass into South Park I was very optimistic about my chances for hitting it big. I was sure I would find enough gold to make it worth all the pain and suffering. I began working the higher springs and small streams using the methods Ned taught me. The third stream I worked gave up several nuggets, so I worked each gravel bar and sand bank up the stream to its headwaters doing well all the way. After that I moved over to the next creek and repeated the sequence. Around the middle of July I found a formation that was similar to one Ned described, so I set up camp and went to work. After several days of busting rock I had not found any sign of gold and was getting mighty disgusted.

In the heat of the afternoon as I headed back to camp I had to cross a steep section covered with shale. At one point the rocks began sliding under me. Everything would have been okay except for sliding over a rattler. The two of us were tumbling on the rocks and at the same time trying to avoid each other. From the sting in my leg I knew he had made a hit. When we quit rolling I could see that one fang had sunk into my leg. The bad part was, his other fang was lodged in my boot.

So there we were, attached to each other, the snake putting poison in my leg and me trying to shake him off. He was not any happier about our situation than I was. He was wrapping and unwrapping around my leg and all the while making that fierce noise with his rattles. The more I shook my leg the more he buzzed. We needed to part company and soon, so I grabbed him behind the head and yanked. Nothing happened. In a panic I yanked again, and again, until at last he came free.

I turned my attention to the pain in my leg as it was beginning to throb. I had to remain calm and stop the flow of poison, otherwise I would die, for sure. I put a chaw of tobacco in my cheek, then cut the pants leg to get at the wound. It was already swelling and turning an ugly reddish black. The pain was getting worse and I knew I had to be quick to cut a mark over the bite and let blood and poison drain out. I was thankful only one fang had gone through the skin because I was not sure I could deal with two swelling wounds.

I was getting weaker by the minute. I placed the tobacco on the cut and bound it tight with my bandanna. I was sweating and shaking so bad I could hardly tie the knot. It was touch and go as I limped and crawled to camp, passing out a couple of times getting there. I removed the wrap, washed the area and poured whiskey on the wound like Dad had taught me. I remembered his caution to pour it in the wound and not in my mouth. I put fresh tobacco on the bite and re-wrapped the area, tight.

Thank God, I had enough tobacco and whiskey to treat the wound. When I took my boot off the other fang fell out. I had yanked the snake so hard the fang tore out of its head and stayed inside my boot. I kept it and later attached it to my hatband as a reminder of my good luck to be alive.

Summer - 1860

By July I was working again, but I was still too weak to work a full day. I was so gaunt that wolves would have passed me up as not worth the trouble. One evening while I was waiting for the beans to heat up, three men came into camp. They were telling about the several hundred prospectors who had come into South Park as word got out about the rich strikes in the area. They knew of a strike along Tarryall Creek and were headed there. I asked if I might join them and they were agreeable.

They were reluctant to give more than first names. Felix, the leader, was a huge burly man with a nose big enough for Kramer to chase gophers in. His voice would drive a wolf to suicide. He told me that the silent partner was called Abe. He was full-grown but his mind was that of a ten-year-old. Maybe he wasn't strong on brains but he sure wasn't short on strength and guts. The third partner used the name Buck. He had long black hair that framed his face. I suspect folks on one side of his family had worn moccasins. He wasn't much of a cook but was better than the others. He could make a chili so hot we didn't dare spill it on the ground or we'd start a fire. After hearing my tale of the rattlesnake bite the men nicknamed me Rattles.

We followed the stream down to more rolling country. It joined a larger creek that we decided must be Tarryall Creek so we followed it, prospecting as we went. We found some promising deposits in one area. We drew up an agreement, plotted a map and went on. Two days later we were on Broadway Street in the town of Tarryall. Miners were lying about resting, washing up, and repairing tools. There were over a hundred cabins and tents, neatly laid out with streets marked off. The business district boasted saloons, shops and a branch of a mercantile store from Denver. Most unusual, all the businesses were closed. I stopped a miner and asked about the closings.

He said that it was Sunday and everything was closed and the men didn't work their claims either. We were taken aback until he explained that many of the men had claims that were producing up to a pound of gold a day. Working on Sunday was not necessary. Needless to say every foot of that creek was claimed for miles. Our group voted to file on the claims we marked, get supplies and go back and start digging.

Once at our claims we set up shelters and began working the dirt and sand. We worked every day because we were not getting a pound of gold a day like those downstream. We were getting better than wages from the claims but not enough to impress the citizens of Tarryall. My partners began to talk over their plans for the winter. After a heated and almost violent discussion, they voted to return to Denver. I did not have enough gold for both a comfortable winter and a good grubstake next year. My plans were to stay and work my claim for as long as weather permitted. After wintering in Tarryall, I would get an early start come spring. When the men packed up and abandoned their claims I sent a note with them to Alex about my plans for the winter.

My claim was producing good color and nuggets. Storms came through, making it uncomfortable for a day or two followed by a week of good weather. I was in a race to put enough gold in my poke to last the winter and I worked like a man possessed by the Devil. One storm dumped a heavy wet snow that quickly melted and caused some minor flooding. I checked the other claims and found one nice deposit exposed by the runoff. After that I checked the claims after each storm with good results. By November the snowstorms came more frequently and the snow stayed longer until I was unable to work the claim for a week. With supplies near gone, it was time to pack up Sarah and seek winter shelter.

Winter 1860-61

Tarryall's population had dropped, but there were enough miners staying for the winter to keep the businesses going. I rented a cabin, which was a little more expensive but the tents were too small for Sarah to stay in. The cabin was crowded with the three of us but we managed, even when it got real cold. It soon became a habit for me to spend the evenings at the Pine Tree Saloon, drinking and listening to the men tell stories and telling a few of my own. Story telling in a saloon in the winter means the truth gets thrown out in the cold to freeze and shatter to bits.

One evening, the bartender decided it was his turn to contribute to the evening's entertainment along with pouring liquor. He told us about Hank Thompson, who had carried out one of the greatest drinking binges in Colorado Territory.

Hank worked a scheme of roaring into a town, shouting that Indians had raided a camp some distance away. Naturally he was plied with free whiskey while he told the bloody tale. Then he would ride off to the next town for more free drinks. He was drunk for more than two weeks before making the mistake of riding into a town for the second time. He was cold sober by the time they got to the feathers.

One of the men doubted the truthfulness of that tale, as did others. The bartender pointed to a man slumped in the corner and said, "Ask Hank yourself."

A newcomer to Tarryall, Frank Butler, rented a cabin next to mine. He hung out a hand-lettered sign that read "Bank." The first day, a man came in and gave Frank one hundred dollars. The next day he got two hundred fifty dollars. Frank told me he was so encouraged by his banking business he was going to put in fifty dollars of his own money.

On Sundays I would read my Bible and write letters. Occasionally a bunch of us would take over one of the saloons for a service. We would sing a few hymns and say a few prayers.

One night Red Dane had taken on more than normal, but had been allowed to stumble home on his own. The next morning we were blasted awake with several gunshots from the edge of town. We rushed to the scene. Red Dane was standing outside the body tent babbling and pointing a smoking gun at the tent opening. During the winter we had a few men die for one reason or another. The disposal of the bodies became a problem after the ground froze. The men voted to put them in one of the abandoned tents at the edge of town, until the spring thaw. That was the tent where we found Red Dane. We took him back to the Pine Tree to calm his nerves and to get it all sorted out.

One of the bodies was that of a man known as McFarland who had been hanged for robbing sluice boxes. McFarland was left hanging overnight and froze that way. The next day two men took the body down and carried it to the body tent. They propped McFarland against the back wall. Red Dane had stumbled into the body tent and passed out on the ground in front of McFarland. When he awoke the next day he saw McFarland standing over him and other men lying around the tent. Thinking they were claim jumpers and that he was about to be killed, Red Dane shot his way out of the tent. After that he wouldn't leave the saloon with out someone escorting him to his tent.

Spring 1861

Prices went up during the winter and when freight stopped altogether they went higher. By March I was dipping into my grubstake gold to feed us. I was concerned that I did not have enough gold to keep up with the price of flour, beans, and bacon. One day, things got real bad for me. I was cold, lonely, and had a bad case of the shakes so I swapped Sarah for a jug of whiskey. The next week I was real sorry I had done that and I was wishing that I had her back, because I was thirsty again. All in all it was a very quiet winter, which was what I needed because I was still mending from that snakebite.

The first supply wagon to make it to Tarryall that spring brought in much needed supplies and the mail. There were two boxes from Alex. It really lifted my spirits to get supplies and tools for the season.

The train also brought disturbing news of the split between north and south and the start of the Civil War. We were far away in terms of miles and further away in attitude. In Tarryall there were men on both sides whose loyalties could start the war out in the territories if we let them. A camp meeting was called to discuss how we would handle the problem. After much discussion and argument the proposal was made that those who started fighting over the War would be taken out and hanged. That was voted down by two votes. The next proposal was to give the fighters four hours to get out of town and never return. That one passed.

As the days got warmer the bodies began to thaw but the ground was still frozen. We decided to bury the accumulated bodies in an abandoned claim and cover them with what loose dirt there was. While we finished the job one of the men shouted a prayer, "Oh God, if there is a God, have mercy on their souls, if any has a soul."

I got Sarah back and left Tarryall. Even with the supplies from Alex, I was starting out with a desperation grubstake. If I didn't hit gold, I was going to be in desperation. I prospected up Tarryall Creek looking for deposits that had been exposed by the winter melt off. I worked the old claims from the previous season for two weeks but they played out. I worked north to the headwaters of Tarryall Creek, then angled west in a big circle, prospecting the drainages along the way. The further we went, the higher and more rugged it got.

Summer - 1861

One night I had a dream. I was camped in the middle of nowhere with no prospects of making a strike and my grubstake was running out. I was wandering in the mountains, breaking rocks and starving. When I woke up I was not so sure it was a dream because that was exactly what I was doing every day. The next day I didn't leave camp. The whole day I lay around feeling sorry for myself and wishing I was with Martha. I got so depressed and lonesome that I was thinking of ending it all. By evening I had come to the decision to return to Denver and hope Alex would have work for me. Rumors of a new camp called Fairplay had found their way to Tarryall during the winter. I decided to go there for the supplies I'd need to get to Denver. I put in a few more weeks prospecting my way to Fairplay, finding only a small amount of gold.

When I reached Fairplay there was news about a big strike on the other side of the mountains to the west. The story was that a group of men went over Mosquito Pass and began working the creeks at the headwaters of the Arkansas River. They made a big strike in an area they called California Gulch. A camp named Oro City had developed and was growing. One of the prospectors telling me the story said that two saloons and a general store were in operation. He remarked that a man and his wife had pulled into Oro City to file a claim and she set up a tent to room and board some of the men. The miners said she could make the best dried-apple pies they had eaten. They were so happy to have a cook in camp, a bunch of them cut timber and built a cabin for her so she could feed more of the miners. Apple pies got my attention, and I asked if their name was Tabor and he thought it was.

It would be a rough trip to Oro City but that was closer than the trip to Denver, and Denver did not have Augusta's apple pies. It was a big gamble to go to Oro City, but gambling is what it's all about when you're looking for gold. I posted letters to Alex and to Mother telling them where I was headed. With renewed hope and energy, I pointed Sarah west over the mountains to look for Oro City. I was sure a brighter day was ahead of us.

Luis pulled out his pocket watch, "That's enough for tonight boys. I'm getting too tired to listen. Even with my bed in motion I should be able to sleep tonight."

When the porter knocked quietly the next morning all three were shaved, dressed, and waiting for the dining car to open. They trooped in and took their places amid good mornings to the other early risers. The boys, now alert to see if the two young ladies were present, were disappointed to find they were not.

Shortly the two ladies entered the car and passed their table. James, with presence of mind, jumped up and made introductions.

"Luis Eaton, this is Kate Barlow and Sarah May Tobin. They have been on a trip to New York and are returning to Denver. Their fathers own the Barlow & Tobin Hardware Company in Denver."

"Nice to meet you. Yes, I know Mr. Barlow and Mr. Tobin," Luis said. "Boys, I'm going to the smoking car. You two can meet me there later. It was nice meeting you ladies. Say hello to your fathers for me."

An hour or so later James and Wilbur plopped down beside Luis. Wilbur was bursting with news.

"James has been bit by the love bug."

Luis leaned over, "Which young lady has caught your fancy?"

"Sarah May"

"Well, your Dad certainly won't object to her name. Why don't you read for a while to take your mind off her."

James opened the journal and began reading.

Fall and Winter - 1861

Oro City was a festering sore on the side of a hill stretching out along the gulch for two miles. As I looked up the main street, all I could see were men, animals, and mud. The town was made up of tents and wagons converted to businesses and sleeping quarters. There were lean-tos scattered helter-skelter along the muddy street.

Instead of taking Mosquito Pass I went over the mountains south and west of Fairplay to explore the streams feeding into the Arkansas River. When I reached the river I prospected it north to California Gulch and Oro City. I stopped at the assay office to cash in what I had panned on my way up the river. I had managed to pick up several more ounces but it was going to be a struggle to get through winter in this end-of-the-world place.

I was able to get shelter for Sarah easy enough, but Kramer and I would have to take whatever was available. Tabor's bunkhouse was full but I was able to rent a bed in a bunkhouse with fourteen other men. The proprietor threw planks down over the mud and erected a large tent. He laid out blankets to make the beds and hung a lantern in the center, though during the winter there was never any oil in the lamp. We walked down the middle and slept with boots pointed toward the center. Since there were only eight beds we slept in shifts so the beds never got cold. A wash pan was set on a box at the door for everyone's use but we had to get the water ourselves.

I got work in a saloon called O'Briens. Con O'Brien was the mean quick-tempered owner of the roughest and most dangerous saloon in the gulch. Removing his conscience would have taken only minor surgery and no painkiller. The saloon was built on one of the few level spaces, with a crude bar set up along one side and a large heating stove in the rear corner. A tent out back was called the gambling room but it was used mostly for the miners to sleep it off and frequently for bodies waiting to be claimed.

Noise, smoke, and gunfire came out of that town twenty-four hours a day. Surviving the dangers of bad whiskey, bad food, and stray bullets became a daily adventure. Any man with a load of liquor could be dangerous in a crowded bar. The best that could happen was for the liquor to knock him down and out before he got his gun into action. We considered any man to be dangerous as long as he could make a noise.

I was hired because I knew how to make whiskey and was willing to do the hard, dirty work of moving beer and whiskey to and from the storage tent. I must have looked a little worse for wear because the bartender offered to feed me before I went to work. He said I looked skinny enough to go bathing in a gun barrel. Working there had its advantages though. Kramer and I ate well from the table scraps and the beer and whiskey was free.

In November, Augusta returned from a trip back east with two wagonloads of supplies for the general store. Even at the high prices Horace charged for the goods we were glad they were available. She also brought the mail, with a letter for me from Alex and Molly. Martha had been there and gone and Alex said she was disappointed that I had not come back to Denver. He had the disturbing news that Conrad Bates was still courting her, with mother Walters pushing harder for them to get engaged.

One bitterly cold winter day at Tabor's we got to talking about what we had done the year before. I asked Horace where they had gone. Horace said that as soon as the snow was gone, they had headed back up the Clear Creek diggings to their cabin. When they got to their cabin they discovered that the miner who had warned them of avalanches had taken it over. It was his because they had abandoned it and he had a right to claim it for his own. Horace said that Augusta was so mad that she would not feed him the whole time they were there. It was harsh enough punishment that he had to eat his own cooking. When word reached Horace about the strike around Buckskin Joe they packed up and went there for a time, then moved on to Breckenridge for the winter. News of the strike at California Gulch prodded Horace to pack up his family again and move to Oro City.

A young lawyer by the name of Luis Elvit Eaton came to Oro City and was trying to get established. It was touch and go, making a living in such a rag tag camp. He spent a lot of time at O'Briens with another lawyer looking for clients. When two men would square off for a fight, each lawyer would quickly claim one of the fighters and offer legal advice. They'd collect a dollar or two from each and then let the fight take its course. With the number of fights that broke out each night they did very well. Sometimes they would collect from the same men two or three times a night.

Luis laughed, "There is one little detail he left out. Newt figured that since it was his liquor that started the fighting, he should get a cut. So for every fighter we consulted we had to pay him ten cents. He had a way of ekeing out a living when he set his mind to it. Go on reading."

One day a traveling preacher came into the saloon and asked if he could hold a service and do a little preaching. I was surprised when Con said he could have twenty minutes. We closed the bar and Con yelled for the men to listen. The preacher went at it with vigor. He had a Bible passage to back up everything he said. Surprisingly, the men listened intently and with respect. While we sang a song I noticed a few of those hard crusty men had moisture glistening in their eyes. The singing was shy on melody but strong on gusto. After the Amen, the preacher asked for donations to be dropped in a tin can. Later he explained to me that he had to give up passing the hat because many times he didn't even get his hat back.

We opened the bar and it was business as usual. Con said the preaching broke up the boredom and made the men ready to drink again. I figured the preaching put such a fear of God in them, they needed a drink bad.

We got snow in September and by October it was snowing most every day. By Christmas nothing could get in or out of town. The snow was piling up in drifts over everything. We spent the long winter days drinking, telling stories, and planning the next season's prospecting. Most of the stories were as solid as the smoke going up the stovepipes.

One morning I was walking over to Tabor's for breakfast. As I got to the door a large man came flying out with Augusta in pursuit. She was hitting him with her skillet, all the while lecturing him on the evils of drinking. He stumbled and fell into a snowdrift and she kept hitting him. He was twice her size but all he could do was cover up and beg for mercy. She relented only when he promised to clean himself up and not squander his gold on whiskey and gambling. Horace said she wasn't against drinking but wouldn't tolerate the men who drank and gambled until their gold was gone, and then came begging for a free meal.

Got a letter from Alex and Molly. They were relieved that Missouri had not voted to secede from the Union. With family and business in Nebraska and family property in Missouri it would have made for a difficult time for the Walters family. As the winter wore on we had more fighting and killing over individual feelings on the War. Some saloons were considered to be Confederate only and others showed preference for those supporting the Union. The rest of us found neutral establishments and tried to drink in peace. Everyone kept an eye out for trouble and many times the entire bar would be on the floor at the sound of someone clearing his throat.

Horace wanted to build a two-story building next to their boarding house for a general store with living quarters above. When the men were putting up the cabin the year before they had put down a boardwalk and floor for the bunkhouse tent. Early that spring he hired two men and me to put the building up over the bunkhouse tent. With every break in the weather we would add to the building's height until the first floor ceiling was on. Then we ran everyone out and took the tent down. The men moved back in, happy to be sleeping in a building and not a tent. When Augusta raised the rates there was grumbling because some of the men were running out of gold. Horace had to let some sleep on credit for a few weeks until they could get back to their claims.

As spring approached, most of the men were definitely getting the itch to get back in the mountains. Rumors of strikes circulated through Oro City every day. There was lots of activity, but no one bought drinks for the house, except on credit. Runoff made the streams and hillsides a slippery proposition and the water was too muddy to drink. The most objectionable or dangerous whiskey in Oro City was safer to drink than the water from the streams which carried mining waste and sewage.

A lot of men were completely astonished that they were still alive when summer came. Enterprising Horace mixed a batch of spring tonic, claiming it would cleanse everyone's winter poor blood. It was a mixture of sulphur and molasses and water. I suggested adding alcohol to make it a better tonic. I helped him stir up a new batch we called Tabor's Tonic for Winter-Poor Blood. We quickly sold out and had to mix up more.

Wilbur asked, "Luis, was Oro City as bad as Dad said?"

"Yes, Oro City was a mighty dangerous place. Those of us who are still alive are very lucky. Your dad had to work hard just to get by."

Summer 1862

It was late in May when I finished working for Horace. In exchange for my labor I got credit at the new Tabor General Store. First thing I charged against my credit was two bottles of Tabor's Tonic. At Augusta's raised eyebrow I explained I needed it to pay off Sarah's feed bill. The next day I picked out my supplies for the season and packed up Sarah.

As usual I headed for the mountains with two pieces of apple pie in my coat pocket. I was starting my fifth season and I had dang little to show for it. I was proof of the prospector adage that expectations tend to be a long way from reality. This I do know: when gold is found in all those thousands of miles of rock, trees, and streams it's luck and nothing more. Some men claim persistence will pay off but I knew many who spent years busting rock and died broke.

I stayed high on the east side of the Arkansas for a few weeks to check the headwaters of each drainage. It was hard checking out each promising outcrop of gravel and sand on the steep slopes. Snowdrifts on the north facing slopes fed the rivulets and small streams. It was wet and soggy every step I took. Between damp clothing and the damp air I was cold a lot. I switched over to the south side of the hills where the sun had melted the snow earlier and was drying things out. Flowers were springing up everywhere with bright yellows, blues, and reds covering the meadows with beautiful designs.

One morning I discovered Sarah had busted her tether and gone off to graze on new grass. I followed her trail for two miles, crossing over two ridges into a hidden valley. When I found her, I grabbed her bridle and started giving her a tongue-lashing. I turned to lead her back but she dug her heels in and refused to budge. She was enjoying the lush grass and was not going to leave. For the next hour I cussed, hit and kicked to get her to return to camp, but she continued to stay put. I flopped down on the stream-bank to rest and think of a way to get Sarah to move. I rested and pondered the cussedness of burros in general and Sarah in particular.

As my eyes wandered over the area I noticed a promising formation exposed by the stream. It looked different from any I had seen. All I had was my knife, so I used it to scrape the gravel into my hand and then swirled it in the water. Then I used the knife blade to stir the sand left in my palm. The third handful produced some color and a few more tries produced a small nugget. That's all it took. I grabbed Sarah, who was now willing to go, and we made a beeline to camp. By that afternoon I was back in the stream with shovel and pan.

A few days later, I was standing in the stream staring down at the gold pan. Raising my head, I shouted, "Sarah, I love you!" Sarah raised her head, showing no emotion or understanding in those soft brown eyes. Then in her usual quiet way she lowered her head to continue to graze. My eyes returned to the nuggets in the pan and I sensed that it was going to be different this time. In the pan was a nugget as big as my fingernail along with several smaller ones. A few hours of busting rock and washing the rubble confirmed that we would at least live well that winter. I built a crude rocker and set up camp. In a week I knew I had found a good strike, or rather Sarah had found it. Five years of pain and grief quickly faded away with each pan of nuggets and flake gold.

Once I was sure I was going to stay the summer, I set stakes, drew up a map and packed for a trip to Oro City to file my claim. I put Kramer on Sarah's back and we walked a mile and a half in the stream to hide our tracks before I turned north. We zigzagged for three days before I could see the smoke from Oro City. I bought a beer at the first saloon I came to and lamented the poor luck I was having that summer. The place had two or three regulars waiting for someone to come in to celebrate a strike by buying a round for the house. They were disappointed when I didn't buy a round. I went over to Tabor's store to give Horace a list of supplies I needed and walked down to the claims office. I had the gold assayed and filed for a deed to The Sarah Mine.

After loading up the supplies, I led Sarah out the way we came in. I watched my back trail for several miles before heading in the general direction of the claim and made camp. The next day I moved slowly until noon and then quickly moved over to the next drainage to make a quiet, cold camp. On the third day, when I was satisfied that no one was following, I headed for the claim.

It was a good summer for us. After a light breakfast at sunrise I would go to the stream and begin throwing dirt into the rocker I had made. It was a crude affair made from sawed slabs of wood and built on rockers at a slant so water and dirt would run down and out the bottom. The rocker was set so that a stream of water flowed out of a trough and over the dirt. The water poured down the rocker and flushed out the bottom. Dirt and light material was washed away. Rocking the contraption flushed the small rocks and pebbles out leaving pea sized gravel and dark sand. This I put in a bag for working over later. It was back breaking work but I was happy with the amount of gold I was getting.

In the morning it was frosty cold and I needed a coat. By noon the heat was so bad I had to strip to the waist. Late each day I would return to camp and fix a light supper. I spent the evening working the gravel and sand with my gold pan. I would pick out the small nuggets, then put the black sand in an iron crucible. I sat in on hot coals and then fanned them until it was hot enough to melt the flake gold out.

Winter - 1862

When the snow drove me out in late September, I headed for Oro City with enough gold to afford the high prices and not have to work that winter. I figured I had not yet found the Mother Lode and Sarah's little valley would produce much more if proper mining work was done.

At Oro City, I discovered that several cabins had been built and could be rented furnished or unfurnished. That's with or without a window. I rented one furnished. I was not going to spend another cold winter in the mountains so I went over to Tabor's and bought a small stove, several blankets and tools. I built a small shelter and corral for Sarah and some furniture for me.

While I was in the mountains, Colorado people had become involved in the Civil War. Confederate troops followed the Rio Grande up from Texas intending to capture New Mexico and Colorado for the Southern cause. That would divert the flow of gold from California and Colorado to the Confederacy. Following that success, the plan was to send troops eastward to attack General Grant from the rear. Word reached Denver that Albuquerque and Santa Fe had fallen to the Confederacy. The Colorado Militia was formed and dispatched from Denver. They met the Confederate Army at Apache Canyon in New Mexico. After a fierce battle the rebels were stopped. After that there were fewer Confederate flags openly displayed.

I received a letter from Alex and Molly. Their business was doing well and if I needed work I was welcome to stay with them for the winter. Alex was expanding the business. In a year or two he expected to have a Walter's Wholesale Company in Denver. They were also happy to report that Molly was expecting a baby in the spring. Martha had been to Denver in July and left in August due to illness. Alex reported that pressure was building for Martha to marry Bates but she was still resisting.

Summer 1863

During the winter I quietly bought equipment and supplies for the next season. Horace knew what was going on but he never asked or speculated on my acquisitions and he never tried to draw me out. From time to time, I would visit Orvil at the assay office to cash in some gold.

It was a long snowy winter. The big difference was I had gold and a warmer place to stay. I spent most of the time at Tabor's. Horace and I sat around thinking up one scheme or another to make money with little effort. I'd shovel snow for him in trade for groceries or peel apples for a piece of apple pie. Maxey, their son, called me Uncle Newt and we used to play horsey and hide and seek. Sometimes we got in Augusta 's way but she never complained.

The first mail that got through that spring brought bad news from my Uncle Frank, that my mother had died in January. She had been staying with my brother and his wife after taking sick. It was several days before I could be around people and not get all stuffed up. I was far away and time had gone by so fast that I had a hard time remembering home.

Alex wrote that he was not ready to be a father and was plumb scared for Molly. He was hoping that Martha would be there soon to help. The store was booming and the town was growing so much that he was going to add onto the store to have more goods to sell. I sent a letter telling them of my plans for the summer.

When it came time to leave that spring, I went over to Tabor's and had a good meal and two helpings of pie. Augusta knew what I was doing. As I left she handed me a small parcel with instructions to open it later. I waited until dark to pack and then quietly drifted out of town. On the second night, I opened Augusta's package and enjoyed two more pieces of her pie. I spent four days crisscrossing the area to make sure I wasn't followed, then I went to the mine.

I worked hard that summer, using a larger rocker to help separate the gold from the dirt. I had a small fire only at night so the smoke would not give my location away. Several times I heard men in the next canyon, but no one suspected there was a mining operation going on in Sarah's hidden valley. After working the surface deposits up and down on both sides of the creek, it was evident the strike was bigger than I had first thought. Soon I would need to start blasting and tunneling to extract the gold. I would have to hire men and haul in mining equipment. That would require partners and selling shares to raise the money for the operation. My knowledge of operating a mine wasn't enough to dig a prairie dog out of his hole. A better idea was to sell to a mining company and let them do it. Best of all, I would be free to go to Omaha and marry Martha.

By late July I had so much gold cached, it was starting to make me nervous. The problem was getting the gold and us to town safely. Bandits watched the trails for prospectors returning from their claims. If it looked like a prospector had made a strike and was headed for town with the gold, they would jump him. I hid some of the gold in with the gear packed on Sarah's back. I couldn't take it all so I buried the rest. Following Ned's advice I shined up my tools and gold pan so it looked like I hadn't been working too hard. I removed my clothing including my long johns and took a bath, the first I had in a year. While in the creek, I washed my long-johns and put them back on to dry. Later, I put on new trousers and shirt and packed the rest of my gear.

Like the year before, I left the Sarah Mine by walking in the stream, then going as far a possible before picketing Sarah and dropping her load. I lay down beside the load and got a little sleep. Before daylight I was up and got Sarah moving along one of the trails leading to Oro City. I walked slow and easy, singing to Sarah and Kramer, acting as if I was heading nowhere in particular.

In the afternoon I met three men watering their horses at a small stream. By their manner and their disreputable looks I knew they could be trouble. A low growl from Kramer let me know he didn't like them either. When I got closer I recognized one of the men as a fighter and troublemaker from Tarryall. Some of the men claimed he was so mean he already had a reserved seat in Hell. I walked up with a big smile and never flinched as I asked them for tobacco.

While I filled and lit my pipe they quietly inspected my outfit. I told them I was flat and asked if they could grubstake me forty dollars for the winter. I even put in an extra plea for Sarah. Satisfied that it was not worth pulling a gun out to rob me, they declined. But as they mounted up one of the men flipped me a ten-dollar gold piece saying something about feeding my partner. I shouted thank you's until they were out of sight. Then Sarah, Kramer and I had a good laugh, while we made hasty tracks the other way.

The next afternoon I was standing at the bottom of California Gulch looking at the town, noting the many new buildings and streets added since I had left that spring. The assay office had moved and I had to ask for directions. The town was so busy with men going every direction that I tied up in front of the assay office without getting so much as a second look. It took several hours for Orvil and the men to weigh and assay the dust and nuggets. Orvil said it was the best strike so far that season. I got a check for five thousand dollars plus seven hundred dollars in Denver Bank twenty-dollar gold pieces. Only then did I feel like I could celebrate my good fortune. Some men start celebrating too soon and lose everything to gamblers or get killed by claim jumpers.

August 1863

I rented a cabin with a window and a stove. I got my equipment in the cabin, bought supplies and feed. I wanted to get everything settled first because I knew Sarah and Kramer would be on their own for a few days. At Tabor's I got some new clothing and carried it over to the barbershop. A bath, shave, cigar and several whiskies later, I was dressed and heading back to Tabor's place.

I had a big meal with lots of steak, whiskey and a whole pie for myself. While I was telling Horace of my discovery and good fortune, Augusta came over. I thanked her for the two pieces of pie that were in the package that spring. Her smile lit up the room. She said she was glad I liked the present. I paid for everything and asked for more whiskey and cigars. Later, when she wasn't looking, I dropped a twenty-dollar gold piece in her apron pocket. I bought several rounds there and many more rounds at other saloons that night and for several days and nights after that.

It took a day to sober up and stop the pounding in my head. It was a struggle to remember what had happened but I was able to piece some of it together. During my celebrating, Luis asked me if I would sell the Sarah Mine. I said that it was possible if the price were good enough. After I recovered, Luis and his partner, Jedediah Taylor, spoke again of making an offer on the Sarah Mine. Then came the problem of getting the three of us out of Oro City, for an inspection of the claim. We did that by leaving town separately and meeting five miles away. Once we knew we hadn't been followed, we made good time getting to the strike.

Jedediah was a mining engineer and they spent two days poking around, inspecting the ground and taking samples. They tromped a mile in every direction, digging up samples and looking at the way the rock formations lay in the ground. I spent my time digging up the gold cached near camp. They were impressed with the amount of gold I had.

After we returned to Oro City they made an offer of five thousand cash and five thousand shares of their new company at a dollar a share. I asked for twenty thousand cash, but we settled the deal for five thousand cash and twenty thousand shares in stock, valued at a dollar a share. Stock deals like this were more in the realm of imaginative finance.

Once the word got out about my strike and how optimistic the new owners were, there was a stampede for the stock. For a few days things got a little crazy. The men were buying me drinks, trying to get an angle on the mine location and on the stock of the new company. In four days Luis and his partner sold enough stock in their mining company to recover the money they paid me and start a large operation at the Sarah Mine.

I sold four thousand of my shares at three dollars a share. Then during the stock fever, similar to gold fever but with less work, I sold a total of seven thousand shares at four dollars a share. Then I sold two thousand shares for four dollars a share and stock in two other mining companies near Oro City. Two thousand shares went for five dollars a share. I kept the other three thousand shares for sentimental reasons. It took several days of figuring and negotiating to complete the transactions. Some of the miners were so desperate to buy stock in the Sarah that they would sell shares in their claims to raise the money. One man offered me one hundred thousand dollars for my stock; the trouble was only five hundred of that was in cash and the rest was in shares of a mine in Nevada. When it was all over, The Sarah Mine brought over fifty-five thousand in sales of the stock and over ten thousand in the gold I had dug myself.

I was getting anxious to get to Denver and visit Martha. As I prepared to leave Oro City I met a horse trader with several good horses for sale. Now when you are dealing with a horse trader you don't have to wonder if he's lying. You just take that for granted. But I did get a good horse I named Misty. He was mostly black with patches of white on his neck and left side. Later that week, Misty, Sarah, Kramer, and I left for Denver.

"Gentlemen, the dining car is open."

"Thank you, Porter. We would like to stretch our legs a bit, then eat in our compartment. Would you serve us a light dinner in an hour?"

"Yes sir. I'll see to that. Thank you."

The light dinner consisted of a choice of cheddar and Swiss cheese along with a meat choice of roast beef, ham, and turkey. The breads included fresh baked rolls, sourdough and rye breads. Luis thought the choice of beer was excellent and consumed four bottles with his sandwiches. After the meal they adjourned to the smoking car. Wilbur opened the journal and began.

Denver - August 1863

Getting to Denver was not so easy. I traveled with a freight outfit hauling gold to the mint in Denver. It was slow and rough traveling but safer that going alone. I stopped at the Denver Bank to deposit my gold and stock. From the bank I headed down California Street, looking around for a familiar face or building but saw no one I knew or wanted to know. The town was busy with miners, merchants, soldiers and every other bit and piece of humanity that existed in the West. It was growing so fast that as many as a hundred wagons a day were arriving from the East. Other wagons went up into the mountains hauling supplies to the gold camps and towns, returning with gold for the Denver Bank.

With Sarah and Misty put up in a livery, I began to look for a place to stay. I had several hotels to choose from, but when I learned that the Tremont House had spring mattresses on all the beds I took a private room for Kramer and me. Then I went over to the Walter's General store. I wanted to see Alex first so I came in from the back street and waited until he came out the back door. I whistled and jumped up on the loading dock.

He was sure glad to see me. He had big news about being the father of a boy named Wilbur Frederick McCall. I also had news to share with him about the sale of the Sarah Mine. I hesitantly asked if Martha was still with them and was pleased when he said yes, she was still there and would be staying until October. The next question was on my face and he answered it with a smile. No, she was not married yet and for me to get cleaned up and come to supper that night.

I went over to the barbershop, got a bath, shave, and haircut. I put on new pants and shirt, telling the attendant to burn the old ones. All except my hat.

Once I was presentable I went back to Alex's store to see Martha and tell her the big news. She seemed pleased with my improved appearance and prosperity from selling the mine. We talked about what had happened to us over the past two years. All the while I was talking around the real topic I wanted to discuss. At one point I blurted out that I had missed seeing her and thought of her often when I was in the mountains. I asked if she would stay in Denver for the winter. Without hesitation she said she had missed me too and would think about staying. Her ready acceptance was a shock as I was sure that Conrad Bates and her mother had probably won her over. If she stayed for the winter I would get to ask the big question. It wouldn't be easy but time would be on my side.

Martha got a letter from her father telling about an accident he had in the warehouse. He was helping the men move crates around when one toppled over and broke his leg. He was in a lot of pain but the doctor said it would mend. Stewart was making sure the shipments were getting out on time.

Alex and Molly were excited about both of us being in Denver. They wanted to open the Walter's Wholesale Company in a rented building and needed Martha and me to help. Alex was sure Mr. Walters would approve of Martha staying. Marie Walters would not approve but that was okay as long as she stayed in Omaha.

One evening Martha and I were talking about the future. I was not surprised when she said that living in the West had not appealed to her. She preferred the eastern cities to the backward towns and gold camps of the West. She said the business and personal opportunities in towns like Omaha or St. Louis were more to her liking. She thought that Denver had possibilities of becoming a large city and hopped it would be a good place to live someday. She looked me right in the eye and told me that I was the most down and out character she had ever met. In spite of that she had become quite fond of me.

I told Martha that she was the first woman that I had any interest in being with and that I enjoyed her wit and intelligence. I told her I was not planning to return to the states. I liked the freedom and excitement of the growing western towns and the expected profits to be made from investing in new businesses. Now that my future was secure, I wanted to settle down in Denver or San Francisco.

Realizing that now was the time for action, I grabbed her hand and asked if she would marry me. Her hesitation was almost too long before she said yes. Only then did I take a breath. I vividly remember that time as if it was yesterday. Martha and I spent several hours talking about our lives and families. When I left by the back door I stood for a moment to enjoy the night air. All of a sudden I heard excited squeals and laughter from Molly and Martha in the room above me.

Five days later, on September 1, 1863, we had a quiet wedding conducted by a Methodist pastor. I agreed to that because I was afraid that if we waited Mrs. Walters might try to stop us. Those first weeks together were a revelation to me. I never suspected what a loving and delicate person Martha was. She appeared to be fragile and yet she was strong in her own way. I would lay awake with her at my side and thank God for putting her in my life. It was a tender and loving time and I did not know that it was going to have to last for such long a time.

Train to Fort Laramie

We had been married almost three weeks when Ben Morrison got to Denver with four wagons of goods from Walters' Wholesale. He also brought bad news. Mr. Walters' accident was worse than he had let on in his letter. He was in a lot of pain and could not walk. The doctor was worried he might lose his leg. Stewart Prosser sent a note asking Martha to return to Omaha with Ben. The Civil War had sharply cut the availability of goods and was driving up prices. Martha's keen business ability and help was needed to keep the business going.

Ben and the two brothers, Jake and Pete Samson, were very happy to hear of our marriage. Jake said that she had done a lot better marrying me than Bastard Bates. I took a peek at Martha to see if she heard the remark but her face did not show any evidence that she had.

Martha and I sat in the kitchen with Alex and Molly to discuss what should be done. Ben wanted to pull out in two days so that they would reach Omaha before severe weather caught them. If they ran into bad weather, they could get stranded somewhere. I wanted to go to Omaha with Martha to meet her parents. Martha pointed out that Alex needed my help to get the building ready for his wholesale company. She was right, of course. It would take the winter for Alex and me to be ready for the spring shipments. I reluctantly agreed to stay, but with one provision. We had been getting reports of Indian attacks on the freight wagons north of Denver. I insisted that I go with her to Fort Laramie and make sure she was safely on the way to Omaha. As we prepared for the trip, several raids were reported north and east of Denver that had resulted in deaths on both sides. I was not happy at the prospect of her traveling in such danger.

Leaving Sarah with Alex and Molly, we left for Fort Laramie in the company of two other freight outfits. Ben and his men were good company and a comfort to us. I bought a wagon for Martha and me to travel in and it suited us fine. Misty and Kramer took a liking to Martha and she liked them. Kramer would ride in the seat between us and lay his head on her lap. If she left the wagon for any reason he went with her and kept a watchful eye for her safety. Martha could ride Misty with ease. Oh how we all loved her. I kept asking myself why I was not going to Omaha too. My answers were not very convincing.

It wasn't long before we realized we were being followed by a small war party. Their presence kept us on edge and sleepless most of the way to the fort. We followed the road north until we reached Fort Collins on the Cache La Poudre River. From there we took the road going to Fort Laramie.

A small freight outfit in our group was in turmoil almost constantly. They had one or two fights every day and most every night. One evening during supper there was a bigger commotion than usual from their camp, followed by gun shots. Later a man from the outfit came around and gave us the details. After leaving Denver the men were convinced they were dying a slow death from poisoning. That evening the foreman saved their lives. He shot the cook.

We passed burned remains of wagons several times. The Indians were becoming a real danger for travelers. I was thankful we were in a large enough group to insure our safety. In spite of the dangers and the cooler weather it was a nice trip for us.

Fort Laramie

Martha's traveling to Omaha with Ben made me feel a whole lot better. It was mighty tough to watch her and the wagons pass out of sight the next morning. Several times I almost jumped on Misty and went after her.

I noticed a number of changes had been made. More soldiers. More immigrants. More Indians.

While I was in the mountains for those years, several tribes had been raiding small trains and outposts, stealing horses and guns. Many people were speculating that an uprising was bound to happen. Soldiers were being dispatched along the Oregon Trail to protect the immigrants. The Seventh Iowa Calvary had built several new buildings and the sutler had a larger store.

I camped near the fort to wait for a large outfit going to Denver. I hoped one would arrive soon as I was anxious to get back.

Traveling alone or in a small group was too dangerous. Hugh Parker, the sutler said there was time for one or two more outfits to go to Denver before the weather got bad. I was more worried about Indians. The soldiers assigned to the fort were a poor excuse for the U.S. military. They were rude to the immigrants and provided them little protection. Some of the soldiers had taken squaws and were handing out Army provisions to their relatives. If an immigrant got into an argument with an Indian, the soldiers would throw the immigrant in the stockade. Drinking, fighting, and shooting were the order of the day. The Indians were getting braver and attacking larger trains but I began to think it was less dangerous for me to face that danger than to tangle with drunken soldiers.

In the second week of October a large outfit came through on its way to Denver. By that time there were several of us waiting and we were all anxious to get started. The weather was our next worry as we watched the clouds building in the north. Three or four days after leaving the fort, the clouds got darker and began rolling in from the northwest. We pushed the animals as hard as we dared, trying to find a site that was sheltered. All we could find was a grove of trees along a dry riverbed. By nightfall the wind had increased and switched to the northeast. We knew it was going to be bad for us and the animals. The snow fell for three days with the wind blowing it up into drifts. Each night the temperature dropped, adding to the stress on us and the animals.

On the fourth day we woke to sunshine and blue skies, and immediately there was dissension among the men. Some wanted to continue south and others thought we should turn back. Those wanting to return to the fort expressed doubt that their animals would last if they continued and got hit with a new storm. The group voted to split up the train and part ways in the morning. Two partners argued heatedly over which group to join and finally decided to split the partnership. The split was made by cutting their wagon in half and making modifications. They parted company each man with a two-horse team pulling a two-wheeled cart loaded with his possessions. I was going on to Denver. My team was in good shape and if necessary I could ride Misty.

After a skimpy noon meal Kramer and I climbed into the wagon for a nap. I awoke with a start. I had been dreaming about being snowbound and that everyone had died due to the cold and lack of food. The dream was very real. I spent an hour playing it over and over in my mind. The suffering and the cold had been so real it was like a warning to me. I went over to the wagonmaster and notified him I was joining those returning to the fort. I couldn't give my real reason for switching so I just said I felt my team would suffer too much if I continued.

Before they pulled out the next morning I gave the wagonmaster a letter to deliver to Alex. It explained my delay and that I would return as soon as possible. The trail back to the fort was going to be hard on us. The snow and cold had already taken its toll on the animals, making it necessary to lighten their loads. We left a pile of goods and two wagons. Four men rode ahead to break a trail for the wagon teams. The snowdrifts caused us to move at a slow pace. At noon we unhitched the horses and replaced them with a fresh team. We continued our march and ate cold food while on the move. The snow was a problem but for that day and the next we enjoyed a warmer chinook wind blowing out of the southwest. That came to an end when new storm clouds began to build in the west.

We weren't prepared for the blast that swept down on us. The temperature drop was frightening. We were in trouble and had to find shelter fast. Three miles back, we had passed a small protected valley with trees and water in it. The rock cliffs on both sides would protect us from the wind. We turned around and pushed the horses to get there. It started snowing and blowing as only it can in that country. It was good that we had our backs to it.

When we got to the valley, we put the horses up in the boxed end and blocked the entrance with the wagons. Tired as we were, we still needed to put up shelters under the wagons and gather firewood. We divided the food, blankets and water among the five wagons. We built a fire beside each wagon and brought in as much wood as possible. Pushed by the wind, the snow swirled around us and through the trees. It was near midnight before we were settled and had guards posted. Everyone was exhausted but our lives depended on staying alert.

I was awakened at two o'clock by the man I was to replace. He said it was getting too cold to stay out there for long. I met with the other men on the watch and we decided it was too dangerous to be out in the cold. We got our wagonmaster up and he agreed we should go from wagon to wagon and wake everyone up and tell them to stay awake. Two men had to be handled roughly to get them aroused.

The storm continued all the next day and we knew we were in danger of losing our lives. The second night I could hear men crying and praying. I did not want to die out there in that desolate place. I shoved Kramer under my buffalo coat and draped the blanket over us. My dream had been a warning all right. A warning to keep going and not turn back. It was a decision I regretted as Kramer and I shivered under the one blanket allowed.

At sunup the third day we could tell the storm was beginning to lessen and in the afternoon the storm passed. We held a meeting to plan our next move. All of us had frozen patches on our faces. Two men were dead and several were in bad shape. Both of my feet and hands were frost-bitten and I could tell my nose and ears were frozen, too. It was important that we get to the fort as soon as possible for medical treatment.

The next morning when the men rounded up the horses, they found three dead and shot four others who would not make it. We loaded the injured men in two wagons and harnessed four horses to each. Four men on the best horses led the five extras ahead of the wagons to break the trail. We pushed the animals as hard as we dared. They had not been able to graze enough in the valley due to the deep snow. Now we needed to find grass and water. When we saw land that had been swept clear by the wind we would go there and turn the horses loose to graze. Water was next on the list. Two men set out for a likely spot and returned with the good news that water was ahead. After getting the horses to water, we hitched up the best teams and traveled until past dark.

Two more days of hard travel brought us in sight of the line of cottonwoods along the Platte. Now it was a matter of turning east and getting to the fort. The Army patrol that found us said we were a sad bunch to look at. One man had died on the trip and one more died after we got to the fort. The skin was falling off our cheeks and noses. I lost two toes and the tips of the fingers on my left hand.

Winter at Fort Laramie

We were in the infirmary for two painful weeks. A young man by the name of Kyle Cobb offered to take care of our horses and put them in the sutler's barn. He worked for Hugh Parker, the sutler at the trading post. Kyle lived in a small shack attached to the barn and Kramer was staying with him while I recovered. When I got better I would walk over to the trading post and sit by the stove to stay warm. It was good to talk with the soldiers and customers. I was self-conscious about my appearance, having lost a lot of weight and still with ugly spots on my face. I'm glad I made myself move around because being active and around people helped my recovery.

One day two farmers were in the store and Hugh introduced us. Zeb had a small place north of the fort and Pete's farm was east of him. Later, Hugh told me those two had kept the fort amused when Zeb bought Pete's sorrel mare for fifty dollars. Pete got to thinking that since Zeb paid the price so willingly, the mare must be worth more. So, the next day he went to Zeb's place and bought the mare back for one hundred dollars. A couple of days later Zeb offered Pete a hundred and fifty for the horse. This went on for some time, with the people at the fort keeping track of the transactions. The mare moved back and forth between the homesteads until the price was up to six hundred dollars. One day a desperate immigrant bought the horse from Zeb for eight hundred dollars. When Pete heard the news he was mad as a hornet. He told everyone at the fort what a fool Zeb was for selling it, when both of them were making a good living off of that mare.

One afternoon a very pretty young lady came in and started talking to Kyle. I could tell by his face and actions that he was head over heels for her. He introduced me to Miss Carrie Swan, the schoolteacher. Kyle explained that Miss Swan had come to the fort on a train bound for Oregon. She had taken sick and needed care and rest. It was decided that the group would go on and she would stay at the fort until she was well enough to travel. By the time Miss Swan had recovered, the people in the area had hired her to stay and open a school.

A few days later, Miss Swan came to the infirmary looking for me. She brought a book for me to read and promised that when I finished it there were more she could let me have. We were bored and needed something to take our minds off the pain. I knew that several of the men could not read so I gathered them around the beds of those who couldn't get up and I read to them. It sure helped us all forget our pain and how ghastly we looked.

The time came when I could leave the infirmary and needed a place to stay. Kyle mentioned that Mr. Parker owned a small place west of the fort that was better than staying in the barracks. He thought I might be able to make arrangements with him. When I inquired about the place, Mr. Parker was very agreeable to my staying there. He had a few head of stock and said I could live there in exchange for taking care of them.

The place had a small cabin, a barn with corrals and a root cellar. The cabin was twelve feet square with a dirt floor and a cooking stove on the back wall. All of it needed repairing and cleaning. In the corral stood five of the worst looking steers I had ever seen. I thought it couldn't be any worse than farming in Ohio, but soon learned how bad it was.

I found a sign in the barn that read;

    5 miles to wood

    10 miles to water

    10 inches to HELL

Looking after livestock is dangerous but in the winter it can be downright deadly. Sometime in February we got a storm that dropped over two feet of snow before the wind hit us. My place drifted in so bad that it was a real effort to reach the barn to feed the animals and the cold air made my face and hands ache. One evening after chores were done I stepped out of the barn into the whiteness. The blowing snow wrapped around me like a blanket. Kramer's legs were too short to walk in the snow, so I picked him up and started for the house. I could not see beyond my nose.

I figured it would be easier to walk straight ahead until I bumped into the side of the cabin then follow the wall around to the door. I struggled for some distance through the snow. When I did not reach the cabin like I should have, I stood peering in all directions. I couldn't see a thing. Looking down I could hardly see Kramer in my arms. Panic was setting in and I was losing confidence that I was headed for the cabin. The snow was suffocating me and the panic was getting worse.

Deciding on a direction to my left, I turned and took a step. Kramer gave a low yip and looked to our right. Another step and he barked. Trusting his instinct I turned right and in ten steps banged my head on the post next to the front door. Without him I would have died in my own yard. On my next trip I tied a rope to the front door post and tied the other end to the barn door. I took Kramer with me every time I went to feed the animals.

I worried a lot about Alex and Molly and their business that winter. I spent a lot of time wondering what I was going to do about getting Martha back to Denver safely. The soldiers were told to expect the Indians to make more trouble for the immigrants. I wasn't strong enough to travel and resigned myself to staying at the fort until summer. At that point, I regretted coming west and doubted the wisdom of my staying here.

As part of the support for the school, the local people pledged food and meat for the schoolteacher. So when one of the cows broke a leg, Hugh had me butcher it and take several cuts to Miss Swan. She told me that some time earlier, little Timmy Jenkins had asked her if she liked pork, but Mr. Jenkins had not brought any pork to her. I wasn't too surprised because old man Jenkins was known as a tight proposition. Later, when I asked Jenkins about the pork he said, "Oh, the pig got well."

Spring 1864

Living at the ranch was real hard on me and everyone at the fort knew it. The winter was even harder on the animals. When I was at the fort for supplies one of the locals, knowing I was down to one cow, asked me if one cow could stampede. I told him yes, but she couldn't scatter much.

In April, Hugh hired me to help Kyle fix up the place. Putting up corrals and fences in Wyoming is real tricky. A rancher has to dig a hole and then quickly put a post in. Otherwise the wind will blow the hole out of the ground and he'll have to dig the hole again. Kyle was worried that because I was so skinny I might step into a hole and disappear completely. I guess I still looked too thin and frail to be working the ranch by myself. One of the men suggested I should carry rocks in my pockets to keep me on the ground.

I was returning a book to Miss Swan one afternoon when I saw two soldiers fighting in the schoolyard. From their shouts and cursing I realized they had shown up to ask Miss Swan to a dance, and were deciding who was going to ask her first. I noticed Kyle standing on the steps, also getting up the nerve to go inside and ask Carrie to the dance. Knowing he did not like the competition from the soldiers at the fort I decided to give him a little help. I walked past the two fighters and stepped through the school door, shoving Kyle ahead of me. The kids turned and stared at us as we marched down the aisle to Miss Carrie's desk. When we got to the middle of the room I whispered to the kids there was a fight going on outside.

Immediately the kids stampeded to the windows. As I handed Carrie the book I told her that Kyle had something to ask her. Later, two boys said it was the very best day they had ever had in school. When the soldiers settled the matter and came in one at a time, each was turned down. They went back outside and started fighting again, blaming each other for losing out to Kyle. The boys enjoyed the fighting and the girls were happy their teacher was going to the dance with Kyle. As for me I had a great time at the dance watching Kyle and Carrie dancing and falling in love.

Once Kyle and I had the barn and corral repaired, Hugh took buying trips for cattle. He managed to put together a herd of ten animals. Though, calling that bunch a herd was stretching it a bit. He hired two cowboys to bring them to the ranch. I didn't know much about cowboys except they are a mighty strange lot. Understanding cowboy lingo is difficult, until you get the hang of it. You have to know in advance what the cowboy means and then you don't have to pay attention to what he says.

The cows were so thin and scrawny I could watch the sun set through them. The herd took to the spring grass like blowflys on a carcass. For the first few days they were grazing, it was dangerous for Kramer to get in their way. Zeb and Pete chided us about branding cows that thin. Said we had to be careful not to cook the meat.

Wyoming is a land of contrasts. We had gotten more snow than we wanted and it was piled up everywhere. Then, from the last snowfall in late March through April, we had very little rain. In May, it got worse and we knew we were going to have a dry year. When it's that bad, you never eat your own beef unless you are invited to dinner at the neighbors. Ranchers brand their stock with a good clean mark so that the fellow who steals it knows where it came from.

As conditions got worse, prayer meetings for rain were scheduled for every Sunday evening until we got relief. Most people in the territories have a casual and informal approach to God. Anything we can't control is automatically under God's providence. God is very real to us. We will argue with him and scold him if he deserves it.

Pete started off the first prayer meeting I attended by shouting; "Lord, if you don't answer our prayers for rain, you have no business in cow country."

One of the nesters followed with, "Lord, I'm bound to round you up for a good plain talk. Now, Lord, I ain't like these fellows who come bothering you every day. This is the first time I tackled you for anything, and if you will grant this prayer I promise never to bother you again. We want rain, Lord, and we need it bad. We ask you to send us some. But, if you can't or don't want to, fer Christ's sake don't make it rain up at Laramie Peak or Scottsbluff. Treat us all alike." After a prayer like that, there was no need for me to add my two bits. I was convinced our drought problem was due to the wind. It rains a lot in Wyoming, but the wind makes it land in Nebraska.

May 1864

One evening I looked out the window to see Alex and Molly pulling into the yard. Their tearful greeting took me by surprise until I learned that they thought I might be dead. The group that had gone on to Denver in the blizzard had suffered the same fate as we had. Only four men out of the group of twenty reached Denver alive. The men figured we had encountered the same storm and believed we couldn't have survived.

Molly kept having the feeling that I was safe and Alex could not convince her otherwise. She wrote Martha that I might be at Fort Laramie and she should write to me there. When they reached the fort Alex asked at the trading post if anyone had heard of me. They were relieved and excited to be told that I was living a short distance away. Molly was smug about having known I was alive. She was expecting their second child in July and did not look well. She claimed she was tired from the trip and the tension from Indians following them.

Their wagon was loaded with everything they owned, including Wilbur, who was about a year old. Tied to the back was Sarah. She seemed to be glad to see Kramer. She ignored me. Alex explained that a terrible flood had hit Denver, carrying away homes and businesses. Their building and merchandise had been lost. He had managed to save only a few items. They were grateful to be alive. They had decided to move on and start over.

We got them settled in the cabin and I moved to the barn. That evening we talked more. That's when I learned Alex was planing to take his family to the gold fields near Bannack City in Montana Territory. He wanted to get there before the baby arrived. I suggested they stay with me and rest for a few days. During that time I intended to talk them out of the trip.

Molly had a letter to me from Martha. It had been mailed in January and reached Denver in April. I opened it and began to read. When I came to the part about Martha expecting a baby I read it out loud. Alex and Molly were excited. At first I was stunned at the news. I was going to be a father. I was too excited to read any further. I was proud and happy about the news but didn't know what to do. I was still too weak to make the trip to Omaha until later in the summer. In fact I was too weak to go anywhere.

Wilbur was just beginning to get active and he was a delight. He had a round face and brown curly hair like his dad. His eyes were deep blue like Molly's. I asked them what they were going to name the new baby. They had picked out John Joseph if it was a boy and Rebecca Ann if it was a girl.

While Alex and I worked on their wagon I kept talking about them staying with me and going back to Omaha together. Alex was adamant about continuing their trip. He was convinced that they could settle in Bannack City or Virginia City and open a general store. My arguments against the trip only bolstered his resolve. We were getting reports of Indian trouble all around the area and along the immigrant road from Nebraska to Idaho. I kept telling Alex it would not be safe for Molly to travel with a small baby. He was sure they would be there long before she gave birth.

As we argued, I realized he was doing a better job of changing my mind than I was of changing his. The talk of finding gold and the sounds of wagon trains heading for the gold fields was more to my liking than the sounds of a cow having a breech birth or soldiers whooping it up. I told Alex I was not going to stay in ranching, even if I was to make money at it. There's a lot of worrying in the ranch business, but worrying about what to do with the profits isn't one of them. Herding cows and fixing fence was not my idea of a good way to make a living.

I was between a rock and a hard place. I wanted to return to Omaha and be with Martha. At the same time I knew that Alex and Molly needed help to get settled. The worse part was that it would be July before I would be strong enough to go in either direction. I was begging them to stay with me and leave after the baby was born but Alex was determined to get to Bannack City as soon as they could.

Alex and I did a little horse trading with Hugh and put together an outfit of six horses and two mules. I gave him the best steer on the place. They found a group heading for Montana and joined up with them. When the time came for them to leave, Molly was not much better. I was worried for her and the new baby.

June 1864

I got a letter from Martha. She had received Molly's letter and was distressed to hear what had happened to me. She wanted to know how I was. She and her father were sorry that Alex and Molly had been wiped out in the flood but were thankful they were still alive. She and Mr. Walters were worried about them going to Montana, afraid they would not make it. The last line in her letter was, "Newt, please go with them and help them get to Montana and get settled. Our baby is due the end of June so I will not be able to come west this year. Take care of them and I'll join all of you in Montana next summer."

For a few days I thought about going back to Omaha. In the end I decided to follow Alex and Molly to Montana. My hands were not completely recovered from the frostbite but I figured I could mend while traveling. One other item in her letter was branded on my heart forever. She wrote that if our baby were a boy she would name him James Newton and if a girl, she was going to name her Molly Marie.

My letter to Martha was several pages long. It was about the storm and how I ended up in Fort Laramie. I told her I was recovering and would be able to travel soon. I wrote at some length about Alex and Molly's visit and my efforts to keep them from going on. I tried to reassure her that they would be safe. I ended with the hope that she would have no problems having our baby and I liked her choice of names. My last line was a promise to catch up with Alex and Molly in Bannack City and help them.

I loaded up the wagon and headed for the fort. None of us would miss that place except Kramer. He got in some good hunting while we were there. We settled in at the fort to wait for a wagon train going west. The wagon I had was too light and would not make the trip so I worked a deal with Zeb for a better one and asked the blacksmith to make it ready for traveling. I would also need a good team of horses.

I heard Hugh had taken in a four-horse team in poor shape. They were fine looking animals, and were recovering with Kyle's care. Hugh was keeping them out of sight until they were in better shape, knowing he would get a good price for them. It would take some fancy footwork and lots of gold to get them for my wagon but I was determined to have them.

Hugh was showing me his stock when a man rode up on a high-spirited mount. Hugh admired the horse and made an offer for it. The stranger accepted. When asked about the ownership of the horse he admitted that it would be best if it were headed west. There was likely to be a dispute over ownership if anyone was to take that horse east. The deal was made and the horse turned out in the corral. Noticing my puzzled look, Hugh admitted that he always made the first offer on a horse as if ownership was in doubt.

I mentioned that the stock he had in the corral didn't suit my needs and I would like to get a better team for the long trip. He admitted he had a nice team he'd been keeping out of sight and would consider selling them to me if we could come to a price. It took two more days of dodging and weaving but I finally got them for as good a price as could be expected. They would require at least two more weeks of rest and oats before traveling. That was fine with me, because I needed to lay in supplies and find a wagon train to join.

Dunlap and Helm Train

More than two weeks passed before I heard about a train headed west that I might care to join. When I got to their camp I did not like their looks, and the condition of their stock showed lack of care. One of the group mentioned another train a mile further east along the Platte. I found their camp and spoke with Mr. Helm and Mr. Sam Dunlap and his wife Kate. They were headed for Bannack City, expecting to pull out the next day. I liked the looks of their stock and equipment so I asked about joining them. They were agreeable.

Going to Bannack City would be a hard trip and all I could do was hope I was well enough to get there. I returned to the fort and prepared to leave with them. I sent a note to Martha letting her know I was on my way to Montana and how excited I was to get in the gold fields again. I promised to find Molly and Alex and make sure they were okay.

We left Fort Laramie on June 19, following the north bank of the Platte River. The Helm's train was going to split off and take the Bozeman Road. They had heard it was a faster route to the Montana gold fields, saving two weeks of travel. At first I was undecided which group to go with, but by the time we got to where the trails divided I had decided that Sam Dunlap was taking the route that was easier on our teams and on us. I was stronger by then but did not want to push my luck. When the time came we were sorry to see the Helm train go.

The day after we parted, our train reached the Platte River station. Fort Caspar was built on the south side of the river to provide protection to the immigrants and to keep the bridge open. We camped east of the fort and rested for a day. Soldiers at the fort reported Indian trouble along the Bozeman Road and suggested the Helm train might be in danger.

After two days of traveling south and west along the Platte, we could see the dome of Independence Rock sticking up above the land. Hour by hour it grew larger and everyone was anxious to make camp along the Sweetwater River. We pulled in on the east side of the massive rock, finding good grass and water. Our camps were placed against the large rock formation to get out of the wind. We built fires against the boulders letting the heat from the fires reflect off the rocks for warmth. After a fried trout supper supplied by some of the men, we settled by the fire, talking and singing.

The next day was Sunday and we had a small service standing at the base of the rock. Later a few of us walked to the top and looked out onto the plains. Sam pointed west to the split rock formation he called Devil's Gate. Our route would take us near the rock tower which had split away from the mountain allowing the Sweetwater River to flow through. One of the men spotted two riders coming along our back trail. We watched for a time and decided to wait for them. It was two men from the Helm's train. They came in all lathered up and beat from the hard riding. The men asked if we would wait and let the Helm's train rejoin our group.

They explained that they had met a group of men returning to the main trail. They told of bad roads and more Indian activity than anyone expected or wanted. Indians had attacked several times with some injuries and stock lost. Their scouts had seen Indians that morning and were sure there was a large war party following them. The Helm's group turned around and was headed back the other direction before someone remembered they needed to take a vote. It was suggested that they would take a vote just as soon as they were in safer country. In two days the Helm's group joined us. We were all glad to be together again.

After a day's rest we left Independence Rock, following the Sweetwater River past Devil's Gate. It was a puzzle that the sweetest and purest water ran through land dotted with alkali poisoned water. Mountain men who long before had traveled in this area called it the Sweetwater for good reason. Again we camped along its banks.

The next day was my day to be on point, scouting for Indians. It's easier than driving a bunch of animals pulling a wagon but a dang sight more dangerous. Indians will lay in wait to whack a lone rider and take everything. I was keeping to open country so I could spot any trouble. The land was mostly sagebrush and scrub cedar brush with large patches of buffalo grass. A summer storm was brewing up ahead and the wind blowing from it was cold. I had a sense of gloom as I directed Misty through the area, watching for Indians.

I rode up a ridge that would offer a good view of the road ahead. When I got near the top I dismounted and walked to the top leading Misty. I eased over the ridge and scanned the area. To my right about a quarter mile I could see burned wagons. Immediately I was alert and looking in all directions. I did not see any danger so I rode over to what was left of three charred wagons. As I got closer I could see several graves scattered about. I dismounted and walked around. I had passed many graves in the past few weeks but what I saw made me retch. It really gave my mind a twitch and made my body go numb. One grave on that barren, windswept land etched itself in my mind forever.

The marker read: "McCall Family. Alex, Molly, and child." They were all gone! Buried together in one lonely grave.

The Bear River Mountains

I'll never forget the desolation that seemed to wrap itself around me as I stood at their grave, praying for each of them and wondering what had happened. When the train caught up with me I explained a little about Molly and Alex and Wilbur. We pushed on until it was time for supper. I sat with the plate on my lap and gazed over the land until time for us to continue. I spent the time grieving over Alex and his family. I slept little that night, thinking about Martha and how she would take the news. For the next few days she was constantly on my mind. I worried for her and our new baby.

The next day we rolled by the South Pass soldier station. I asked about the burned wagons back along the trail. The officer did not know the details of the attack. We reported our intentions to take the Landers cutoff road through the mountains. The officer suggested we stop at Big Sandy for a rest because it had good water and plenty of grass for the animals. When we got to the Big Sandy River, the men took advantage of the time to stock up on trout, antelope and sage grouse. Kate did a lot of cooking and baking for the tough days ahead. I was anxious to find someone who knew about the Indian attack. Each day I visited trains near us to ask about Alex and Molly. I wore myself out for nothing.

We knew the trail ahead through the mountains was rough and grazing would be a problem once we started. On the last day of our rest stop another train pulled in and camped. Their stock was in worse condition than ours. They were going to take a week of rest before tackling the mountains. On the morning we pulled out the other train treated us to a Sunday service conducted by a Canadian Methodist missionary. He was a little too stuffy for my Baptist background but it was good to hear Christ's name used in a gentle and proper manner for a change.

The mountains put us all to the test. The road got rougher and narrower as we climbed toward the pass. The men and teams were not getting proper rest and the grazing was poor. For two days, darkness overtook us before we got to a campsite and we had to park on the road. Some of us spent the night taking the teams to water and feed and returning by daylight. The animals were beginning to suffer from the conditions and we were worried that some would parish. It didn't get any better going down the other side.

While crossing the mountains many in our train and the other trains were bothered by mountain fever. One morning a young man from the Helm train we knew as Will came up missing. We guessed he had gotten out of bed and wandered off. We lost several hours looking for him. Sam said the sickness could make a person get so crazy they would just wander off and die. When we found him, he was leaning against a tree, staring off as if in a trance. For the rest of the trip in the mountains we tied his leg to a wagon wheel at night and watched each other for signs of the sickness.

We were lucky to have Sam and Kate in our group. He was a druggist with medications to help us fight off all sorts of ailments. Sam said there were a lot of maladies called mountain fever but the worst one was from the bite of a tick. He said the mountain fever we suffered from was mostly due to high altitude, fatigue, and not getting enough to eat.

We heard reports of Indian trouble with the trains ahead and behind us, but luckily our group was not bothered. We occasionally lost stock but found no evidence that it was due to Indians. We felt very lucky to escape the Indian trouble, and were sorry for those who lost lives or stock.

In the evening of the 20th of July we reached Black Foot Junction, Idaho Territory. At that point the Landers cutoff road met the road from Salt Lake City. The valley below the junction was covered with wagons, tents and animals. From then on we saw a steady stream of wagons going to Bannack City or to the new gold strike at Alder Gulch near Virginia City. I wanted to visit some of the trains to inquire about the raid on Alex's group. The Dunlap train went on ahead and said they would ask around as they traveled. I stopped at the Pleasant Valley stage station and met Ben Holladay, the owner of the stage line. He had not heard of the attack and doubted that the remainder of the group had come north. He thought it likely they went on west to California or Oregon.

"Boys, I think that's a good place to stop. Let's see what's on the menu tonight."

When James turned to mark the next page a folded scrap of paper fluttered out. "It's a note that was stuck in the book." Wilbur read the note, written on thin paper showing age and wear.

I have observed the pluck and grit of the women that followed their men west. Like them they endured trying times, danger, and hardships. The women did the same work as the men and in addition were responsible for the care of the children and feeding everyone. Kate was an angel of mercy to all of us. Sam had the medicine but Kate had the healing touch. Like most of the females out in the West she was handy with the tools and animals. More important she was always quick to encourage the men. She was ready to pitch in and help with every chore and faced danger like everyone else. To save the horses she walked alongside the wagon as much as possible. On rest days she cooked, cleaned, doctored, and helped with the animals. When we got tired or discouraged she would get us to sing one of our favorite songs or gather us up for a prayer. When we had an especially hard day and the men were feeling overwhelmed she would present us with a pie she had been saving. There wasn't a man in the group that wouldn't give up his life to save hers.

God bless you, Kate.

While walking to the dining car, James asked Luis if he knew the Dunlaps.

"No, I don't know them."

Everyone on the train lost sleep that night due to an unscheduled stop for repairs. The noise of the repair work was less than the argument as to how the repair should be accomplished. Once the train was on its way, James slipped out into the corridor. In the dim light of early dawn he could see ghostly features of the land floating by. With each mile west he was feeling better about looking for his father. Every word and sentence from the journal strengthened a bond between them. For the first time James felt anxious about meeting his father.

The dining car that morning was nearly empty. While they waited for their breakfast to be served the two ladies entered the dining car. They sat across the aisle and the four had a lively conversation during their meal.

When he finished, Luis excused himself. "I need to walk and relax for a while and later I'll go to the smoking car." As he left he heard their conversation gravitating to plans for further meetings.

Later James and Wilbur joined him in the smoking car. James continued with the journal.

Bannack City - August 1864

Sam and Kate Dunlap had arrived safely and rented a place west of town. Since I was planning to move on shortly, they made a place for my wagon and animals in exchange for work. I was to help Sam with fences and repairing the cabin while I looked for someone who might know about the attack. First I needed to notify Martha and her family. I spent an evening and a bottle of whiskey trying to write a letter about Alex, Molly, and Wilbur. I spent most of the next day rewriting it, again and again. I started over several times before I accepted the fact that there was not an easy way to write about a tragedy. You just have to jump in and keep going.

My way to meet people is to buy a round or two and then let things take their course. I usually get friendly with the man who will thank me for the drink and offer to buy me one. Well, I was in four saloons before I even got so much as a thank you. Later in the Goodrich Saloon, I was offered a drink from a man who introduced himself as Tom Doyle. He had been in Skinner's Saloon when I bought a round and now wished to buy me a drink in return.

Tom had been in one of the first groups to arrive along Grasshopper Creek in the summer of '62. He talked about his first year in Bannack City and how it was just as wide open and dangerous as any camp he had been in. He said an old timer in Montana Territory in '62 was anyone who had come into the area in the spring and was still alive that fall.

Men were living in tents, wagons, and makeshift lean-tos. Some were sleeping on the ground just wherever they decided to flop. Bannack City's first saloon was on the back of a wagon that traveled up and down the area selling whiskey and cigars. The story has it that the wagon broke down and while making repairs the bartender opened up the bar. Other wagons began to park alongside and a camp grew up around them. Soon it was considered a gold camp.

Gold was everywhere. The men were sagebrush mining by roping a large sagebrush and pulling it out of the ground. They would shake off the roots and then pan the loose dirt. Some did quite well for very little work. When things got tight and a man needed some money he would get his rope and horse and go work the sagebrush for a day. In that year the population grew to over a thousand men. Claims were staked up and down Grasshopper Creek for ten miles. Gold from the claims was assaying out at ninety-nine percent pure, giving many of the prospectors better than wages for their efforts. Now Tom was selling his share in the claim and heading for Last Chance Gulch.

I told Tom of the Indian attack and the loss of Alex and his family. I admitted new strikes and new camps were exciting to me, but at the moment I wished to continue my search for information about the attack. He suggested several people I could talk to in Bannack and Virginia City. We parted, wishing each other good luck. If I decided to come over to Helena, he said I should look him up.

It wasn't long before Kate was feeding the men working a claim near us and making good money. Sam made a deal with George Miller to open a drug counter in his general store. Sam had been there about a week when two men walked in with masks on. The taller one had a gun drawn and demanded the cash. Sam reached into the cash box with both hands and drew one hand out with cash in it. Both looked at the cash first and too late noticed the Colt .44 in his other hand. The unarmed man whirled and ran for the door, bumping his partner in the process. The partner and Sam fired at the same time. The bandit's shot missed, but Sam's bullet hit him in the leg. His scream brought the partner back to help and they made their get-away.

Since the shots did not come from one of the saloons, the sheriff came running to check on things. He followed the trail of blood to a small shack and arrested the two. He sent a deputy for Doc Reitz to come and patch up the wounded man. The deputy found Doc in a poker game over at Skinners. He was holding a flush, so he told the deputy that as soon as the hand was done he would come. The other players figured he must be holding good cards and promptly threw in their hands. Doc was so mad at the robber for spoiling his game he demanded fifty dollars before he would care for him.

The next day Sam showed us the bullethole in the wall. If he had been an inch taller he would have been dead. He made us swear never to tell Kate how close the bullet came. Soon the story about Sam and the robbers was known up and down the gulch, earning the respect of the miners. They were faster at paying their bills from then on too. George Miller said that if he had know that's what it took to get bills paid he would have shot someone years ago.

Sam and Kate invited a preacher by the name of Reverend Thompson to their cabin for dinner. He's what they call a brush college preacher. All his education and training was done in sagebrush country. He was well liked by the people in town and was known for preaching to the men while they were working. Reverend Thompson would get down in the streams with the miners to preach and read the Bible while they worked. He'd help them shovel the dirt and clean the sluices while reciting phrases from the Bible. The miners nicknamed him Hell Thompson. After dinner I told Reverend Thompson about my search for information on Alex and Molly's death. He said he would inquire among the miners as he visited the claims.

Sam mentioned the Goodrich Hotel had an opening for a bartender. Said it was paying two hundred a month and washing. The next day I followed up on his tip and talked with Mr. Jackson, the owner of the Goodrich. He said I was hired if I could start that evening, working each night until 6 a.m. Fighting and shooting was not allowed and he had men hired to keep the peace. There would be a brief dust up once or twice a day but the men would settle down and I never saw a gun out of the holster the whole time I was there. I was glad to have the job and his saloon was one of the best I had ever worked in. I decided that if I was to run a saloon I was going to run it like Mr. Jackson did.

Saloons and restaurants were always in need of fresh meat to feed the miners. One time when supplies for the kitchen were particularly short Old man Crisman was dealing with a man for meat and requested that it be delivered. "Can't." said the man. "I've got a wagon but you just bought the horse."

It was not unusual for us to have some of the local characters in the saloon every day. The assortment of men always had a story to tell or embellish on. A miner came in the saloon with mud caked on his boots. Charlie Leach wondered how much gold might be on those boots so he had two men hold the miner down while he scraped off the mud into a gold pan. The mud bought the man his meal and a round of drinks for everyone.

Reverend Thompson made a deal with Mr. Jackson to preach in the saloon for a half-hour every Wednesday. We would close up the bar and turn the place over to him. He was well received by the miners, who felt that if God called a man to do the Lord's work, then he was ready to preach and they were ready to listen. His style of preaching reflected his nickname. He preached on two themes only. Heaven and Hell. His sermons were like riding a runaway horse. Once he got going all you could do was hang on tight until he ran down or reached the barn.

I asked the Reverend one time why he didn't write out his sermon. He said, "When I get up to preach, the devil himself does not know what I am going to say."

Winter - 1864

The fortunes of men rose and fell overnight in Bannack and Charlie Leach was no different. He arrived in Bannack with no money, no food, and very few possessions. Three months later he was on a stage bound for New York with ten thousand dollars in his poke. Some said it was acquired through economy, perseverance, and hard work. Charlie told me it was because his uncle had died and left him fifty thousand dollars and that he was lucky to get out of town with what was left. We heard later that his stage was held up and he went home broke.

In September I started working extra hours at the Dart Hardware Store. One day we got an order from Doc Bissell over at Virginia City. When none of us could read it I took it over to Sam at the drug store. He said it was for ten dollars worth of pills and he would send them to the Doc. Two weeks later we got a letter from Doc Bissell asking about the rattraps he had ordered.

The engineer applied the brakes with enough force to jostle the passengers. James jumped up and looked out the window. "Why are we stopping. We are nowhere near a town?"

"James, look over on this side. There is a herd of buffalo crossing the tracks. Wow, look at them run. Luis does this happen often?"

"Yes, it happens frequently that we have to stop for animals or derailments. Boys we can stretch our legs a bit while they wait for the tracks to clear."

Mining in Bannack was becoming hit and miss. There was still a large amount of gold coming from the claims, but it was dwindling and there were fewer new strikes. Men were pulling out for Virginia City or Last Chance Gulch, the latest strike in the area. A prospector by the name of Howard Ross came in the store asking for a grubstake to go to Last Chance Gulch. I had seen Howard around town and judged him to be honest and what they call weasel smart. I put up forty dollars for a half interest in whatever he found.

Mr. Dart went over to Virginia City in November and contracted for a building to be built on Wallace Street next to the Allen & Millard Bank. He asked me if I would move over there in April and run his new store. He offered a salary that included living quarters in the back. I wrote Martha about moving to Virginia City. I said I was missing her and that I wanted us to be together soon.

By December it was taking three to four months for a letter to arrive from the states. The Indian raids in August and September were so fierce that the mail and freight was held up along the Platte River Road from Nebraska to Utah. It was considered a miracle when mail got through. Many times we heard of mail being burned or scattered by the Indians. Immigrants were forced to travel in larger trains and to keep the stock close at night. I had been in Bannack for three months and had not received one letter from Martha. I had not seen her for over a year and with all the troubles going on it looked like it was going to be a lot longer until we would be together. I still did not know whether I had a son or a daughter.

To celebrate the new year of 1865 Sam Dunlap, Hard Luck Ray, and I went with a few other men to Virginia City to watch a prize fight between Hugh O'Neil and John Orem. O'Neil was a six-foot husky Irishman known for his drinking and woman chasing. Orem, fifty pounds lighter and the owner of several saloons, had a reputation for being a quick-tempered teetotaler. Some in the crowd thought the quick temper was a result of being a teetotaler. The fight went one hundred and eighty five one-minute rounds. It ended up being a long fight as it started at 1 o'clock in the afternoon and had to be called off at dark. Both men were a mass of smashed, bloody flesh and bruises. We had a grand time on our little outing. We didn't have much to say when we were asked about the trip. We were drunk for the whole six days.

Hard Luck Ray had been on the wrong end of several claim deals, and as they say, was hard pressed to put two coins together. He came in and badgered Mr. Dart about getting a little more on credit. Mr. Dart was holding about three hundred on the books but said that he was willing to go fifty more. Hard Luck said, "Okay, let me have that there forty-dollar rifle and five dollars in ammunition and put it on the bill." We heard that he took the rifle over to Skinner's Saloon and sold it for enough money to get out of town and head for the strike at Last Chance Gulch.

Gold fever strikes every man at least once in his lifetime. A man can have gold fever for a short time or it can last a lifetime. Too often, a short time and a lifetime are the same. A mild case of gold fever is when a man says he is going to bust rock for a day or two and is gone for three weeks. Sometimes a man will suddenly disappear for a week and return to his old habits without explanation.

Then there is the gold fever that turns men into idiots. I remember a man came into Goodrich's Saloon and announced that he was looking for his hog. If anyone was to see it he wanted that hog back. One of the regulars was sure that man didn't own a hog. Besides as far as we knew there wasn't a hog within a hundred miles. The men speculated that he was not looking for a hog but for something else. But what could it be?

There were a few suggestions made and then rejected. Then, almost in unison they shouted, "Gold."

The miners, thinking the man was really working on a tip about a gold strike, downed their drinks and stampeded out of the saloon. For three days there were twelve miners loaded with picks, shovels, and gold pans following that man as he looked for his hog. Sure enough, he found his lost hog. The red-faced miners returned to the saloon and drank quietly for the next few days to let the fever dissipate.

At last, I got a letter from Martha. She wrote mostly about our son James and what he was like. The loss of Alex and Molly and Wilbur had deeply affected her father and mother, and they were having a hard time dealing with their deaths. News of Indian trouble made her reluctant to join me and she was needed to help her father run the business. The tone of her letter troubled me. There was something else she was not telling me. I sat for a time feeling lonely and the saddest I had ever been.

Spring - 1865

In April I made arrangements with Sam and Kate for Sarah to have a home and good grazing for as long as she should live. I loaded up my effects, said good bye to Sarah, and headed for Virginia City. I still had Misty and Kramer to keep me company. Kramer had slowed down some but was aging nicely. He was more inclined to stay in the seat next to me and bark rather than go streaking across the prairie as he had once done. The road was rough and slow going in spots. Late in the day we met three freight wagons heading to Bannack. We were meeting on a particularly rough spot so I slowed and pulled to one side so they could pass. Kramer and a dog in the middle wagon saw each other and the chase was on.

It ended as quickly as that. As Kramer bounded off my wagon it lurched and he hit the ground wrong, stumbled and went under the wheel of the passing wagon. I was holding him when he died. I had never lost something so precious to me in my entire life. All I could do was hold him and rock back and forth. The teamsters standing around us had tears in their eyes, knowing my loss. Finally I got up, wrapped him in a blanket and laid him in the back of my wagon.

I camped on the Stinking Water River then I carried Kramer up on a rise and dug a place for him to spend the rest of his days chasing coyotes and rabbits. I stood looking down at him for the last time, remembering the great times we had. I thanked him for being the best friend I ever had. I laid him in the grave, filled it up and then piled rocks on top. That night the moon rose early, casting its pale light over an empty prairie. I thought of my family so far away and was feeling sorry for myself because no one was there to comfort me on my loss. I wondered what kind of future lay ahead for Martha and I. The next morning as the sun edged over the horizon pushing back the coldness of the prairie breeze, I said goodbye to Kramer and bid him good hunting.

Three weeks after I arrived in Virginia City I got a mysterious letter from Kate Dunlap. On the evening of the day we had left Bannack, she wrote Sarah had started to bray and carry on, kicking the barn and corral poles. She kept it up for most of the night, her noise and agitation keeping Sam and Kate awake. It was the same evening I had stood over Kramer's grave.

The men building the Dart Hardware store expected to finish by mid-May, just in time to start working their claims. The unusually hard winter brought high drifts to the mountain passes, delaying delivery of lumber and supplies to town. I got word that fixtures and inventory for the store would be shipped via one of the first boats of the season. Its arrival in Fort Benton was expected in May.

When word of the steamship arrival got to me, I arranged for the Conover Freight Company to take me to Fort Benton to pick up the shipments. When we got to Fort Benton, they were still unloading the cargo, expecting to be done the next day. It took two trips with six wagons to get everything to Virginia City.

The excitement and energy of a gold camp of over eight thousand miners, gamblers, and lawyers can be so overpowering it seeps into your bones and infects your mind. All of that was mild compared to the excitement and celebrating that went on when word was received that the Confederate Army had surrendered. The war was over and that was very good news to us all.

A newspaper called the *Montana Post* had been established in Virginia City. The editor, Thomas Dimsdale, was a man of integrity, but not shy about using words to sting, prod, and educate the readers. Most of the men in gold camps and towns have little understanding of politics. Mining law was all the law we needed or cared about. Like it or not, Dimsdale changed all that with his editorial comments on politics, politicians and vigilantes. Dimsdale wrote "Twelve Reasons Why I cannot Vote the Democratic Ticket." There's only one I can quote from memory. It went like this. "Because I want no hungry politician in office - I want a just man; and the Democrat candidates look to the fleece and not to the flock."

Virginia City - 1865

One afternoon, I was having dinner at the Silver Palace when Crazy Bob came through the door and headed straight for the bar. He was more agitated than usual and his bugged eyes were spinning. He obviously needed a drink and an audience. I signaled George to set him up with a drink to prime the pump. Appearing to be a down and out miner, Crazy Bob was a lot smarter and craftier than people suspected. He was always mooching food and drink from the townspeople, all the while selling bits and pieces of information to certain highwaymen. No one knew for sure where he lived, but I knew he had taken over a shed behind the Star Billiard Hall. While I bought, he drank and talked.

Bob was hunting along the road to Salt Lake City when he heard unusual sounds coming from a grove of aspens. They were sounds he had never heard before and it sounded like several animals were in there. He worked up enough nerve to check the grove out. Before he reached the trees he spotted one of the animals. His description began to falter until George poured another drink. The animal had a funny looking head with a long nose and a big mouth with a long tongue. The body was about the size and color of a cow elk but it was horribly deformed with a large growth on its back. When he saw several of the deformed beasts, Bob took aim and shot. He missed because he was shaking so much. The animals made the horrible noise again and that's when he decided to hightail it back to town and get some nerve medicine.

Bob timed his story so that he got two more drinks before he finished. Several men had gathered at the bar to listen and they decided to check things out. They grabbed

Crazy Bob for a guide and a bottle of whiskey for reinforcement. As they headed out the door, two strangers were coming in and they had to make way for them. The two men ordered whiskey before asking what the mob was up to. With a wink I repeated Bob's story and description of the terrifying animals.

We had a good laugh when the strangers proceeded to tell us about the twenty-three camels they were driving to Helena. The U. S. Army had auctioned off the animals in Austin, Texas. They had been used in an Army experiment to see if camels would do better than horses in the desert. Problem was, no one could throw a diamond hitch on the beasts and they had a tendency to run off, destroying the loads they carried. They would bite drivers and soldiers at every chance, but the worse part was they couldn't be mixed with horses and mules. The animals would stampede every time a camel came near them. A freight company in Helena bought them to be used as pack animals at the mines.

Apparently someone in the expedition knew what the mysterious beasts were, for it wasn't long before the men returned to the saloon. All except Bob. They said he disappeared while the men were laughing. When I asked if the bottle of whiskey had disappeared too, there was a brief silence and then a reddening of faces. The next day the camels moved through town on the road to Helena. I will say, they were the scraggliest bunch of animals I had ever seen. At first the townspeople were enjoying the parade but the smell and dung quickly took all the fun out of it.

One afternoon I looked out the window and saw Hard Luck Ray coming toward the store. Dang'd if he hadn't come back to pay his creditors. He was very tightlipped as to his sudden wealth. He'd got a job hauling freight from Helena to Virginia City and came in to pay off his old bill. I could not get him to admit where he got the money to pay us. Every time he was in town I tried to get him to talk about his windfall. I tried whiskey and threats but he wouldn't fess up.

Summer 1865

When the Territory Legislature voted in January 1865 to move the capital from Bannack to Virginia City, we had politics dropped right in our laps. I was too busy with the new store to take much interest in politics myself but the Post kept me apprised of the political shenanigans that went on. When a candidate got up to speak, he could expect all manner of ridicule and back talk from the crowd and later have it reported in the newspaper. One politician running for Governor claimed that all Montana needed was good people and good water. Someone in the crowd yelled, "That's all Hell needs, too."

During one campaign that was louder and sharper than usual, Dimsdale noted that he didn't print the Democratic speeches out of mercy to the politicians. Just before voting day he wrote, "Vote the people's ticket once, and then look out for those who vote often." Once, while explaining the nature of Montana politics, he wrote, "Politically Montana has three factions: A small aggressive group of Republicans. A small group of copperheads (those Northerners who sided with the South during the war). And a strong majority of Democrats, most of whom are secessionists and brought their rebel war cries, and songs of Dixie to the Montana gold fields."

I have heard another Montana legend that says, "The left wing of the Army of the

Confederate, under General Price in Missouri, never surrendered: They retreated to Montana."

I think it was sometime around June of '65 that I hit a detour in the road of my life. It was a pleasant distraction in the person of one James K. P. Miller. The K. P. stood for Knox Polk but it didn't take long for me to decide that the K. P. stood for "Keep Pouring." I met him one evening at the Missouri House where he was lodging. He had recently accepted a clerking position with Rockfellow and Dennee, owners of several grocery and general stores in the area.

We hit it off right away, owing to a mutual liking for billiards and liquor. When it came to business dealings, James was quicker and more experienced than I was. He was a go-getter in business as well as in the social life of the town. He helped organize a Social Club that was well attended. I began spending more time at the billiard table and in the Oyster Palace to ease the loneliness. Our daily routine changed as the social club functions increased and the membership grew to over twenty-five members, myself included. We spent Christmas attending a milk punch social with James, George Hill, John Ming, James McShane and other business leaders. It was a grand time and I stayed drunk enough so I wouldn't miss Martha so much.

James had a working agreement with Mr. Dennee for the right to purchase goods from his connections in Salt Lake City and have them shipped to Virginia City. He would sell the goods on the side and realize the profits for himself, referring to them as his "little investments." I was impressed with James' ability to buy the right goods two months in advance of demand, take care of shipping and then sell at a profit. Most times he sold for a good profit, but he admitted at times he was lucky just to get his investment back.

I kept after him until he agreed to help me start an investment club with Albert Hanauer, a local banker, and Mr. Higgins, who owned a dry goods store. We met several times a month for supper, drinks, and cigars. Then, over a table at the Star Billiard Hall, we would discuss the investment possibilities. Between the Social Club and the Investment Club I was playing and drinking most every night. With as much drinking and playing James and I were doing at the Star, we were thinking of buying it to save money on our socializing. Virginia City's economic conditions being what they were, we soon came to the conclusion that the best investment would be to move to Helena or somewhere else.

The Virginia City Literary Society was formed by several of the leading ladies. Their endeavors were an instant success. The inaugural ball they held in December was a big hit with everyone. The speech by Dimsdale and readings by others were entertaining as well as informative. Of particular interest to several gentlemen was the attendance by Miss Boice. I wrote Martha that I spent the evening standing at the bar and wishing she would come West to be with me.

In January, the Vigilance Committee held a grand ball at the Adelphi Hall in Nevada City. It was well attended with decorum maintained due to the influence of the ladies in attendance, especially the unattached ones.

Spring - 1866

By March, things were getting so bad in Virginia City it looked like I was gonna have to give up drinking because my friends had given up buying. News of large gold strikes near Last Chance Gulch continued to draw men from Virginia City to Helena. Newspapers reported increasing amounts of gold shipped from Helena mines to eastern banks. Every news report on Last Chance Gulch meant more men leaving for Helena. Businesses were following the miners to the new diggings, leaving vacant stores and offices behind. I could see it wouldn't be long until our store would have to be closed or moved.

Cascade Smith badgered me for two weeks about a grubstake to go to Last Chance Gulch. I was not reluctant to put up the money. It was because he was offering only a sixty-forty split. We finally agreed to a fifty - fifty split and he would not have to pay back the amount of the grubstake.

It was about that time I got a letter from Martha with still another cancellation of her plans to come West. She still talked like she wanted to come but it was getting harder to believe. I wrote back that my situation in Virginia City was not going to last much longer and that I was planning to move to Helena.

We got a handbill telling about a bull and bear fight scheduled for Helena. I decided to go over and take in the excitement. Stagecoach travel is an adventure but mostly hard on the tailbone. The fare was twenty dollars for first class; ten dollars for second class; and five dollars for third class. I figured that since we all got there at the same time I'd go third class. I learned my mistake when the coach got to the bottom of the first hill and the driver yelled out "first class stay in the coach, second class get out and walk, third class get out and push." By the time we got to Helena I was plenty tired. I was the only one traveling third class.

The next day I attended a bull and bear fight that was being staged at the edge of town. A bull and bear fight is usually predictable. The bull wins because the grizzly is chained to a post. But this time we had a little more excitement. The bear made several lunges at the bull and managed to pull the chain off the post. The grizzly stood up, sniffed twice and went for the crowd.

There was lots of activity in Helena. The gold camp was growing larger every day and even the big strikes were greeted with minor interest. I'll admit I was starting to get a gold fever itch that I needed to scratch. But, just as most gamblers and hurdy gurdy girls know, it's easier to get the gold after a miner has dug it. I rode back first class, pondering my next move. One thing I knew for sure, I wanted to run my own business.

A Chilling Tale

One afternoon a man walked into the store and asked for Newt Harvey. I nodded that he had found him and asked what he wanted. He hesitated for a moment then asked for a drink. Puzzled, I turned and headed for the back room and he followed me. He was short and stocky, dressed in miners' clothes and wearing a sweat stained, wide brimmed hat. His hands were large and rough from working the dirt. I motioned for him to sit on a keg of nails while I got the whiskey down and pulled the cork.

A box of salted herring became a table for his glass while I poured the whiskey. He reached out, licking his lips. He wiggled his fingers over the glass before tenderly picking it up with thumb and index finger. Slowly he lifted it to his lips, took one small sip — paused - and then downed the rest in a quick motion. He held the glass up looking at it for a moment as if expecting the glass to tell him something. He lowered his hand, gently setting the glass on the herring crate bar, and nodded for a second shot. I poured again and watched him repeat the process.

Men have different drinking habits in the West and I was sure that this man's actions occurred when he had something troubling his mind. Something was bothering him so bad he was having a difficult time putting words together. He was drinking with slow and deliberate actions while trying to find the way to start the conversation. When a man did that in a saloon, everyone watched his gun hand. This man did not have a gun so I felt safe about that. While I poured the third round he started. I have written his story as I remember it.

"My name is Silas Anderson. My wife Woah and I traveled with the same train as the McCalls. We moved to Bannack City last month and met a man and his wife by the name of Dunlap. They said you were looking for information on an Indian raid west of Devil's Gate two summers back. So we come here soon as we could.

"When we left Fort Laramie, the McCall's wagon was next to ours. My misses and Mrs. McCall became friends while Alex and I was helping each other stay up with the train. The trip was hard on Molly, with a baby on the way and all. By the time we got to Independence Rock for a rest stop she was having problems with the baby. She'd been staying in the wagon ever since Platte River Station and looked plumb wore out.

"When she went into labor, Woah helped as best she could and soon Molly and Alex was parents of a tiny baby girl. She had come a bit early but she seemed to be okay. The men voted to stay an extra day to give them a rest. The rest seemed to help and it looked like they was going to be all right when we pulled out. We stopped early that day and camped west of Devil's Gate.

"The next day we continued on towards South Pass. About noon a scout came back with two arrows in him. The wagon master picked out as level a spot as he could and began to circle us up. We were about to get the last wagon pulled up to close the circle when the savages attacked.

There was thirty or forty of them heading for us and some were heading for the opening in the wagons. Alex and I ran over to where the opening was and began shooting the Indians horses. We wanted to build a pile of horses in the opening so as to keep the rest of the Indians from riding inside. As it was, three or four got through and were riding around shooting at us. Our men started picking off the ones inside until they were all dead.

"The problem with shooting his horse is that the rider will keep coming on foot. Alex and I shot two or three Indians as they ran at us. We had several close calls. I got nicked in the arm and Alex was roughed up a bit. Once that was taken care of, it looked like we would be okay. We had plenty of guns and bullets to make a stand until troops could arrive from South Pass station.

"At that moment, Molly began to scream and we looked over to see that Alex's wagon was on fire. So was the one in front of his and it soon spread to the next one. Alex was running to help Molly when several Indians jumped from between the wagons. One shot Alex and turned to shoot at me. I shot him first and began to shoot at the others. The warriors ran outside the wagons and leaped on their horses. By the time I got there, the wagons were burning so hot it was too late to do anything. Molly wasn't screaming any more. It all happened so fast that no one could help her. It made us all sick just to stand and not be able to do a thing.

"The warriors bunched up and we prepared for another attack. They looked at us, talking and gesturing for a time, then they whirled around and rode off, whooping it up. Alex was still alive but hurt bad. He kept trying to tell me something and all I understood was the name Newt and Fort Laramie. We promised to take care of Wilbur until we found you. We buried what we could find of Molly and her baby in the same grave with Alex."

I had started to pour another drink when he began his story. From that moment on, I stood there unmoving, the neck of the bottle just inches above his shot glass. Silas reached out and repeated his drinking ritual. I poured myself a shot and sat the bottle down. In a shaky voice, I asked what had happened to Wilbur. Silas told me that Wilbur had been staying with them so Molly could take care of her new baby. He said if I wanted to see Wilbur he was outside in their wagon.

I poured and drank another shot then followed Silas outside. As we approached the wagon I could see Wilbur sitting in the back, watching people go by. When he saw us he focused his attention on me and never wavered. I stopped in front of him smiling and looking at his blue eyes and curly brown hair. I was worried that he would not like me or worse be afraid of me, but I was soon put at ease. He smiled right back and asked if I was his Uncle Newt. I told him I was and that I was happy to see him.

Mr. Anderson introduced me to his wife. She was a pleasant woman holding a small baby. I invited them to come inside and tell me more. Silas said there wasn't much else to tell. They had dug through the ashes, finding only a few articles that could be used. They found a metal box with personal papers and a small amount of money, which they used for Wilbur's care.

As he handed me the box I saw Mrs. Anderson turn away with tears in her eyes. I knew it was hard for her to give him up but times were bad and they had their own new family to raise. I told them I would see to it that Wilbur got to his family in Omaha and that I would tell them about the fine folks who took care of him. Silas knelt down and took Wilbur's tiny hand in his large rough hand and told him goodbye. Wilbur then ran to Mrs. Anderson and hugged her leg. Silas took the baby from her so she could pick Wilbur up. She stood there hugging him for a long time. I looked at the two of them and tried to express the gratitude of the family for their sacrifice and love they gave Wilbur.

A bit shaken by what he had just heard, Wilbur got up.

"I'm getting hungry."

"So am I," said James.

Luis shook his head. "You two go ahead. I'm going to our compartment and take a nap. I think I overdid it at breakfast this morning. Eating every meal in a fancy dining car is too much for my system. You can spend a little time stretching your legs and maybe you'll meet those two ladies again."

While the boys explored the train for the ladies, Luis sat in their compartment, thinking of Newt and wondering where he was or if he was still alive. Later the boys joined Luis in the smoking car. From the expression on James' face it was obvious they had found the ladies in the dining car. Wilbur continued reading from the journal.

Omaha with Wilbur

There I was, responsible for a three-year-old boy who had just lost his second set of parents. I was turning many things over in my mind as to what to do next. My life was going to change and for the better I thought. That evening after prayers I tucked Wilbur in with the promise that I would someday tell him about his mother and father. He wanted to know when I would tell him. I said it would be soon.

In the light of a lantern I opened the tin box and started taking things out one at a time. Mostly there were receipts and bills of sale that reflected their short life together. Near the bottom I came across a letter from Martha.

She wrote about how upset their mother was about our getting married. Their mother was still convinced Conrad Bates would be a better husband than a dreamer who wandered around looking for gold at the end of a rainbow. Mrs. Walters had tried to get Martha to annul the marriage. When Martha announced she was expecting a baby the subject was dropped. Mr. Walters was proud as could be that he would be a grandfather. Martha wrote that their cook Irene said she was just happy the father wasn't that sneak Bates. She wrote about sending several letters to me about us having a child on the way. Martha was very upset that I had not answered the letters. She complained of not receiving letters from me for many months.

Later that week, the investment club met at the usual meeting place. James remarked that Virginia City looked like a very large town minus the people. Mr. Higgins said he was pulling out for Helena and making his next investment there. I announced that I was leaving for Fort Benton in two days and within two weeks I planned to be in Omaha. I was going to bundle up Martha and a son I had not seen and bring them west. James wanted to know what I was going to do if she refused to come West, which he thought was likely to happen. I said I would demand she come West with me. After the laughter died down I changed the subject.

Two days later we took the stage to Fort Benton, only to find the river was still too low for the steamboats to get past Fort Union. '66 started out a dry year so the first boats were not expected until after the twenty fifth of May. I was now so impatient to get Wilbur to his family, and to see Martha and my son, that nothing was going to stop me.

I hired a boat that could make the trip to Fort Union. It was a shallow draft freighter designed to go in shallow waters like the Yellowstone River. It was used for carrying freight so there was little room for passengers. I was able to convince the captain to make the trip with his load and us. He wanted two hundred dollars for passage. I said okay and an extra one hundred dollars if we were to leave immediately. In two hours we were underway. As the boat headed downstream I noticed that most of the men were standing around above deck. When I started asking questions, they told me if the boiler blew they didn't want to be below deck.

We had two encounters with Indians. The first was not too serious as we stayed in the middle of the river and outran them. The second time, Blackfeet attacked as we were landing to get wood and hunt for game. We had to shoot our way out. Two days later we were at the Fort Union dock booking passage on the Octavia, leaving the next morning.

When we arrived in Omaha we were walking down the gangplank before it settled on the dock. I hired a horse and buggy to take us to the Walters' Wholesale Company. There was so much construction going on the confusion and activity reminded me of an anthill. As we drove through the business area I did not see any recognizable building or landmark from my first trip. We turned a corner and before us stood the warehouse. It was larger now with a new building attached to the old one.

We drove up to a door in the new building and I asked to see Mr. Walters. When we met he was amazed at our sudden appearance. We shook hands and instantly liked each other. His smile and the sparkle in his eyes were the same as I had seen in Molly. Wilbur was holding on to my hand and hanging back a little. Mr. Walters looked at him and seemed to freeze a moment, trying to sort out his feelings and premonitions when he saw the face and blue eyes.

I said, Grandpa Walters, I would like you to meet your grandson, Wilbur McCall. Wilbur, this is your grandfather I told you about. I am sure that the men standing nearby had never seen their boss at a loss for words and they had never seen him cry like he did that day. After a time he recovered enough to suggest that we all go up to the office. As we approached the stairs to the offices, the office door opened and there stood Martha. I looked up at her and gaped. Then 'Ol' man Walters laughed and said, "Uh, by the way, Newt, in all the excitement I forgot to tell you Martha was here."

I went up the steps two at a time. As I got to her, something warned me that things were not right with her. She was so frail and delicate! I stopped and looked deep into her blue eyes and knew something was wrong. All I could do was take her hand and point to the little boy walking up the stairs and explain that it was Wilbur. She nearly fainted.

I do not have the ability to describe the events that took place for the next few hours. Mr. Walters, Martha and I were quickly asking questions and giving answers to catch up on two years of separation. After a brief time at the warehouse we rode out to the Walters' home. It could properly be called an estate. The large home sat with trees and flower gardens around its stone walls. The property was surrounded by twenty acres of trees, ponds, and hedges. The servants were not prepared for the noise and confusion generated by the master of the house when the drove up to the front door. For a time it was a combination of laughter, crying, and talking. Meeting my mother-in-law would have to wait as she was visiting in St. Louis.

I was never so nervous as when I met my son for the first time. Already James was tall and thin for his age. He was shy with me at first, which was understandable. After a few hours he and Wilbur forgot I was there and he acted more at ease with my presence. It was fun watching them talk and play. We were becoming a family. It would take time but I wanted my boy to grow up having family memories like I did. I remember what a preacher said about families arriving in the gold camps. "Culture comes with the sunbonnet, and civilization comes with the cradle" I was returning to civilization.

That night after supper Martha and I took over the library for some time together and to catch up on the news. The room allowed us privacy and comfort. Best of all the liquor supply was kept there and I was going to need it. I told her about what had happened to me and the information I got from the Anderson's about Molly and Alex. It was evident that each of us had received only a few of the many letters we had written over the past two years.

We talked for two hours before I could ask the question that was in my mind earlier but dreaded to hear the answer. I wanted to know why she was so frail looking. Her face got whiter than it already was and she was silent for a long time. She admitted that she had a heart condition and the doctors in St. Louis were taking care of her. She had been cautioned by the doctors to limit her activities and be careful not to over exert herself. She had been born with the condition and had always been weak physically. Her pregnancy took all the strength she had and it further weakened her ability to regain her health afterward. We talked well into the night. Most of the next day was filled with making arrangements to go to St. Louis.

St. Louis - 1866

The Shaw family home was located in a fashionable neighborhood, reflecting the wealth and status of the family. Previous generations had settled there in the early part of the century to invest in the growth of St. Louis. Mrs. Walters's brother, Levi Shaw, lived in the family home and he was happy to see us. Levi preferred investing the family money rather than working. He was a social climber like his sister, associating with bankers and investors including Old Man Bates and his son, Conrad.

Mrs. Walters was cool to me and let me know that she had not changed her mind about me and probably never would. However she sincerely thanked me for bringing Wilbur back to his family.

It was likely that we would live in St. Louis due to Martha's health. We made plans for me to return to Montana long enough to sell my holdings, transfer my bank accounts and then return to St. Louis. Mr. Walters had expressed the idea that we might establish a wholesale company in St. Louis and I thought it was worth considering. Although I would have preferred to live and work in Colorado or Montana.

I began looking around St. Louis for a bank to handle my accounts. I had the list of the banks that Martha's family was connected with and began to look for a bank that was not on the list. At the Merchants and Miners Bank I knew I had found the place for my money. It was an old bank, with the original furniture, desks and cages that had been installed when the bank was built.

After a short wait I was ushered into the office of Amos Steck, president. Right away I could see we were going to get along. Amos looked like a miner in a fancy suit. He was a barrel-chested man with large arms. His hands were more suited to using a pick and shovel than a pen. He had been in Gregory Gulch the same year I was and had been lucky to get out alive. He admitted his fortune came a few years later when he took money from a small inheritance and speculated in railroad stock.

On the wall behind his chair was a mural of a miner throwing dirt into a sluice box. When asked about the mural he was pleased at my interest, admitting that he was proud of the acquisition. On a trip back east he had seen the painting and purchased it. It hung in his office to remind him of the hard work it takes for some people to earn their money and that he should be thankful for his thrifty bachelor uncle.

I told him a little of my adventures in the territories and the circumstances of my being in St. Louis. I explained my family ties and that I wished to bank with someone who was not connected with the family. He understood my reasoning and was pleased I had chosen him for my banker. I told him I needed him to help me with investing my money in St. Louis. In the future I would do a little grubstaking or whatever term he would use, but for now I was looking for land investments for a home and a warehouse. Any information on available land for sale was to be telegraphed to me in Helena.

For most of a week we lived like a family and it was good to see how well the boys played together. Martha had to be careful not to do too much but I could see improvement in her energy and she smiled a lot. The steamboat company informed us that the season would be short this year and I would need to leave soon to get all the way to Fort Benton. I boarded the boat in St. Louis with the same apprehension as when Martha and I had parted in Fort Laramie.

I got off in Omaha to spend a few days with Mr. Walters to discuss working for him. I was only worried that I would not be able to do the work he needed. I was not a bookkeeper or accountant but if it was loading or working with the teams I could do that. He had other projects in mind for me. He was making plans to expand, using the railroad to ship his goods west. They were already shipping to the railhead towns in Nebraska and Wyoming and he wanted be ready for the increased business when the Union Pacific would connect Omaha with California. I was given a grand tour of Omaha and visited with business friends of Mr. Walters. We spent the evenings discussing the work he was doing and his ideas for the future.

One day, after spending the afternoon and early evening at the Walters' Company I was tired and decided to go back to his house while he finished his office business. Instead of bothering someone to drive me home I decided the walk would do me good. It would give me a chance to think about things and to see the town. I was walking along a dark street when I was stopped by two rough-looking men who seemed to know who I was. There was a third man standing in a dark doorway. The two made remarks about my character and my western ways. They suggested I return to the territories and take up with a squaw and leave their fine Omaha ladies alone. While one confronted me with his tirade the other was edging around to my side. The man in front pulled out a pistol and pointed it at me. I realized this was not going to be a dust up. They intended to do some real harm, maybe kill me.

Glancing around, I saw no help, and no escape. My best bet was to be the first to make a move and surprise them. When the thug moved again, I lunged, grabbed his arm, and swung him around to get a hold on his neck. The other man fired, hitting his partner in the back and he collapsed in my arms. I leaped at the dazed shooter, punched him twice in the face and took off running hoping the third man wouldn't try to shoot me.

The sound of the gun aroused men nearby and they shouted for the police as they headed for the two men. I took a roundabout way to the Walters' home. I got to my room to clean up and decide what to do. I discovered the bullet had passed through the man and grazed my arm. I cleaned up and put a bandage on it.

An hour later Mr. Walters came home with the news of a shooting in the area. I took him aside and showed my wound and told him what happened. He decided I should wait for him in the guest house until he could get information from his friend at the newspaper office He returned with the bad news that the police were looking for me. The police reported that a stranger had tried to hold up two citizens, shooting one in the back in cold blood and beating on the other. The description by men who had seen me running from the scene was of me or mainly my hat. We decided that I would return to Montana until it cooled down and Mr. Walters could get to the truth. George, the butler, drove a wagon to the rear of the house and I got in and he drove me to the docks.

I booked passage to Fort Benton on the first boat going up the river and boarded immediately. I stayed in my cabin and did not mingle with the passengers even after we pulled away from the dock. If the captain was suspicious he never let on but at each port I nervously watched for police or deputies coming aboard. Not until I got past Fort Union would I be able to breathe easier and not fear arrest. When we docked at Bismarck I watched every person coming on board and sure enough an Army officer approached a deck hand and showed him a paper. At that moment there was a knock at my door and a whispered, "Mr. Smith, I have a message from the captain."

The sailor on the other side of the door was calm as he explained the captain was a good friend of certain people in Omaha and would help all he could. The captain felt I needed to take up residency elsewhere on the boat and to get my gear and follow him. We walked through narrow passageways stacked on either side with freight. At the rear of one compartment the sailor moved boxes to expose a door. He instructed me to stay there and keep quiet. He promised to return and let me out after we were underway. I stepped in and he closed the door. I could hear him put the boxes back and walk away.

The smell was horrible and I could hear small feet scurry around the room. It seemed like hours before the whistle blew and we got underway. Soon I heard steps and boxes being moved. The door was opened and I followed the sailor back to my cabin. A tray of food was waiting for me. While I wolfed the food down he explained that not every man on board could be trusted and some might report my presence at the next stop. I was to remain quiet and not show a light.

We got to Fort Benton with out further problems. I was in civilization less than fifteen days and got into more trouble than in the entire eight years I had spent in the lawless frontier. I would not be able to return to my family until I cleared my name. Martha wrote there was a witness who described me as the killer. The witness was not being identified and Mr. Walters smelled a frame up. Her letter indicated that Mrs. Walters felt the fight was my fault and further proof that I was not a good husband for Martha.

1867

Mr. Rockfellow married Molly McNiel. To the bride and groom it was a solemn occasion and the ceremony was conducted in the proper manner. Fellow members of the Virginia City Social Club conducted themselves in anything but a solemn manner. During the second day of celebrating the sheriff should have put a stop to the revelry. He didn't because he was one of the participants. Later fines were levied all around and quietly paid.

By March, James and I were reflecting on our future in Virginia City. Our spirits were so low we tried to raise them with whatever bottled spirits we could find. I was missing Martha something awful and lamenting that everything was against us being together. During the winter, I worked and schemed on how I could set Martha's family straight and clear my name with the police.

In May, James was asked by Mr. Rockfellow to make a business trip to his stores in Argenta, Bannack City and Salmon River. This was a chance for James to look for any opportunities in those areas. I suggested that he contact Sam Dunlap for help. James, with Sam as a guide, spent part of a day checking out quartz leads in the area but found nothing worth the risk.

When things began to happen, they happened fast. James returned from Bannack City on May 12. Three days later he announced his decision to return to the East Coast and then possibly on to Europe. He began selling his possessions and packing the rest. The going away party between the two of us started then and lasted until the 26th when he boarded the stage bound for Helena and Fort Benton. He was financing his trip by carrying gold for the Hershfield and Co. Bank for a fee.

I got a bad case of the lonelies and gave serious thought to going to Omaha and St. Louis even if I had to dodge the law. But when the time came for him to leave I stayed behind. The official Virginia City Social Club party for him ran for only one night and one day in order to reduce the amount of damage and complaints from the city fathers.

By July, I was making plans to move to Helena. I wrote the bank in Denver to have some of my money transferred to Helena, the rest to be sent to my bank in St. Louis. A large envelope arrived from Luis Eaton. Luis and his partners had sold the Sarah Mining Company to eastern investors. The eastern investors wanted to purchase my remaining shares for fifty thousand dollars. The money had been deposited with the bank subject to my signature. Luis wrote that Horace and Augusta were still in Oro City but times were getting tougher as the easy gold had played out and many of the men moved on. Only two or three mines were still in operation. He felt that most of the stock I had in the other mines looked doubtful.

I signed everything and sent it back. I asked Luis to quietly buy promising claims before they would be abandoned and to keep the titles up to date. I did not want to let the claims be abandoned. Somehow I had the feeling there were riches still buried in those mountains.

I got an invitation to go hunting for a week which I gladly accepted. The group was going to a hunting camp near Butte. The drinking started the day before we left and never let up. We took three wagons piled high with gear, food and whiskey. That week I had the best luck I'd had in years. I filled two inside straights for a half interest in a bar in Helena. Later, the owner suggested we high card for the other half and I won. At least I thought I won. That's all the push it took for me to give notice to Mr. Dart, turn over the store and pack up. I had my possessions shipped while Misty and I headed for Helena. I wrote to Martha about the developments and that she could write to me there.

The Sarah Saloon - Fall and Winter 1867

I discovered I was the owner of a rundown, dirty saloon that catered to a dangerous bunch. A snake wouldn't bring his mother in the place. The brass rail was loose in places and broken in others. The back mirror was cracked from previous fights and flying furniture. Glasses had not been cleaned in months and the white apron on the bartender was a dingy shade of gray with dark, mysterious stains all over it. I had not won much, but it was a start. The most valuable part was the land it sat on.

The restaurant next door was owned by Katie Gilbert, a widow lady with two boys and a girl to raise. She ran a clean establishment and served good food. Her business was poor because of the disreputable saloon next door. Namely my place. I offered to buy her business and then hire her to run the restaurant for a percentage. Her acceptance doubled the size of my business. I ordered a fancy bar and all the fixtures from a supplier in Kansas City. They confirmed the order would be shipped by steamer next spring.

While waiting for the arrival of a new bar and fixtures I started remodeling. After tearing out a wall I had enough room to put in several gambling tables and a piano. It was costing a lot of money but I was going to offer the very best food, whiskey, and pleasant surroundings that I could afford. I offered two whiskies that first year, one I purchased from the whiskey drummer and the other I made myself. The whiskey drummer made claim that his Montana Lightning was the best around. One nip of this brew would make you steal your own clothes, two nips would make you bite your own ears off, and three nips would make you save your mother in law.

The house whiskey I made was very popular with the old timers who had acquired a taste for Tiger Spit, Red Death, Widow-Maker, or worst of all Taos Lightning. They did not expect a refined taste, all they wanted was a jolt.

I posted a sign over the back bar that read:

Welcome to Sarah's Saloon.
No riding your horse in the saloon.
No shooting at my dog.
No spitting at the stove.
I serve good whiskey in here.
It won't kill or maim.
The first drink of the day is on me.
Newt Harvey, prop.

Above all, Sarah's Saloon and Gambling Hall was going to run honest games of chance. A lot of men made money from gambling but it wasn't the miners. It was mostly the dealers. I knew I could run honest games of chance and still make a lot of money. I figured, with the name of Sarah on the outside, I couldn't miss. It was a busy first year owning a business, especially a saloon and gambling hall. I only got two letters off to Martha and she sent three to me. We had been married for over five years and had been together for less than two months.

Many of my customers were men I knew from Bannack and Virginia City who had moved to the new diggings. Little excuse is needed to pull the cork in a gold camp; the men would call for a round when we got visitors, if a man died, or when there was a business opening or closing. A marriage or a birth was enough to declare a holiday.

There was always a celebration when someone made a big strike and the men seemed to come up with a big strike most every day.

Every morning, Three Fingers Putnam came in and threw the dice to see whether he got a slug of gin or if his horse got a bucket of oats. That's the unluckiest mare I have ever known. The poor thing had one stretch of bad luck where it didn't eat for more than a week.

Three Fingers got his name over in Idaho Territory. He got bit on the hand by a rattler. The only thing he could do was grab an ax and chop off two fingers. I know he has pain in the lost fingers and it must bother him still. It's an experience you never forget. Even now when I hear a rattler buzzing my leg begins to twitch.

Howard Ross was in for a grubstake. The summer had been a washout and he was broke. I didn't hesitate a moment before giving him a hundred dollars. He is such a strange man. He stood just over five foot but when it came to strength he was like a mountain. There was lots of muscle under his shirt. Besides his honesty there was something about Howard I liked. He kept me entertained by thinking up new locations to go look for gold. The gold strikes in Nevada had taken his interest and he talked about going there to avoid a winter in Montana.

Hard Luck Ray came staggering in one morning and I had to run him back out into the street. The smell came in through the door before he did. His shirt, pants, and beard were covered with dried tobacco spit. I yelled at him to stay out until he was cleaned up. He shuffled and swayed over to a horse trough and fell in. Later he returned explaining he had been in an all night poker game that was so fast and so crooked that he couldn't afford to turn his head to spit. He was flat busted broke as usual, and begging for whiskey money. I told him I would pour him a drink only if he told me how he came by the money to pay off Darts Hardware two years before. He got a funny look on his face and then he edged to the end of the bar. He pointed his finger at the empty glass and with a sly grin he told the story.

He had been drunk for three or four days and had crawled into a loaded wagon to sleep it off. They were five miles from town before the owner discovered him. He rolled Hard Luck off and drove on. Hard Luck woke up that afternoon hearing distant gunfire. A little later he heard hoof beats headed his way and prudently hid. Soon, two men rode up and stopped for a breather. Dust in the distance showed they were being chased. They rode over to a large tree and tied a sack high up in the branches and galloped off. Hard Luck stayed hidden and sure enough a posse came by tracking the two riders. When it was safe to come out he climbed up, cut the sack down and lit out. In the sack was almost five thousand dollars in gold from a stage holdup. He used that to pay off the debts and have a spree for most of a week. He told me that he recognized both of the robbers and had been afraid to talk. He felt safe in telling the story now as both had been hung by the vigilantes.

I had grubstaked a few men over the years, sort of to ease my conscience over being lucky at finding a gold strike. But I decided that Hard Luck Ray was not a good prospect for grubstaking. He had been on the wrong end of claim deals so many times we couldn't help wonder what was going to happen to him next. One look at his down and out appearance would keep a dying man from feeling sorry for himself. He did get lucky one night though. He came into The Sarah one morning spreading the tale that Sam Parker had come home that night and found his wife Mary in bed with his friend Oscar. Sam up and shot Oscar dead and then Mary shot her husband. Hard Luck said it could have been worse. He was there the night before.

The porter entered the smoking car. "Gentlemen our chef is preparing a special steak tonight. I suggest you don't wait too long. While you're eating I'll prepare your compartment for the night."

"Thank you, porter. Would you wake us for an early breakfast?"

"Yess Sir."

Wilbur stood, "I'm tired of reading, let's quit until tomorrow."

Breakfast was taken early the next morning and they returned to the compartment. Wilbur picked up the journal. "James, it's your turn to read."

"Okay but, I'm going to stretch out and get comfortable before I start."

Summer - 1868

It is said that if you see a rabbit and no one is chasing him then times ain't too bad. In the summer of '68, The Sarah Saloon and Gambling Hall was just like that rabbit. It was doing quite well. There were times I would leave town and visit other cities to look for businesses and mining companies I could invest in. During those trips I thought about Martha and the boys and what they might be doing. The years were going by too quickly and we were no nearer a solution.

In July, I got a letter from Mr. Walters. He had been talking to the police about clearing up the charges. I was to think it over and decide if I wanted to chance it with the police. He suggested that Martha and I consider adopting Wilbur since he and James were being raised as brothers. When I got Mr. Walters's letter I decided to take some time and think on things. I rode the two miles over to Marysville to visit the Belmont and Savage mines, more for the diversion than for business.

Returning late, I left Misty at the livery and walked to The Sarah to check on things. The men fell silent and turned to look at me as I came in the front door and headed for the bar. Now, I really did not sense trouble, but the room was crowded with excited men who were expecting a show. When I reached the bar, Mike stated in not too low a voice that I had a visitor up in my office. I got two steps toward the stairs when the office door opened. It was Martha. She was more radiant and beautiful than ever. She came down the stairs towards me, with the silent men parting to make a path. The air in my lungs was exploding and my mind had melted. After a moment of just looking at each other we hugged and I began to breathe again. The men set up a cheer when we kissed. They got to cheer for quite a long time.

When Martha got off the stage that morning, she had come looking for me at The Sarah. Mike thought it too dangerous for her to be wandering around Helena so he suggested the comfort of my office. Meanwhile, the men had jumped to several conclusions about who she was. The news got around town about my visitor and the men came in to see her. The betting was that she was either my wife or my lover. Either way the men were there to see us meet. I quieted the crowd and introduced Martha as my wife. Amid shouts of approval I saw money change hands. I signaled Mike to announce a round was on the house while we slipped into the back room and out into the street.

We went over to the hotel and sat by the window in the lobby. While Martha was talking I was looking at her and struggling to listen. Being around her beauty and hearing her voice was a big distraction. I had been living alone a long time and now I hoped it was about over.

Over the past year her health had gotten stronger and she had decided to come to Montana to see if the climate and altitude would suit her. She had taken the steamboat from Omaha to Fort Benton and had arrived in Helena on the morning stage. She was planning to stay until the last boat would be leaving Fort Benton for Omaha. If I couldn't live in Omaha then she was determined to live in Helena. The trip had been tiring so we decided she should take it easy for a few days while she told me about James and Wilbur. We went to my lawyer and got the papers drawn up so that Wilbur was officially our son. I sure would liked to have been there when he found out he had a family again.

Once she was rested, we spent a week riding around town and looking over the country. She showed no signs that the altitude and climate were affecting her. One day we headed west of town so I could show her a place that I knew was for sale. It was a log house built at the edge of a grove of aspen and lodge pole pines. A stream crossed the yard in front. It had a nice pasture and garden plot to one side. From the porch we could see snow capped mountains above the trees. It would be a beautiful place to live the rest of our lives together.

The next day we found Frank Heiser and told him that we wished to buy the property. He was hoping to sell before winter and move to town with his son. He was very happy to sell it to someone who would love it as he had.

Martha and I spent many days looking through the house and making a long list of what needed to be fixed by next summer. There were three rooms on the second floor. She picked the room with windows facing south for a sewing room and the other two I would fix up for Wilbur and James. I knew where I was going to be spending my winter days.

By the time we got word that the last boat would leave the next week we had made a lot of decisions. The day before she was to leave we drove around Helena one last time. She was impressed with Helena and thought it might be a good place to settle down after all. Those words were good to hear but would it ever happen for us? She was pleased that we had an Episcopal Church. A library association was raising funds to build a library and Helena had a fine school started. Church?! Library?! School?! I had been involved with my own business so much that I had not noticed that people really were making Helena a good place to live. With a lot of misgivings, I put her on the stage for Fort Benton, wondering what the future held for us.

Fall and Winter - 1868

Before 'Ol' man Heiser was able to move out, I had men working on the corral and others building a barn. I began to spend more and more time at our home in the woods. I had never known that I could enjoy hammering and painting. I got a letter from Martha about how excited the boys were at coming to Montana next spring. Wilbur was happy with his name change. Mr. Walters was pleased with our decision to adopt Wilbur and our determination to be together. The trip had been hard on Martha, requiring several days' rest when she got off the boat. She reported that the doctor had advised her to come out next year just for the summer and return to Omaha in the fall so he could make sure she was doing okay.

We got a heavy snow in January. I went out to our house to inspect the roof and do some work. It snowed for three days straight and the wind blew up large drifts around the buildings. I awoke on the morning of the fourth day to blue skies and bright sunshine. The sun reflected through the snowflakes as they fell from the trees, filling the air with diamonds. Everything was covered with a bright, clean, white powder. It was a beautiful sight to see as I sat in the living room having coffee.

In the distance I could see a horse and rider coming from town. They struggled against the drifts for a long time before reaching the road to the house. The horse was played out and having a time getting through the drifts. After the man got off I could see it was my bartender Mike. He came in, out of breath, with red cheeks and ice on his beard. I told him to get a cup of coffee and stand in front of the stove while I took care of his horse. When I got back to the house he was standing at the front window not moving or saying anything. He had such a funny look on his face when he turned and handed me a telegram from Mr. Walters. I opened it and saw three words: Martha died today.

Losing Kramer, or Alex and Molly, or my mother did not prepare me for my sense of loss at that moment. I must have sat in that house for three or four days without eating or sleeping. I couldn't shake the despair and the feeling that God was out to hurt me. I went blank for a time and I still have only fleeting recollections of what happened. The most I remember was standing out in the snow, watching our home burn to the ground. I was not wearing a coat or boots. If the neighbors had not seen the blaze I would have frozen to death. The rest of the winter I was downstairs getting drunk, or upstairs in my quarters above the saloon, sleeping it off.

Spring and Summer - 1869

By April, I was looking forward to going to Omaha to see the boys. The weather for most of March and the first week of April had been unusually mild and sunny. By the middle of April I was hit with a mild case of gold fever that I could not shake. I decided to go over to Anaconda and look around. A week away from Helena wouldn't hurt the business and the hurting inside me was never going away. I found nothing around Anaconda that I would consider for investment. I decide to check on Cascade Smith's claim near Butte. I had a sack of supplies for him including a bottle of his favorite whiskey. We discussed some prospects and he showed me the gold he had gotten so far.

On my way back I started getting a feeling something wasn't right. When I reached Montana City I heard the news that a fire had started in the gambling house at the corner of West Main and Bridge Street and had destroyed Helena's downtown district along Main Street. When I got to town, The Sarah was gone. There was nothing but a hole in the ground, piled high with blackened timbers. It was another big blow in my life. I had lost Martha and now The Sarah. Life was not fit to live anymore.

I was thankful no one had been hurt or killed. Luckily my bank had escaped the fire so my cash assets were safe. I lost all of my personal belongings because I was still living in a room over the saloon. The only things I had left was the clothing I was wearing, my hat and my journal.

I had a decision to make. I could rebuild, or take what little money was left, sell the land and go to Omaha. I would not have much to show for all my years of hard work and I would have to face my mother in law as a failure. That I could not stomach.

Tom Doyle suggested that rebuilding The Sarah might be good for me. After stirring my brain a bit, I decided he was right and I should stick it out rather than give up. I hated to make that decision and hated even more telling the boys I would not be coming to Omaha that year. I posted a letter to them explaining the fire and my plans to stay and rebuild. In my letter, I included a list of the supplies and materials I would need. I said I would appreciate it if Mr. Walters would ship them to me as quickly as possible. I didn't know which hurt the most, losing The Sarah or not getting to see the boys. I sent word to the bank in Denver to transfer my entire balance to Helena.

Once I had decided to tough it out, I made a quick trip to Marysville, secured two empty buildings and arranged for them to be dismantled and freighted to Helena. If The Sarah was open again by the first of July, with a makeshift bar and gambling tables, I would make it. We began cleaning up the mess and salvaging what we could. We processed the ashes and dirt from the cellar, recovering nearly four thousand dollars in gold.

In May I got a telegram from Walters' Wholesale that the first shipment was on the steamboat Alabama and was expected to dock at Fort Benton on the eleventh of June. While waiting for the Alabama we put up the temporary saloon. It was built so that when the workmen put up the outer walls of the new building they would not interfere with business.

Freight was being unloaded from the Alabama when I got to Fort Benton. Captain Guizot had a message for me that there was freight on the Cora and the Imperial too. I could expect them to arrive over the next ten to fifteen days. That was good to hear because the water levels were dropping and by the first of July it might be too low for the steamboats to go further than Fort Union.

Another problem chewing at my stomach was the shortage of freight wagons to haul my goods back to Helena. I was lucky to get the first load headed for Helena, but it was going to be some time before the next loads would reach town and that would delay the opening of the saloon. Sure enough, when I returned to Fort Benton two weeks later, freight was filling the warehouses and piling up on the docks. My cargo from the Cora was in the warehouse and the Imperial was unloading. I looked for Captain Weinshank of the Imperial to see if there were any further messages for me.

He was curious about how I got such a big company like Walters' Wholesale to give my shipment priority handling. He had been ordered to unload enough cargo in Omaha to accommodate my shipment and ordered to unload my cargo first if possible. I told him I was a friend of the owner. If I had told him about me and Martha the story would have reached Omaha and St. Louis before his boat did.

There just weren't enough freight wagons to handle the large amount of cargo being unloaded. I was going to be delayed for weeks and it was going to cost me a lot of business. I spent a few days talking to freight companies and found demand for their services was high and so were their rates. I was getting desperate when a strange message came that there were several wagons coming to haul my goods. The next day a train of ten wagons pulled up to the docks. It was a group of my regulars at The Sarah who had volunteered to help get my shipments back to Helena to reopen the saloon. As one man put it. "The sooner we have our Sarah back the sooner we will have Tangle Leg to drink." Once again I escaped going broke.

With the freight came a letter from Mr. Walters saying he was sorry that I had lost my business. He was sure I had made the right decision to rebuild. The boys were doing fine and I needn't worry about them. Along with what I needed for The Sarah, he had sent merchandise to start a general store. He knew I could sell any of the items I didn't need and make a profit, which is exactly what I did.

Christmas - 1869

The floor above The Sarah was completed with small quarters in the rear for me and offices for a doctor and two lawyers up front. By November The Sarah was running smoothly but I had a troubling problem. It was obvious that by the bank's January fifth deadline I was going to be short five thousand dollars.

I was reminded of my first year in Colorado and what a difference that peddler Wooton had made to our desolate camp, with his whiskey and supplies. I began thinking about the men in Helena, working hard to build a new and better business district. There was going to be more money in the men's pockets for Christmas celebrating. All they would need was the tiniest of excuses to spend it.

When I told Katie of my idea she was all for it. We decided to throw a big celebration starting the week of Christmas and running through New Year's day. I ordered extra gambling tables to offer Faro, Roulette, Chuck-a-luck, and Poker. We put in a large stock of whiskey, beer and food. Using James's old connections in Salt Lake City, I got oysters, hams, and turkeys shipped in along with other delicacies that Katie suggested. She had two ladies cooking pies and cakes in their homes. I was taking a gamble but I couldn't think of a better way to raise the money and have fun doing it.

When news of the party got around, I soon had volunteers to provide music and entertainment just for the food and drink. The ladies of the library and the literary society offered to make and hang decorations for a generous donation. Josephine Airey volunteered her hurdy-gurdy ladies to help entertain the men, and we would split her profits. I accepted her offer because she employed decent ladies, treated them fairly, and above all didn't tolerate any nonsense from the men. The men got excited at the prospects of such a grand party and the news spread from mine to mine.

Many of the men arrived shaved, cleaned and wearing new clothing. Some weren't recognizable. The celebrating ran twenty-four hours a day for ten days. The men wanted to enjoy the party for the entire week and acted like gentlemen. On Christmas day I shut the gambling operation down and closed the bar. I allowed each preacher in town fifteen minutes to hold forth and give us all something to think about. Two church choirs combined and we all sang Christmas carols.

When it was all over I jumped up on the bar and called for quiet. I said we all had a lot to be thankful for and challenged the crowd to donate to the fire relief fund. We had a bucket at the end of the bar and it clanked day and night for the rest of the celebration. People came from miles around to celebrate the New Year and the return of

The Sarah. Profits from the party put me back in the black and I beat the payment dead-line by two days. More important, I was back to my old self and glad to be alive. Tom was right, as soon as I started with the rebuilding I began to feel better about myself.

Spring - 1870

On March 24, downtown Helena was hit with another bad fire. The Sarah was spared, but some of the businesses who had been just recovering from the last fire were burned out again. Many who didn't have the money to rebuild so soon after the last fire had to sell their land and leave. I had all of my assets in the building and business and would have suffered the same fate if I lost The Sarah again. The Helena Brewery saved their buildings by using beer to wet down the walls. Some said it was the next best thing beer could be used for. Next to drinking it, of course.

One of the saloons had just received a brand new piano when the fire struck. Some of the men got real excited when the fire jumped across to their block. They were afraid it would reach the saloon and burn their new piano. Excitement and fear grew as the flames got closer. They decided if the fire got much closer they would go into action. Sure enough, when the fire reached the next building four men grabbed the piano and hauled it out in the street to safety. The fire changed directions and the saloon was saved. When the time came, it took eight men who struggled to haul it back into the saloon.

Howard Ross was back, asking for a new grubstake. I didn't mind. I figured that someday he'd hit a good strike and I'd get my money back plus a profit.

Summer - 1870

The Sarah attracted a close knit group of prospectors who had been chasing the golden mirage since the '49 rush to California. Many of those who claimed to have made it to "Californy" couldn't be pinned down as to the details, however. One part-nership that lasted through thick and thin was two old timers known as Norm and Virgil. Over the years they had gotten tired of eating the same food day after day, so Norm had sent away for a cookbook. Virgil was telling me that Norm had that book for more than two weeks and the food still tasted as bad as ever. He wanted me to take a look at the recipes to see what the problem was. I quickly discovered their trou-ble. The recipes all began the same way. "Start with a clean dish."

One young man by the name of Jack Wilson was working for me doing odd jobs, cleaning up the place and such. One day he asked for a few days off to go visit his fiancée's family over near Silver City. Now that was going to be a "for better or for worse" marriage. He couldn't have done better and she couldn't have done worse. But things must have gone well because he sure was busting with joy over his future father-in- law's way of treating a guest. When it came time for a toast, Jack said he took down the whiskey jug, pulled out the cork and threw it away.

I got a letter from Amos Steck at the Merchants and Miners Bank in St. Louis with news about Martha's family. Her uncle Levi Swan had fallen in with Old Man Bates on several bad investments. He had started using the family property as collateral to cover his losses. My mother-in- law and her brother were about to lose the family home and a forty-acre parcel of land adjoining it. Bates was going to acquire the property and then sell it and other land he owned to eastern investors. The key property was the forty acres and the land the family home sat on. Amos suggested I purchase the forty acres for enough money that Levi could pay off his debts and escape from the clutches of Old Man Bates. I wrote back to do whatever was necessary to secure the property and I would send the funds to him. I also requested that no one know of my part in the transaction and the property be put in James' and Wilbur's name.

Captured

Along with rents from the doctor and lawyer on the second floor, The Sarah was making good money. That summer I decided I was not going to work so hard. I was going to some time off and travel around the territory. Montana Territory was growing and a lot of folks were prospering in many businesses besides mining. I had another reason for getting away. One of the ladies had decided that it was time I settled down and got married. She had decided she was the right woman for me and I could not convince her I was not interested.

I took the stage to visit the Dunlaps at Bannack City. I spent some time with them, talking about Martha and what had happened over the past year. After a few days, I borrowed Sam's wagon, intending to explore the mountains over in Idaho Territory and get in some fishing and prospecting. I did too much wandering and after a few days, I had lost track of my whereabouts. Two more days of traveling and I was still in unfamiliar country. I knew I was in Idaho Territory and needed to turn east to find my way out.

One morning I awoke looking down the barrel of an old 40-cal Sharps rifle. A fierce looking Indian held the other end. Four other braves backed him up with assorted knives, spears and arrows. I didn't move or talk, in fact I was afraid to blink. I noticed they were all very young bucks, probably Nez Perce on their first war party. From the looks on their faces, I knew each one was itching to make a name for himself by killing me and taking my equipment and hair back to camp. I wouldn't have been in that fix if 'Ol' Kramer had still been alive. He'd have given me a warning. It was a staring match for a while until another warrior came up to us. By his manner and dress I guessed he was the leader of this fierce little band. He said something I didn't understand and motioned for me to get up.

What I did next was out of habit developed from years of sleeping on the ground. I sat up, reached over, put my hat on and stood up. All hell broke loose when they saw a Colt .44 was under my hat. It's a wonder they didn't kill me right then and there. There I stood, over six foot all in my long johns, boots and hat. While they stood a little higher than five feet tall, I was the one in trouble. At that point I was lucky to still have my hair.

The leader began to shout and gesture at me with all of them chiming in. I was sure it was some sort of a death chant. My death. I didn't understand a word, but he was worked up about something. Yelling and gesturing they would draw back their bows with the arrows pointed at my heart. Spears were thrown to see how close they could come. All of a sudden the leader stopped in mid-yell and began looking at me with interest. Saying something to the others, he stepped up and grabbed my hat. With more words he pointed to the spirit bag on the band. The other braves began to talk back and forth, gesturing at me and the equipment. They were arguing about something and it appeared to be the leader against the others. The words "seve nakohe" came up several times. When two of the braves made a move toward me the leader jumped between us, shouting a long string of words that must have stung. They backed off as he spit out a tirade with all the authority and malice he could muster.

Whatever he said got action. Two of them tied my hands and put me on a horse while the others leaped on their ponies. We rode out of camp, following the leader who was carrying my hat like a trophy. We rode hard for hours, taking only one short rest. I was worn out trying to stay upright in the saddle. Even with hands tied in front, it's hard to stay in the saddle. We followed a trail higher and higher in the mountains over a narrow pass above timberline. The narrow trail led over a ridge to a camp hidden in a small canyon.

My captors galloped in, yelling and gesturing to draw a crowd of women, children and a few older braves. The bucks acted up for a while to entertain the home crowd. They must have been a little too boisterous for the older men. The disdain on their faces was clear. Eventually they pulled me down off my horse and shoved me into a small tent. It wasn't long before the young warrior returned and led me through the tribe to a ceremonial lodge in the center of camp. It was adorned with eagle feathers and decorated with symbols and pictures. My hands were untied and I was prodded into the dark interior.

As my eyes adjusted to the dim light I could see the chief and one older brave. Behind the chief, wisps of smoke drifted from a smoldering fire adding to the dinginess. The sweet smell of sagebrush mingled with the smell of fat and rancid flesh. The chief sat facing the door. Long jagged lines of red paint adorned his chest, neck and head. A single bear claw hung around his neck. As my eyes adjusted I could see that the designs on his body were made by painting over large ugly scars. To his right sat the older brave who motioned for me to sit on the chief's left.

The chief reached behind and pulled out my hat and placed it in front of us. He spoke for a moment and then motioned to the brave, who repeated his words in halting English. "The one who speaks is Raging Bear. His people lived in the mountains far to the south of here."

The chief spoke again while gesturing to me and pointing to his chest. I did not feel any danger from all this so I watched and listened with interest. "Raging Bear tells of a young warrior on his vision quest. He built a sweathouse near a spring and for many days he prayed and fasted for a vision to guide his life as a warrior. While he sat in the sweathouse, the vision of a large grizzly appeared. The vision roared and tore at the house until Raging Bear realized it was not a vision but an angry grizzly. He shot an arrow as the bear lunged to claw and bite him. Fearing he had little time to live he began running. Looking ahead he was dismayed to see a white man pointing a gun at him. Raging Bear fell and began his death chant as the bear stood up over him. Then came the noise of the white man's gun."

Again the chief spoke, this time tracing the scars with his finger. The interpreter repeated. "The white man's medicine was strong. He killed the bear and then cared for me until I was able to go on my own. The scars on my body remind me of that time. Before I returned to my tribe the man gave me the pelt, claws and teeth. It was a great gift. I prayed to the Great Spirit and asked for him to protect the tall white man. I put one claw and one fang in my spirit bag and gave it to the white man as a token of our friendship and as a sign that he was protected by the Spirit of the Great Grizzly. I returned to my tribe with a vision that my name was Raging Bear. The bear's hide was my robe and the claws my necklace. We now sit on the robe of the great bear we killed."

I looked down, and sure enough, we were sitting on a bear rug, bullet holes and all. I looked up and smiled at my warrior friend. "Tell Raging Bear I am full of joy at seeing my friend again. Ask why he has come so far north from his hunting grounds."

The brave relayed my greetings and question. The chief paused for a time, in obvious discomfort, before answering with a few sentences. The brave listened then spoke. "The elders said that I brought dishonor to my vision as a warrior by letting a white man help kill the bear. I was banished from the tribe with what I could carry. My horse was given to another. I followed the mountains north to this place and the Nez Perce accepted me."

The interrupter paused then added, "From that time on he has fought with honor for his new family." He pointed to the opening. "Now we must go."

We got up and walked outside. In front of the lodge stood the entire tribe of about forty men, women, and children. Not a sound or a movement came from anyone. For once even the dogs were quiet. They were a starving and haggard looking bunch, with no sign of arms except the one Sharps rifle which I suspected had no ammunition. They were not a menace to anyone.

The Gift

As everyone including me watched, Raging Bear reached inside a large beaded bag tied to his belt. He pulled out his hand, raised it high and opened his fingers. There in his palm was a spirit bag that looked like mine. He open it and produced a bear's tooth and claw. As he spoke the brave repeated his words. "Many times I have stood before the council and told the meaning of this bag, how the fang and claw inside bring me power from the spirit of the great grizzly."

Raging Bear then stepped forward and held up my hat. He removed the spirit bag and opened it. Again he raised his hand and opened his fingers to show the bear's tooth and claw to everyone. "I have told you of the white man having big medicine to cool the heat in my body. He stands with me now and we are glad to have this friend with us."

After replacing the items, he attached the bag to my hat and handed it back to me. I put my hat on and smiled.

He shouted, "Seve nakohe! Seve nakohe!"

I shouted back, "Seve nakohe!"

The roar from the tribe was thunderous for such a small bunch. It nearly knocked me down. Their delight in this little ceremony was unbounded. I was happy because I realized I was going to live. We stood and grasped arms like we had done many years before. We did a dance around the others with such glee they must have thought the chief and I were crazy.

Our celebration continued that night with feasting and games of skill. At one point we were watching the young braves skillfully throwing spears at a furry target. I asked Raging Bear where the older braves were. He became serious for a moment and then answered in two sentences. The interpreter was quiet for a time before repeating his words. "Raging Bear says they are all living with their Spirit Father. He says only old warriors and women protect us now."

Later, I asked the interpreter about the young bucks that had brought me here, especially their leader.

"He is Raging Bear's son, Black Otter. I hope he will live long enough to see a new family started."

A disturbance behind the line of older squaws caught my attention. Two women were beating a young girl. Her howling and screaming brought the hair up on my neck. It sounded more like a wounded animal than a child. She was fighting back with all she could muster. I was amazed at the scratching, kicking, and biting she was doing all at the same time.

Finally they got a leather thong on each leg and tied them to stakes. I walked over to where she was tied to get a better look at her. She appeared to be seven or eight years old, although due to starvation and poor food she could be older. She was so dirty I was not sure where the dirt stopped and the skin and tangled black hair began. Her dress was a discarded rag with holes in it. She wore nothing else.

I spoke to her and got no reaction. Like most captives she looked away, having learned that to look someone in the eyes was to invite a beating. One of the squaws returned with a stick and began to beat the child with blow after blow. I raised my hand and she stopped. The girl let out a string of words and sounds that were full of hatred and vile feelings. I caught a mixture of Nez Pierce and Sioux spewing out against her captors.

My interpreter walked up motioning for the woman to leave. I pointed at the girl and asked about her. He explained that she was received in trade with the Sioux. The Sioux called her Sky. Later his tribe called her ma sa nee or crazy one. She was thought to be crazy because she fought them constantly. He started to say something, hesitated, and with a smile said, "Come."

I followed him around the celebrating people and to the lodge. He motioned for me to stay outside. He entered. There was a long conversation within. When the flap was thrown back, Raging Bear stepped out and walked to the fire and shouted. After every one quieted down he turned and spoke to me. I was trying to understand what he was saying by the reaction of the tribe. They started laughing and gesturing. The brave looked pleased as he told me Raging Bear's decision. A gift was to be offered to mark the occasion. And the gift? It was to be the girl!

I was in a fix. I didn't want her and couldn't keep her. Yet to refuse her would insult the tribe and might get her killed. The people quieted down waiting for my answer. I was so surprised at the turn of events I could not think of a way out. Reluctantly, I gave the sign of acceptance and the roar of laughter was unsettling. The girl was quickly untied and dragged into a tent.

By sun up, I had my horse saddled and ready to go. The young warriors led by Black Otter were preparing to take me back to my camp. I was sure they were going to make a show of our departure like they had when we arrived the day before. After we were mounted, four squaws brought the captive girl out and put her up behind one of the braves. Instantly, the girl grabbed the brave's knife and slid off his horse. Everyone watched as she ran screaming through the crowd directly at her victim. With a howl and a new outburst of words she leaped at a squaw and knocked her to the ground. They fought hard, hitting, scratching, and pulling hair as they rolled in the dirt. All the time the girl was yelling words of hate at the woman. The others understood and were encouraging her. The old woman's resistance eased and the girl quickly grabbed a small beaded bag from around her neck. The blade flashed in the sun as it came up and back down. In an instant, the knife cut the thong and the girl was on her feet with the bag raised high above her head. With a burst of words directed at the woman, she spat on her and kicked her before backing off. The girl eluded a few halfhearted attempts to catch her as she ran into a tent. Two squaws went in the front as she slashed the back wall and stepped out carrying a small bundle. She walked back through the tribe with head held up and glaring at everyone. With a satisfied smile, she returned his knife and allowed the brave to lift her back on his horse. They raced out of the camp followed by the braves, yelling and waving weapons.

It was a good thing they knew the way because I had lost my bearings coming in the day before. Once out of the camp, we settled down to a fast pace in silence. I spent the time pondering what I was going to do with the girl. I couldn't keep her and it was likely she would escape at first chance. I could try to find another tribe to take her but she would be a slave again. I didn't want that to happen. It looked like I was going to be stuck with her and there was something about that girl that made me very uneasy. Her behavior was unsettling and I was not sure I could handle the little wildcat even for a short time.

For some time the train had been slowing down and now it came to a complete stop. James opened the compartment door just as the porter came into the car. "Everything is okay. We had a derailment here last week and we have to wait for the crews to get the track clear before we can continue. Its best if you don't leave the train 'cause we'll only be stopped for a short time." The porter turned to leave. James spoke, "after we get underway we would like our dinner here in the compartment."

"Yassir, I'll see to it as soon as we get past the wreckage. It was not long before the whistle blew and steam was applied to the wheels. Slowly they crossed the damaged area. The men could see two mangled box cars and a passenger coach scattered along the railway bed. Once they were beyond the damage the engineer gave it more steam and they were underway again.

Luis returned to his position. "Okay, James, go on, and we'll stop when the food arrives."

Returning to Civilization

When we got back to my camp the girl was tied to the wagon. I let Black Otter know they were to take some food back with them. Black Otter turned to the brave who had pointed the rifle at me the day before and said something. It was obvious that he did not like what was said. A second threatening command from Black Otter got results. The defiant brave produced my Colt .44 and handed it to me.

We ate and smoked before they left. Black Otter motioned to their lone rifle and signed they had no ammunition for it. I explained as best I could I did not have shells that fit. When Black Otter and his braves mounted up to go, he rode up to the girl and talked to her in an almost kindly way. It was as if he were telling her something important and that he wanted her to understand what was happening. She sat, staring at the ground, showing no sign she heard.

After the braves left camp I squatted by the fire and made lines in the dirt while I thought about my situation. Once I had decided how I was going to treat her, I went over to the wagon and got out my knife and stuck it in the ground next to her. I was taking a chance but I wanted her to learn that she was in control of her life. I placed some food just out of reach so that she would have to cut the thong to eat. I returned to the fire to watch what happened. She looked at me, then the food and then the knife.

Three quick movements and she was eating the food with both hands and looking at me with wide-eyed curiosity. A flash in my head and I knew what had been gnawing at my brain to get out. This wild creature, a captive of two or more tribes, had blue eyes! She was a white girl! That was why Raging Bear had given her up. If the soldiers found white captives in a village they destroyed it, killing everyone. Raging Bear knew that eventually they too would be caught with her and he did not want his people punished any more.

I had been talking out loud and she had been listening, probably thinking I was crazy. Now I had a different set of problems. People in some towns would not accept white children who had been with the Indians since they were babies. They believed these captives to be more Indian than white. That was a problem we would face later. Right now I just needed to figure out how to talk to her. She was looking at me and I could see she was working something over in her mind. I hoped she was not planning an attack, as I was not sure I could fight her off for long. There was a whole lot of wild cat in that child.

The first way to communicate was to know her name. I pointed at my chest and said "Newt" several times. I got no response. Then I pointed at my chest, said "Newt" and then pointed at her with a questioning look. Still no response. I decided that I would work on her from time to time to see if she would catch on.

Another problem was what to do about sleeping. I didn't want to tie her up but if I left her untied and fell asleep it was likely I would wake up with a knife stuck in my chest. It was also likely that she would run at first opportunity. That was a chance I would have to take. I threw a blanket to her and said nothing.

I took my blanket and rolled up near the fire to spend the night thinking, planning and staying awake. I was glad for the friendship of Raging Bear and his family but their future was not hopeful. One thing for sure, our past has a way of catching up with us. Sometimes help given in human friendship can be repaid years later in mysteriously wonderful ways. Being saddled with this wild girl was more of a burden than I thought I could handle. I was sure going to need advice on what to do with my new responsibility.

Out of the corner of my eye I saw her crawl under the wagon and roll up in the blanket. A good sign, but I had a long way to go. I called across to her saying good night, thinking that I should treat her as if she understood. Prospectors always talked to their animals, knowing that the sound of their voice had a calming effect. It's good to hear a voice, even if it's your own.

The next morning I stirred up the coals and laid small twigs and leaves on them. A glance told me that she was no longer under the wagon. I sensed she was watching me from further back in the trees. I went to the wagon and got out the coffeepot, skillet and my sack of food. I turned and there she was, laying some wood next to the fire. I said good morning and smiled while laying things out to fix breakfast. She kept me supplied with wood but made no other effort to help or talk. I talked a blue streak to no avail.

When I set the plate in front of her she grabbed the food and ate with her hands. That set me to thinking about how I was going to civilize her. Getting her to take a bath and wear new clothing was going to be an experience for both of us. While I packed up the wagon I continued with my name game to see if she would respond. I loaded the wagon and hitched up my horse. By pointing and gesturing I tried to get her to get in the back. It didn't work so I picked her up, blanket and all and placed her in the wagon. I expected a fight, but she was quiet until the horses started. Then, she hopped out and walked alongside, as she had been used to doing.

After three days of following Black Otter's directions we topped the ridge south and west of Bannack. I headed for Sam and Kate's place with apprehension. This was going to be the first real test. I was not sure if being in a town would frighten her and she would run. I pulled into the yard and waited for Sam and Kate to come over to the wagon. They had been worried about my absence and were now worried about my presence. After a quick explanation Kate turned toward the girl who was now standing at the rear of the wagon.

She shrank back when Kate approached to make friends. I told Sam more of the story of how she came to be with me. He said that I was lucky to have been carrying that bag around with me all those years. He wondered if it worked as a pass through all Indian territories. I wasn't game to go find out.

When Kate gave up and backed away, the girl quieted down. I asked for clothing and a hairbrush. Kate did not hold out much hope for me to get her to bathe or change her dress. She thought it unlikely that I would have much success with her hair either. Sam helped me load up supplies and we headed for Helena.

The trip to Helena allowed me time to think of what would be best for the girl. I couldn't keep her with me and there weren't many people around who would take such a wild animal. After a week I was no closer to an answer. I made three attempts at bathing and changing her dress all with the same result. She would start spitting words increasing in volume and intensity and then would come the scratching and kicking.

As dirty and smelly as she was, I sure understood her reaction to my efforts, but I was determined to clean her up. As we approached Helena and I still didn't have a plan of action. I came to the junction were the road turns west into Helena or east to Sadie's place. I was about to go into town when the idea hit me. I was so happy and relieved, I stood up and waved my hat and gave out a yell. "Sadie's."

I swung the team east a half mile to a large ranch house. There were a few horses tied up out front, but it looked like a quiet afternoon at Sadie's and that was just what I wanted. I drove around to the back, chickens scattering as the wagon passed through the yard. I could see Jake pitching hay up in the loft as I stopped near the barn. Washing on the line was flapping in the breeze. Another quiet day at Sadie's.

While I made for the house, the girl ducked under the wagon to sit in its shade. Just as I reached the door my favorite cook, Belle, opened it. Belle was a beautiful woman and I told her so every time I came out to Sadie's Place. Sadie catered to a wide variety of customers. Through the back door a man could dig into the best food anywhere in the territories. Entering by the front door, a gentleman would be served up with the most refined female companionship he could ask for. No one was turned away. Even if he was broke, a man could at least get something to eat and a safe place to sleep. I was always trying to get Belle to cook for me at Sarah's but so far had not had much luck in luring her away. Sadie was always trying to get me to come through the front door but in all the years, I had never strayed.

No one was in the kitchen except Belle. We sat at the table and I told her about the girl under my wagon and the predicament I was in. If I was going to be the one to get her cleaned up I needed help and I figured this was the place to start. Belle walked to the door and looked at the dirty little girl for a long time, while I told about my efforts to gain her confidence and Kate Dunlap's failed attempts to help.

She turned back to me and said she would help, but it was going to cost me something in return. I had never known her to put a price on helping people and said so. I said she charged plenty for her food and it was worth it but never had she asked for payment to help someone in need or was broke. The look on my face must have been something because she started to laugh. She explained, that if she helped me I was to never again ask her to come work at The Sarah. That was a lot to give up as I really wanted her to come work for me. I reluctantly agreed to her terms.

Belle picked up a plate and piled on biscuits and a jar of honey. She told me to stay inside no matter how bad the ruckus was and not let any of the men come out to watch either. By the time Belle was starting down the steps the girl was looking at her. A few steps closer and the girl was out from under the wagon standing and looking at Belle. She was not displaying the same hatred or fear as she had for Kate, just a quizzical look. Belle continued to walk, saying nothing, but holding out a biscuit. The girl did not move until Belle was a few steps away. She took a step toward Belle and looked at the biscuits. Belle put honey on one and gave it to her. She ate it and several more.

Belle set the plate down and pointed to her chest and said "Belle." The she pointed at the girl's chest with a questioning look. The girl pointed at herself and said something I could not hear. I was astounded at what I had just watched. Belle returned to the house and the girl went back to the shade under the wagon. Belle had a smug look on her face when we sat down at the table. I was fit to be tied. Laughing, she pointed at her chest and said "Belle" then pointed at my chest and said "Newt" in such a mocking manner it made me mad.

She explained that sometimes a colored woman could get an Indian child to respond. She just took a chance it would work with the little girl. For two weeks I had been talking my self blue and had gotten nowhere. In two minutes and with a couple of biscuits she had tamed the wild cat. In spite of everything, I knew the girl was going to have a bright future. I asked about the girl's response when asked for her name. Belle said she did not understand what the girl said but predicted she would soon have it figured out. Belle suggested I leave the girl there to get cleaned up and presentable and she would let me know when to come back. I handed Belle two hundred dollars for boarding expenses and said to let me know when that was gone and I would give her more.

When I got back to The Sarah I took a ribbing about getting lost and taking so long to get back but no one suspected the real story of my trip to Bannack City.

A knock at the door interrupted the reading. The porter brought in the food and left. Luis poured three beers. "James, as soon as we get something put together, you can read on."

Fall - 1870

I took a trip over to Virginia City before winter set in. When I got there it was almost a ghost town. Nevada City was worse. Things were so bad I could have bought several claims for the price of a round at the saloon. A miner I knew from Nevada City came in the saloon. I set us up for a drink and we talked about who was still in the area. The bartender asked if we had heard about the latest prank that Frenchie Durand had pulled on George Pike. Frenchie has a playful streak when he's drinking, which is most of the time.

Frenchie owns a saloon in Nevada City, but he is more widely known for his practical jokes. George Pike was selling his claim and heading back east before winter set in. When it comes to George, any accusation of overworking would die for lack of evidence. Frenchie and his pals decided to have a little fun with George. They made up a supply of counterfeit gold and headed up to his cabin. Fake gold is made by melting copper and dropping small amounts on a stone. It comes out looking real enough to fool some prospectors and all greenhorns. The men told George that they had an investor, but he wanted the claim checked. George said that was fine as long as any gold recovered was his.

The pranksters took a large bucket to the diggings, filed it with ore and salted it with the fake gold. They went back to the cabin and panned the ore. When the fake gold popped up, 'Ol' George was bug eyed, but kept a straight face when he assured them that he was getting nuggets like that all the time. The boys handed over the fake gold and said they would talk it over with the investor. The jokesters stopped at several saloons in Virginia City to boast about their little prank before going back to Nevada City.

Finally, in the wee hours, they staggered back to Frenchie's Saloon for a few more drinks. When Frenchie opened the cash box he discovered the fake gold. "Where'd you get this gold?" he asked. The bartender said, "George Pike came in here claiming you boys helped him find that gold. He paid his bill and got a gallon of whiskey."

The easy deposits along Alder Gulch had played out and now other mining methods were needed to remove the gold from the rock. That took lots of money and professional mining engineers. I looked up a lawyer who was putting together claims to sell to eastern investors and told him if mining got going again he should send word to Tom Doyle. From Virginia City I went to Cascade Smith's claim, but it was abandoned, so I headed back to Helena.

When I got back, there was a message from Belle. She was ready for me to come out for dinner on Sunday. It had been three months since I had dropped the girl off and I was curious as to the progress Belle was making. Also, I was missing her cooking. The girl's presence was known in town but where she came from or who she was had not come to light. I hoped that I could keep my part in this as quiet as possible.

On Sunday I put on my best shirt and pants and announced I was going to visit Sadie's. Of course everyone thought I was going out to eat and try to ask Belle to come to work at The Sarah. It was just before one o'clock when I guided Misty past the front door and around to the back. There was no other buggy parked there or horses in the barn. That was surprising because on Sundays, with the front business closed, Belle was usually busy. I turned Misty loose in the corral and went up to the door.

Sadie and her ladies, dressed for the occasion welcomed me and led me to the dining room. Sadie explained that Belle had been working hard with the girl and she was doing very well. Her ladies had taken the little child into their hearts. This was to be a special day, with a private party for her to meet the man who saved her. Belle came into the room and said I was to sit quietly and do what I was told. By then I was so curious that I had trouble keeping my mouth shut. I turned to say something to Belle and my mind went blank. I forgot to close my mouth.

Standing at the door was a little girl in a white dress. Black hair hanging down in ringlets framing a face of alabaster, brightened by a shy smile. Overshadowing all that beauty were her eyes. They were a blue that defied description. I could not take my gaze off her. I started to speak, then remembered my orders. The child came over and stood in front of me. She pointed at herself and said "Sky". Then she pointed at me, and I whispered "Newt" in a shaky voice. She repeated "Sky," then "Newt." By that time everyone was crying and I mean everyone.

The transformation was a miracle. While we ate my attention was on Sky. I was thanking God for this little one to be alive and doing so well. I asked about the beaded bag hanging around her neck. Belle said that it seemed to be very important to her. When she or someone else had shown interest in it Sky would clutch it and not let anyone touch the bag. One of the ladies mentioned that there were times they would catch Sky looking in the bag but the contents were still a mystery.

Afterwards, Belle and I talked about what needed to be done. I asked what was best for Sky and what I could do. Belle said she had become very attached to Sky and wished to raise her. She found Sky intelligent and quick to respond. I was more than happy to continue to pay for Sky's support.

Winter - 1870

Just after Christmas, Katie Gilbert announced she was leaving Helena. The boys were grown and gone. She had decided to go live with relatives in Kansas. I told Katie if she needed a grubstake to open a restaurant, I would get the money to her. Over the years we had become good friends and her kids thought of me as an uncle. Her leaving made me homesick for my own family.

I got a letter from Amos that my purchase of the forty acres had cost Old Man Bates two hundred and fifty thousand, and he was plenty mad. The last line in his letter read. "As soon as Old Man Bates finds out who is responsible for this we will all have to watch our backsides. Your being out in the territories may not save you from him."

Katie Gilbert had been gone less than two months when I got a letter from her. She had arrived in Cheyenne and had found a saloon and restaurant for sale. They needed ten thousand and would appreciate it if I could send that much. Which I did.

Josephine Airey sent word she wanted to discuss a business matter. The next day we met at her place of business and she explained her proposition. Josephine had been in Helena for about three years and the hurdy-gurdy house was very profitable. The house was too small for her needs. She and a silent partner were prepared to buy my business and building for forty thousand dollars. I could think it over and give her an answer in a few days. All she asked was that I keep her offer quiet. The strain on my brain was about to set my hair on fire so I headed for the billiard hall to think.

On Friday, I made a counter offer of fifty five thousand. Josephine responded with fifty thousand. It was done. I sold The Sarah and one week later I was turning the business over to her. I wrote Mr. Walters that I was definitely going to be in Omaha in June. Tom Doyle offered to look after my claims and other property and I made arrangements with Mr. Wier at the bank to receive payments from my investments and grubstakes. Like my friend James Miller, I made decisions quickly and planned to head downriver with the first steamboat of the season.

Summer - 1871

Two or three weeks before I was to leave for Omaha I got a letter from Mr. Walters. He reported that Old Man Bates knew of my purchase of the forty acres from Levi Swan. He was so mad at my interfering with one of his land deals that he hired a bounty hunter to go to Montana to get me. The orders were that I was not to get back to Omaha alive. I was skeptical about the danger I was in and decided to stay. Tom thought it best that I disappear for a while just in case the reports were true and the killer was to get lucky.

Some months before this, Belle had received word from her sister about a restaurant in a fancy hotel in San Francisco that was for sale. I was putting up the money for a half interest in the restaurant. Belle and Sky were preparing to leave the next week. It seemed like a good idea for me to help them with the move. I could spend time with them and return when it was safe.

We took the stage to Utah and the Union Pacific to the coast. San Francisco was a cross between St. Louis and Oro City. It was a place of culture thrown in with a rough and tumble collection of men and women, all looking to get rich and having fun doing it. With so many people coming to San Francisco there were only a few nice accommodations. I got Belle and Sky moved into a nice boarding house near the hotel. I had to stay at a miserable hotel down by the docks. Luckily it wasn't too long before I got into the hotel where our restaurant was. We finished the negotiations and bought the restaurant. It concerned me that the banks might be less accommodating to Belle because of her color and being a woman. I was wrong. The President of the Golden State Bank was most helpful and we got everything set up properly. I stayed for two months to make repairs in the kitchen and dining room. By the time I left I knew I had made a good investment in Belle and Sky.

Fall - 1871

Cascade Smith had a claim near Tonopah, Nevada. I went there from San Francisco to see how he was doing and maybe collect my share. After enjoying California, I was beginning to like the warmer climate. I found his claim and learned he was no longer doing the work. He had hired a bunch of men to do the digging and was sitting in the shack taking care of the books. He claimed there was plenty of excitement in Tonopah to keep me entertained and my share of the claim was enough to keep me fed and in whiskey for as long as I wanted. If I got bored, I could spend time throwing dirt in a box.

I rode into Tonopah one evening to get supplies and look the town over. A small group of people had gathered in an empty lot. They were there to break ground for their new church. I was across the street watching when I recognized the preacher. I had to rattle my brain a little before I came up with his name. I walked across the street to the crowd. His preaching hadn't changed. When he saw me he came over and said he was sure he knew me from somewhere else. I asked if he was still known as Hell Thompson. He laughed and said that he had not been called that since leaving Montana. I reminded him my name was Newt, a friend of the Dunlaps.

Inside of twenty minutes he had me roped into staying the winter to help build the church. We went out to Howard's mine and got my gear. Two families "adopted" me so I had a place to stay and plenty of good food. I was a part of their family and it did me a lot of good to be helping someone and not worrying about getting shot at. It did curb my drinking somewhat, but that was not a hardship. Sometimes it was just Reverend Thompson and me hammering and sawing, but it was worth it. When we had a wall ready we would gather some of the men from town to put it up and secure it. The men would go back to their work and we would continue with ours. We finished the church in the spring and began to hold regular services. When I announced I was leaving, there were offers of work, so I would stay, but I felt I needed to get on. I left with a good feeling about the work I had done and learned a lot about the Bible too.

Spring - 1872

I took the Union Pacific to Cheyenne for a visit and to catch up on the news with Katie. I stayed around there for a few weeks, then got itchy feet again. A letter from Tom Doyle finally caught up with me. He wrote about the bounty hunter that had come to Helena looking for me and suggested I stay clear for a bit longer. I wrote him that I was going back to San Francisco to visit Belle and Sky and maybe look for gold there.

After the train left Cheyenne and started up Sherman Hill I settled in the smoking car for the trip. I hadn't been there long when two scruffy looking characters come in and sat off in the far corner. An hour of watching those two talk and draw and argue convinced me they were plotting something. All my years of experience as a saloon-keeper and a gold prospector told me that whatever it was, they were up to something. I thought if it was a gold strike I would get in with the first wave which is the most profitable. My interest heated up a bit when they told the porter they were getting off in Rawlins. I had not heard of any gold being found in that area but I decided it was worth the loss of my train ticket to follow them.

The two lost no time getting to a livery and arranging for horses for the next morning and went next to the mercantile to get outfitted for a week's trip. They checked into a hotel and then went for supper and drinks. While they were having supper, I was getting my own outfit ready and making arrangements with a young boy to get some information for me while I was gone.

The next morning, I followed the two conspirators as they left town. They followed the railroad tracks west for two days. On the third day they went south, wandering around looking for some spot or another. Shortly after noon of the fourth day they tethered the horses and set up camp. We were about seventy miles southwest of Rawlins.

I watched them work for several hours, taking something out of a bag and scattering it around the area. Then they stomped and walked around on the stuff they had scattered. It was then I tumbled to their scheme. They were salting an area with gold or some other mineral. I was amused at myself that I had not caught on before. Those two swindlers had lured me out on the desert for five days over worthless treasure. There was nothing to do then but let them get their work done and check it out after they were gone. They left late that day so I waited from my vantage point until the next morning before going down to look around.

I couldn't believe my eyes. The land sparkled with flashes of sun light off glass or metal. I began to scrape and kick the dirt around and picking up gemstones. I found diamonds, rubies and emeralds scattered all over the area. It appeared they had salted the area with real gems though it's known diamonds and rubies and sapphires do not come from the same rock formation. I pocketed some of the better specimens and left for Rawlins.

Back in town I located my young informant and for twenty-five cents in candy and a dollar I got the information I wanted. He reported that as soon as the two hit town they returned the horses to the livery and stored their gear. The next morning they took the train for San Francisco. I told the boy that I might need him again in a week or so.

I spent the evening in my room with a bottle and my thoughts. I decided that their next step would be to bring the suckers out to Rawlins and let them see the acres of riches. Then they would let the suckers talk them into selling a few shares of their mine. I spent my days and nights at the depot waiting for the train from San Francisco with the two swindlers aboard.

It was ten days before five well dressed men got off the train with the two scruffy prospectors. From the look on their faces and the sound of their voices I knew the five men were hooked on a different form of gold fever and were about to be plucked of their money. They put an outfit together and left. I knew what was up so there was no need for me to go tramping out in the desert when I could stay close to a saloon.

I waited eight days before I saw them again. They came out of the desert with dusty clothing and skin all caked with dirt. The next day they were at the restaurant clean, dressed up and ready to do business. Those two men and done a good job of setting the hoax up and the greed in the banker's hearts was causing total blindness to the reality of the scam.

I watched them board the train for San Francisco wondering how much they were going to lose. I telegrammed Belle to watch the papers for a story on a large diamond strike. I took my gems to the local jeweler to see what they were worth. To my surprise I got three hundred dollars for just one diamond and one ruby. I kept the rest of them for future needs.

"Hey, that's the last entry! The rest of the pages are blank!" James leafed through the remaining pages looking for some clue to the ending.

The men sat in silence. The train had been slowing down to enter the station until it jolted to a stop.

"Cheyenne! Gentlemen, I'll see to your luggage."

Luis and the boys stepped off the train and shouldered their way to the depot to meet Sarah May and Kate. The boys escorted the ladies to the Denver train and helped them board. James promised they would visit them in Denver soon.

Chapter Eleven
Luis Remembers

After making arrangements for their luggage to be delivered to the hotel, James, Wilbur and Mr. Eaton walked the one block north to the Frontier House. The boys complained of sore butts and stiff joints but Luis kept quiet, though like them, he was hurting all over. After they registered, Luis suggested James and Wilbur take a look around town while he got some rest in a bed that was not in motion. They could meet in the saloon that evening and have supper.

Over supper, the boys and Luis puzzled over the journal and what may have happened to Newt.

"Boys, my memory is a little shaky but in '73, July or August I think it was, I walked in my office after lunch and there was your dad in fine new clothes in the latest New York fashion. He had my office girl Elizabeth and the other workers in giggles and pounding hearts. He was telling a big tale about that diamond and gem mine hoax in Wyoming."

"What happened after that?" Wilbur asked.

"Newt spent the winter of '73 in Leadville with the Tabors. From the stories Augusta told, they had a good time. When he wants to he can be one hell of a charmer with the ladies. The summer of "74 was spent throwing dirt in a box, as he would say. He didn't make much but it kept his claims valid and him out of trouble. In September, Newt came to Denver planning to stay the winter. In five days he had gotten wind of a gold strike and was all fired up to check it out. He put on that crazy hat he wears when he smells gold, and left, saying he was going to join Tom Doyle.

I didn't see Newt again until November of '75. I gathered his summer in the Black Hills was an adventure but he didn't give many details. He was in town for a week or two before going to Leadville. Newt and Horace got suspicious about some eastern investors who were buying up abandoned claims. Those two were sure they smelled an opportunity, and began buying claims to merge with theirs to form a mining company. It was a busy winter for them but they were as happy as two young otters playing in a pond.

"Now boys, what I'm going to tell you is the Lord's truth. Newt, Horace and Augusta came to Denver in April of '76 for fun and shopping. The very next day Newt walked into my office wearing that damned old hat. Said he wanted to get in on the excitement up at Deadwood.

"He was back in the summer of "77 with lots of stories about Deadwood. Horace had written to him about the silver boom at Leadville and he was there to see it for himself. Newt and Horace sold their holdings for over a million dollars plus a percentage of the first two year's production. With the news of the silver strikes, Leadville boomed again, making Horace and Augusta busier and wealthier than ever. Horace was investing in everything he could, buying business lots in Leadville and claims anywhere in the territory.

Newt came to Denver and talked like he was going to take it easy for a while. It wasn't long before he came in the office one morning and announced he was returning to Deadwood. We had lunch before he left and that was the last time I saw or talked to him."

"No hint of what happened to him after that?"

"From time to time I would hear that he was at one strike or another but no confirmation. Over the years he moved around between Rapid City, Cheyenne and Helena. I heard he had opened a saloon in Rapid City but have not heard if he still owns it. If no leads turn up here then I suggest you go to Helena and talk to Tom Doyle. From there you might have to go to Rapid City."

The next morning Luis climbed aboard the train for Denver, promising to look for Newt in Colorado. "A word of caution, stay away from the hog ranches. They'll skin you, and throw you to the wolves."

"Hog ranch? What's that?"

"Wilbur, explain that to your brother."

As the train pulled away from the station James asked Wilbur, "What is a Hog Ranch, anyway."

"It's a dangerous place for a man to visit if he's alone. Its one of those places near the forts for the soldiers to go drink and carry on with women. It's a good place to get robbed and killed."

The boys found no leads on Newt in Cheyenne so they decided to go to Helena as Luis had suggested.

James and Wilbur stood on the platform and watched the train being loaded. Behind the passenger cars and smoking car the yard master had coupled up two boxcars bearing U. S. Army lettering on the sides. In the gathering darkness, they watched four soldiers get in one of the box cars and set up for an evening of poker while "guarding" the shipment. The boys were disappointed when they noticed the closed sign across the steps of the smoking car. As James and Wilbur helped a lady and her baby up into the car, they failed to see a tall man with a black dog approach the train. He climbed the stairs to the smoking car, ducked under the closed sign, and entered.

A short time later the conductor began swinging his lantern and yelling. "All aboard."

The Union Pacific crossed southern Wyoming connecting Cheyenne, Laramie, Rawlins, Green River and Evanston at one hundred mile intervals. James and Wilbur were asleep when the train pulled into Laramie. They did not see the tall man from the smoking car walking his dog to pee on the wheels. Later, they did not see him come through the car to talk with the conductor.

After pulling out of Laramie, the car's occupants settled down to get what sleep was possible. In the early morning hours the train made an unscheduled stop at Fort Steele. The conductor announced it would be thirty to forty minutes before they would resume the trip. James and Wilbur stiffly stepped to the platform and wandered into the small station with some of the passengers. Even at that early hour, the station was busy, with civilians and soldiers milling around. If they had stayed out on the platform a little longer they would have seen the tall man come out of the smoking car and step off on the opposite side of the train. They would have heard him calling for his dog Kramer as he headed toward the fort saloon.

"James, this traveling is beginning to affect my mind. Last night I dreamed that a black dog was sitting and staring at me. Then a voice said. 'Leave the man alone.' The dog grabbed a bite of my food and disappeared. We had better find Dad soon before I start having nightmares and seeing ghosts. Let's get some air and look around a bit."

Wilbur stopped a soldier and asked. "Can we get something to eat at this hour?"

The soldier pointed. "Yes sir, at the saloon on the other side of the train. Go around the front of the locomotive and you can see the saloon. Ask Chugwater Charlie if he has any chili left. You'll have to hurry if you're gonna eat before the train pulls out."

James and Wilbur walked around the train and to the saloon. They were about to enter when three soldiers and a civilian tracker came tumbling out, crashing into them. James got the worst of the collision and was knocked down hard. Wilbur, being stockier, was able to stand his ground. Behind the soldiers, a lieutenant banged the doors open and yelled for attention. The sheepish privates gathered their wits and got to attention. The tracker used the railing to stay upright and was cussing everyone in sight. The language even shocked the soldiers to silence. The lieutenant apologized to the boys for their injuries then gave orders for the three soldiers to apologize and help them back to the train before it pulled out. Turning to the buckskin clad tracker he yelled. "Calamity, no more for you. Find a bed and sleep it off or I'll have you escorted to Cheyenne and put on the stage back to Deadwood."

James and Wilbur dusted off and followed the soldiers back to the train. Lieutenant West returned to the table and continued drinking with his guests, Kyle and Newt. "Someone warned me about hiring Calamity on as a tracker. I should have listened to them. She has been more trouble than she's worth. I suppose I'll have to ship her out before someone gets killed."

For James and Wilbur it was an uneventful trip to Corrine, Utah. After a day's wait they boarded the train to Helena.

Chapter Twelve
Arrival in Helena

Helena could be described as a long golden ditch with a busy town built on it and eight thousand people digging in it. James and Wilbur stood on the corner, watching the inhabitants of Helena going about their business. They had just arrived on the new railroad line from Utah and needed to walk around to get the kinks out. James looked north along Last Chance Gulch for some business sign or building that they would recognize.

Wilbur spotted an old timer sitting on a boardwalk bench in front of Reeves Jewelers and walked over to him. "Sir, we're looking for a saloon that was called The Sarah back in '69. Could you help us find it?"

"Sonny, that's a lot of years back. I don't know if there is anyone here that would know about it. Check at city hall. It's that building over on the next street. You can see the top of it there."

First inquiries at city hall produced no leads. Then James had an inspiration. He asked about Josephine Airy. Immediately they had directions to the Josephine Saloon and Gambling Hall. The Josephine was in a plain two story brick building of recent construction. The boys stepped into the saloon and stood there, struck by the beauty and opulence of the interior and it's owner, who was lounging on a red velvet love seat.

"My, you boys look lost, and thirsty. Mike, set these boys up."

"Are you Josephine?" James asked, knowing the answer.

"That's me, what's on your mind."

"We're looking for Newt Harvey. Heard he used to own this saloon and we thought someone here could help us?" In the silence that followed the atmosphere chilled fifty degrees. In mid wipe the bartender stopped to remove a cold three-day-old cigar from his mouth.

"Who's ask'n?"

"I'm James Harvey and this is my brother Wilbur. Newt Harvey is our father."

"If that's so, then you would know what he used to call this place."

"The Sarah."

"How'd he come to name it that?"

"His mother's name was Sarah," answered James.

"Yes, and that's the name of his burro that found his first big strike," Wilbur chimed in.

"That's enough, Mike. I have been observing young James here and I would say there was more than a little family resemblance."

Wilbur spoke up, "We know why you are suspicious of strangers asking for Newt Harvey. But you don't have to be cautious now. He was cleared of the charges in Omaha several years ago and we can prove it."

The bartender looked skeptical. "That may be true enough, but what about the two men that's after him?"

"We don't know exactly what that's about, but we hope to find him before something happens." James turned to Miss Josephine. "We know where Dad was in '76. We are hoping someone here would know where we could find him."

"James, there is only one man in this town who might know where he is. I'll have my clean up man take you to him."

Tom Doyle stood looking out his office window, letting his mind drift back a few years. After introductions and an explanation about the search, he was happy to talk about his friend.

"I had some wild times with that man over the years. Gold hunting with him was profitable and drinking with him was dangerous. I don't know exactly where Newt is now. The last I knew, he was in Rapid City, Dakota Territory.

James spoke, "Dad was planning to come to Omaha before he heard the bounty hunter was coming to get him. What happened then?"

"When he heard a bounty hunter was after him, Newt wanted to stay and fight. I was afraid that the man would get in the first shot. I talked him into leaving for a time. I know for sure he took a trip to San Francisco to help Belle and Sky get settled there."

James said, "We read about that in his journal"

"A month after he left, the bounty hunter showed up. Boys, that man was no bounty hunter, he was a professional killer. We wouldn't tell where Newt was, but he stayed for a week just to be sure. Mike, down at Josephine's, reported the gunfighter began visiting mines in the area looking for Newt. The miners wouldn't talk to the man. They were a little edgy with a gunman around and wanted him to leave. I heard later that at one of the mines, a man told the gunman he knew where Newt was hiding. For twenty dollars he would point out the cabin. The gunslinger said he would pay ten dollars before and ten after. Later one of the miners came to town to report that some dumb easterner had gotten into a dynamite shed and accidentally blown himself up. The Josephine began taking up a collection for the informant so he wouldn't be out the other ten dollars and the cost of the dynamite.

"I didn't see Newt again until the fall of '74. He showed up talking about the rumors of gold over in the Black Hills. Stories were circulating that the U. S. Army had sent General Custer and his troops to escort an expedition to the Black Hills. The expedition was to determine the extent of gold deposits in the area. General Custer allowed reporters to travel with the expedition, thinking they could report on him and his activities. Instead they printed stories about gold deposits and riches in the Black Hills. The newspaper articles had Newt fired up to dig rock. He spent the winter putting an outfit together.

The Black Hills belonged to the Indians and the U.S. Army was supposed to keep the white man out. Newt heard that the government was going to change the treaty to open up the Hills for exploration. He intended to be among the first to go in. I admit, it sounded good and knowing Newt's instincts for gold were usually accurate, I went along.

Newt and I bought a mule to haul the supplies and we each had two good horses to ride. Our supplies would have to last for the summer, as we would not be able to get provisions there. For firepower we purchased two '73 Winchester lever action rifles in 44-40cal. We added two Colt 'Peacemaker' pistols in the same caliber. That way we only needed one bullet for all four guns. Then we bought lots of ammo. That map up there on the wall shows where we went."

Chapter Thirteen
Prospecting in the Black Hills

"Now, what we did the summer of '75 was illegal, and dangerous as hell. During the entire trip we were on constant lookout for Indians and the Army. We were particularly worried about meeting up with the Blackfeet so we angled across the section of no man's land between the Blackfeet and the Crows. The Blackfeet would torture us for a few days then kill us. The Crows would steal our horses and leave us die on our own. Unpleasant prospects, either way. My hair was standing up even when I was asleep. When we reached the Yellowstone River, we followed it downstream looking for a spot to ford the river. We were told there was a good river crossing where the river curved to the north and met Alkali Creek. Today, the town of Billings is located a mile or two upstream from the crossing. We stayed a mile or two north of the river up in the rocks and bluffs to keep from being spotted by the Indians.

"The Yellowstone was running cold and swift from spring runoff. We had no choice but to plunge in and go for the far bank. Crossing in the high water nearly ended our expedition. The mule lost its footing and the current began dragging it downstream. I kept the other animals going for the far bank and Newt went for the mule. He managed to get the halter rope and guided it to the bank. The water was so swift that it nearly took Newt off his horse. He said he didn't want to lose that mule because it was the one carrying the tobacco.

"We rode to the top of the ridge and stopped for a rest in the trees and to make sure we had not been spotted. We kept out of sight in the trees, rocks and gullies as we proceeded south away from the river. We'd gone maybe five miles when Newt spotted a cave in the sandstone bluff. We watched the area for signs of life before going up to have a look around. We discovered three caves. One had lots of strange pictures painted on the walls along with some carvings, too. I was worried it might be a sacred place and we'd be in big trouble if caught there. Newt seemed to think it was used for living in because of the items and flint pieces laying around. We thought about camping in the smaller cave but decided it would be easy for Indians to trap us in there and smoke us out.

"We had seen game in the area so we made camp about a mile from the caves. We shot two deer and jerked the meat. Once in the hills we would only be able to fish and catch small game in snares.

"From the camp, we headed southeast toward the Black Hills. When we got close we pulled sagebrush behind us to cover our tracks and stayed on alert for Indians and the blasted Army. A couple of times we spotted troopers before they saw us and we hid out." Tom walked over to a large overstuffed chair and settled in.

"As soon as we were safely in the Hills we began to prospect for a stream that might be worth the effort. We worked two weeks before finding a stream that produced enough color and small nuggets. Once Newt decided it was worth working, we looked for a safe place to make camp. I found a large cave that we could use to hide in. We discovered we could light a small fire deep inside and not be detected. The cave was hidden by a stand of pines and aspen, allowing us to keep the animals tethered close by.

"For the entire time, we couldn't smoke or have a fire outside and we had to work as quietly as possible. It was hardest on Newt because we didn't bring any liquor with us. Several times we heard gunfire but our luck held and we weren't found out. Twenty-four hours a day we had two horses saddled and loaded with provisions, ammunition and the gold. If we were discovered we could jump on our horses and hopefully get away.

"By early September it was time for us to get out. Before leaving, Newt wanted to look over in the next two or three valleys in case we wanted to return the following year. We prospected every stream we came to, without getting any color in our pans. One morning, we sensed we were being followed. We didn't know which we preferred, the Army or the Indians. It wasn't long before we knew it was Indians and they were going to jump us soon. Before we could find a place to hide, they attacked, shooting from behind rocks and trees. There were six of them. They had good weapons but our new Winchesters equalized the battle and we were better shots. We shot three of them and that scared the rest off. After they were gone we found one of our horses dead which was a blow.

"We were surprised when we checked the bodies and found that two of the braves had Winchester 66's with fancy brass casings. The Indians prized that gun for its shiny metal parts and shooting ability. They had put designs on the stocks using brass tacks. One rifle had a lightning design that matched the painted markings on one of the warrior's face. The other rifle had a half moon design that matched the other's face. I took the rifle with the lightning design and Newt took the one with the half moon. While I searched the third Indian, Newt took his gold pan to check the stream nearby. He was gone about fifteen minutes and came back with nuggets that showed the area had promise. We drew up a map and rode double back to our camp. Deciding it was time to get out, we took the Indians' rifles apart and wrapped them in a poncho. When we loaded the mule, we hid the weapons in with the equipment. We divided the gold and carried it under our gun belts.

"We were out of the Hills three days when the hair began to rise on our necks. Before we had time to find a place to hide, ten or twelve Blackfeet set up a howl and came for us. We had to make a run for it. Searching for a place to make a stand, Newt saw a ridge of rocks in the distance that we might be able to use. We whipped up the animals and headed straight for the rocks with the Blackfeet in pursuit. Newt was ahead with the mule and I followed with the extra horse. The warriors were far enough back that we would make the ridge okay, but I wasn't so sure if that would save us.

"Newt shouted something and pointed ahead. We were heading for a dry riverbed with six-foot high banks. We couldn't change direction and we had no time to look for a better way to the bottom.. We plunged off the bank at full speed, our horses nearly going down, but they managed to stay on their feet and we kept going across the river bottom. Then I saw two men running for their horses. We rode past them, through their camp and up the other bank without missing a step. We kept going until we reached the ridge and stopped to take a look back. The Blackfeet were attacking the men instead of following us. We were discussing whether to go back and help, when we saw the two men going south on one horse chased by the Blackfeet We left, going west, figuring it was their fight now and there was no sense of us interfering. Later, as we rested, Newt mentioned that the men looked familiar but couldn't be positive about it.

"We continued west looking for a trading post we'd heard was operating north of a giant rock formation. It took several days to find the unusual mountain of rock rising above the plains. It looked like a giant tree stump hundreds of feet high. It would take half a day just to ride around it. We camped nearby to clean up. Newt has a trick he learned a long time ago. We each had new pants and shirts that we put on for the rest of our trip. With our equipment cleaned and shiny it looked like we were new to the area and inexperienced.

"The trading post turned out to be two dug out buildings. Lumber was scarce so the men had dug back into the hillside. The available lumber was used to make the front wall and covered porch on the trading post and the saloon opening had canvas hung up for a door. We gave the owner our order and said we would be pulling out after we reduced his liquor supply.

"The saloon was dark and smelled of damp earth and smoke. Light was admitted by tying the canvas door back. The cooking stove was at the front so a short stovepipe could reach the outside. Furniture consisted of an eating table and benches. The bartender set us up and went about his business. When we asked about meals we got a surly reply that the cook had been killed by Indians and for us not to expect much. Later when we ordered another bottle, the bartender brought it over and sat to tell us what happened. He told a story that made us jump out of our skins.

"A month back they had a load of supplies coming in with an Army escort. They were attacked by Indians, losing two wagons and two men. One was their cook. Three wagons made it safely including the whiskey supply, which was good news. The bad news was that one of the wagons they lost was full of guns, ammunition, and other supplies. He said his partner Ivan was really mad about that because there were two of those brass casing Winchester '66's in the wagon. They would have fetched a good price out here. Ivan was so mad that he vowed to kill whoever got those rifles. Hearing that, we decided it was time to move on. We hastily paid up and left the saloon to get our supplies from Ivan.

"Just when we thought we would get away with out suspicion, an army patrol rode in. The officer came over to ask were we were headed. We lied, saying we had started up the Bozeman Trail and got lost. We said we were going to Helena to work in the gold fields there. He thought we were crazy to have come this way alone and insisted we wait until the next day. They were going beyond Helena to Fort Shaw. We could travel with his soldiers as far as Fort Baker, then go the remaining distance to Helena. To avoid calling suspicion to ourselves we agreed to travel with them. We spent a nervous night, afraid we would be searched and they'd find the rifles and the gold. Our nervousness lasted for several days but we managed to keep our secret hidden. I think the new clothing and shiny equipment helped to fool them.

"The soldiers did not stick to the trail like we thought they should. They took us more to the north, looking for sign of Indians. When we reached the Yellowstone River, they turned us west. A few days later we could see a large rock bluff that sat all by itself along the river. The lieutenant asked if we knew about the Lewis and Clark expedition. We said we knew they had been through Montana but that was about all we knew. He told us the bluff we were heading for was called Pompey's Pillar. One of the soldiers said it was also use by the Indians as a signal tower. It had names and dates carved in the rock. We camped at the rock and looked around. Apparently the expedition had stayed there to camp and rest. We climbed up to see Clark's name and the date 1806 carved in the rock.

"From there we followed the Yellowstone to the crossing point we had used in the spring.

We crossed and followed the north bank a few days then turned north toward Fort Baker. We left the troops there and came on to Helena.

"By the way, do you want to see those guns? I have them in the next room. Newt left his here because he thought the rifle would draw too much attention."

"We learned that Dad came to Denver in November of that year," James spoke. "He must have come from here."

"Yes. He went to Fort Laramie first to visit a family by the name of Kyle and Carrie Cobb. They heard the sutler at Fort Steele was sick and had his store for sale. Newt was putting up the money for the purchase."

"The last trace we have of Dad was in early '77 when he left Denver." James remarked.

"Boys, my guess is that someone in Rapid City will know where Newt is. He was in Deadwood in '76 and by '78 he was in Rapid City. He built a new saloon and gambling house there. Called it The Sarah. He still owned it three years ago when he wrote he was coming to see me some day to pick up his rifle. Newt is a wild, crazy man who could outtalk and outdrink us all. He was generous to everyone to boot. Every saloon he owns is called The Sarah for good luck. By now you've heard about his hat and the stories behind the trinkets on the band."

Wilbur said, "Yes and that hat should be easy to spot, but we've not seen it or him so far. At first we thought he might be dead but I have a feeling he's alive"

"Wilbur and I would like to thank you for telling us about Dad and for your suggestions. We'll be going to Rapid City in the morning."

"The train will stop in Billings long enough for you to ask around for Newt. Check with Jake Wallig at the Blue Grass billiard hall or see Andy Hanson at the Brewery Saloon. They might be able to help you."

James said, "Thank you for your help and we'll let you know when we find him."

Chapter Fourteen
A Precious Package

Newt let Misty walk at his own pace as they approached Fort Steele from their hideout in Benton. Rounding the quartermaster stores, Kramer saw Lewis and dashed ahead. By the time Newt and Misty had reached the corral, Kramer and Lewis were chasing imaginary foes. Carrie was standing at the wash line watching them.

Newt led Misty into the barn and took the saddle off. He let him munch on oats while giving him a good brushing. Finished with that chore, Newt walked across the yard to the back door of the Cobb house. The air had that yeasty smell of fresh bread baking. Newt stood, taking in the aroma and the sight of the golden crusted bread, still warm from the oven. "It sure smells good in here, it could make saliva run from the mouth of a statue. I should have build my hideout closer so I could have fresh bread every day."

"Sit, and I'll cut you some bread. From the looks of you, the work at Benton is getting tiresome." Carrie placed a loaf on the table and cut several thick slices.

"It is. I'm getting too old for this nonsense. But it's worth it if I can get those men off my tail." Newt spread pale butter on a slice then ladled on two gobs of strawberry preserves. He ate four slices while they talked. "Where's Kyle today?"

"He went over to the Browns to deliver feed. Mr. Brown got kicked by a horse and he's laid up. Lewis and I are minding the store until he gets back. Newt, there's mail for you over at the store, a letter from Rapid City and one from Cheyenne. Then you got a letter and a small package all the way from Australia."

"It'll keep until I finish this bread. Did you say Australia?"

When Kyle returned that evening Newt helped with the team and chores. Later they spent time in the store discussing business until Carrie rang the dinner bell. The two men closed up and walked to the house.

After dinner the three sat at the kitchen table and talked. Newt pulled the letters from his shirt pocket. "These provided some interesting reading this afternoon. Dotty writes that three men were looking for me in Cheyenne. One of the three left for Denver, and the other two hung around for a few days before leaving on the train. They were clean cut men, she thinks they are lawmen or Pinkertons."

"After all these years, why would the law still be looking for you?" Kyle asked.

"I think it's Old Man Bates trying to even the score after I stopped his land grab and cost him all that money."

Carrie asked. "Did Dotty know were the two were going next?"

"She said they took the train to Rawlins about the same time I came back here, but that's all she knows. I sent word to Alice to keep watch for them there.

Newt got out the letter from Rapid City. "Delaware says Bates and O'Toole showed up in Rapid again. They must have got the birdshot out of their pants. They haven't been too quick to move on. They must think I will come back there. I 'm going to have to take care of those two if I'm ever going to have peace of mind. What concerns me is that you two are involved as much as you are. Carrie, does Lewis understand what he is to do and say if someone comes around asking for me?"

"Yes, he does. He knows how important it is."

" My hideout is about ready. In a few days I can start living at the cabin." Newt picked up the other letter. "This is an interesting bit of news from my friend, Howard Ross. I've grubstaked him several times over the years and expect some day he'll hit the big one. A few years back he showed up in Rapid City asking for a two thousand dollar grubstake. That was a large amount for a grubstake and he was very secretive about where he was going. I gave him the money, figuring I'd never see him again. Now he writes that he used the money to book passage to Australia. I remember a rush to Sidney in '51 that lasted a few years but had heard nothing since. Howard says he got word of a new strike and decided to follow up on it. He joined up with three other men and they've found good paying claims that should last for several years. He wrote he's sending a small package with something I would find interesting."

Kyle pointed at the package. "That came only a few days ago. The letter has been here over a week. From the markings it has taken five months for them to get here."

The package was two inches square and an inch deep. Newt cut the wrappping and opened the box. "Well, let's see what kind of treasure Howard sent me." Reaching in with two fingers he pulled out a small leather bag and a piece of paper. Newt unfolded the note and read it aloud:

"I acquired these from a convict who traded them for food. Don't know exactly where they came from. Would you check these out and let me know what they are worth? By the way, the bag is a pebble case made out of a kangaroo's scrotum. The man claimed it was from a very fine 'fighting buck.'"

Newt inspected the bag then opened it and poured the contents out in his large calloused hand. "Well, I'll be go to Hell. Look at these."

Kyle plucked one out of Newt's hand and squinted at it for a moment. "I think these are opals."

"That's exactly what they are. Fancy that. I wonder what these are worth? Next time we're in Rawlins I'll take these to the jewelry shop and have them looked at."

"Opals from Australia. What an interesting country that must be." Carrie was talking out loud to herself. But it was Newt who had a far-off look in his eyes.

Chapter Fifteen
A Shot of Tangle Leg

The Northern Pacific line across Montana was newly laid, reaching Helena from Livingston just the month before. The trains had been assembled from old passenger cars, acquired from defunct east coast railroads. The cars were falling apart piece by piece and should not have been put in service. The train left Helena for Miles City pulling thirty-six new ore cars carrying over a million dollars in gold ore. Coupled on the end were two passenger cars with their uncomfortable and frightened passengers. They kept to the usual schedule of arriving three hours late to Billings.

The boys had only enough time to find the Brewery Saloon and ask for Mr. Hansen. He had not seen Newt for a few years. One of his employees was sure that Newt still had The Sarah in Rapid City. As the boys climbed into the rail car, James remarked. "Billings is the first town since Cheyenne that seems to be growing and prospering without the dirt and grime of mining around it. Look at the beautiful cliffs there to the north. I'll bet this valley looks grand from up there. I wish we had more time to look around."

"We'll have to look for the crossing at Alkali Creek that Mr. Doyle mentioned. That ridge over there south of the river must be where they found the caves. I heard the conductor telling another passenger that we can see Pompey's Pillar from the train when we go by there.

The Miles City ticket agent gave them bad news. The only transportation going on to Rapid City that day was the express stage. They hurried over to the express station and pleaded with the driver to let them on.

The driver said, "Its okay with me but I ain't gonna slow down just so's you two can enjoy yer selves."

Two hours from Miles City they knew they had made a mistake. Speed was king and the driver seemed to be aiming for every rock and bump in the road. The boys spent their time hanging on to keep from hitting the roof and avoiding the shifting freight stowed in the coach with them. Stops during the eighteen-hour trip were for changing horses only.

Arriving in Rapid City, the driver swung the team at full speed into a large building and then yelled for the team to halt, dumping the boys and the packages on the floor. With an ill hidden smile the driver opened the door and announced, "You can get out now, this here's Rapid City."

They picked up their bags and stiffly walked out into the sunlight, aware of the snickers and laughter coming from the freight men as the driver recounted the trip.

James and Wilbur asked for directions to a good hotel from an old man sitting on the boardwalk whittling a stick. He pointed at a four-story building and said. "That's the best in Rapid City for sleeping. In the next block y'all find The Sarah. It's the best place fer eat'n. They's got the best whiskey there too, but watch out for the one called Tangle Leg, it'll get'ch."

The boys checked in at the hotel, wondering what the other hotels must be like if this one was the best. They dropped their bags in the room and headed for The Sarah with high hopes that this would be their last stop in the search.

James and Wilbur stepped a few feet inside The Sarah and stood looking around. Two rough looking men stood at the bar quietly talking. When the patrons grew quiet and fidgety, Wilbur nudged James, and they moved to the bar. The bartender at the other end did not move or look at them. He kept on reading a paper while he asked, "What's your drink, men?"

Wilbur got an inspiration and said. "A bottle of Tangle Leg."

The bartender slowly lowered the paper and looked over at them. Then he busted out laughing. "TANGLE LEG? You two don't know what yer ask'n for. A whiff is mor'n you could handle." At the mention of Tangle Leg the two rough looking men at the bar turned and walked toward James and Wilbur. The smaller of the two had red hair and beard. The other man had large muscular arms and chest from a lifetime of digging and lifting. The bigger man spoke, "You're too wet behind the ears to know about Tangle Leg."

Wilbur looked them straight on and said, "We're looking for the man who owns this saloon and is known for making Tangle Leg."

"Who's ask'n?" The man raised his chin slightly and tensed up.

"I'm James Harvey, this is Wilbur. We're his sons."

"Sons? What if I was to say Newt was never married. I guess we'd know what that would make you."

"It'd make us bastards. If you think that rips any hide off us, your wasting your breath. We've taken worse from high bred boys in a private military school." Out of the corner of his eye James saw two men get up and start for the door. Raising his voice a little, he caught their attention, "Gentlemen, please don't leave. We promise not to talk about bastards again. Unless of course one of you happens to be a man known as BASTARD BATES," his voice rising to a yell on the last two words. The bigger of the two men stopped, then turned toward the group. James started to chide him again.

"I'll bet..." Bates drew his gun. In a split second several shots were fired, filling the air with bullets and smoke.

Chapter Sixteen
A Swindle

James came to, with a knot on his head and flashes of light in his vision.

"Are you okay, son?"

James opened his eyes a little and sorted out the pain before he let them go wide open. He started up asking, "Wilbur?"

The big man said, "He's okay. It was you that got hit." The man stood up and yelled to the backroom. "Wilbur, your brother's awake now."

James asked, "Who are you?"

"Name's Delaware son, and my red headed partner is known as Josh."

"What happened?" James asked, still trying to reduce the buzz in his head.

"That stupid jackass drew on us! A man never pulls a gun on a bunch of men standing together. None of us knew which one he was gunning for, so we all shot him."

Wilbur and the redheaded man came from the backroom, "James, it was crazy! I've never seen anything like it. It took thirty minutes just to clear the smoke out."

"What happened to me?"

Wilbur answered, "When the men began shooting, Bates' shot went wild and hit the chandelier. It spun and fell on you, knocking you out like a dead fish."

"Here, have a drink." Delaware handed James a glass of brown liquid. The jolt cleared his mind a little more.

"Thanks. What about the other man?"

Delaware answered. "Oh, he won't be a bother. We shot him too. He's alive, but he's not likely to cause trouble for a while. Doc Fiske is working on him in the back room. Those two weasels made enemies with several of us. We did what we should'a done the first day they came in here looking for Newt. "

The red headed man spoke up, "Wilbur said you're looking for your dad. You're Newt's kid all right, I can see it in your face."

Wilbur helped James to his feet and they walked into the back room. O'Toole lay on a board placed on two barrels. His breathing was raspy and his face was as white as chalk. The doctor was wrapping a bandage over a wound in the leg.

"Just a minute, boys, and you can talk to him. He's got a bullet in this leg and a wound in the shoulder. He's lost a lot of blood, but it's okay to give him a drink."

James pulled a box over and sat, while Wilbur hopped up on the counter. James leaned over and asked, "Do you know who we are?"

The man nodded, " Yes."

"Wilbur and I would like to know why you and Bates were after our dad."

O'Toole lay quiet for a moment. "The best I can do is tell you what I know but it ain't gonna help you find your pa. You know how Bates was always scheming to marry your mother? Well, when Newt started getting in the way he got madder and madder to the point I thought he was going to kill him. When Martha went to Denver in '63, some of the men began poking fun at Conrad about Martha marrying Newt. Conrad vowed that if she married Newt Harvey he would just have to marry the widow Harvey later. That fall, when Martha came back and announced she had married Newt, Conrad was in a rage for days. Mrs. Walters wanted Martha to marry Conrad so she tried to get it annulled. Mr. Walters kept her from doing that, but she tried everything she could to keep Martha and Newt apart.

"Conrad saw his chance when Newt came to Omaha in '66 with that kid." He pointed his finger at Wilbur and said, "I guess you're the kid. While Newt, Martha and you boys were in St. Louis, Conrad went to Omaha and worked out a plan with my brother, Irish, and his partner Loupe. When your dad came back to Omaha, Conrad waited his chance. One evening Newt was headed to the Walters home alone and the three of them jumped him. Things got all messed up and Irish was killed. Bates and Loupe claimed to the law that Newt did the shooting and the police went after him. Somehow he managed to escape back to Montana Territory.

"Things were quiet for a while. Conrad went back to St. Louis to work at his father's bank. He'd return to Omaha once in a while but figured there was nothing more could be done. In '69, Bates learned that Newt was coming to Omaha to clear his name and work for Mr. Walters. He was worried that the police would learn the truth. He heard later that Newt's saloon had burned and he was staying in Montana."

James asked, "How was Bates able to learn what was going on?"

"There was a maid working for the Walters family who was sweet on Bates. He strung her along so she would send him reports of what was going on in Omaha. She was reading letters between Martha and Newt and telling him what was happening.."

"That dirty weasel. All right, go on."

"While this is going on Old Man Bates had dealings with Mrs. Walters' brother Levi Swan. He intended to swindle Levi out of the family home and the forty acres of prime land next to it. Somehow Newt found out about the deal and bought the forty acres so Levi could pay off the mortgage and keep the family home. Without those forty acres Old Man Bates couldn't work a deal with eastern investors. He lost two hundred and fifty thousand dollars."

"So, Dad had both Conrad and his father out to get him. Is that when the pressure was put on the Omaha police to be on the lookout for Dad should he return?"

"Yes, and it was Conrad who decided to hire a bounty hunter that could be persuaded to bring Newt back dead. The gunman never came back for the other half of his money. Later we learned he was killed in an explosion and Newt was still alive.

"I guess it was in '72, Conrad heard from some big banking and investing men on the west coast. They invited him to invest in a new mining company being formed to mine diamonds and other precious gems in an area that was worth a million dollars an acre. Ol'' Man Bates smelled a swindle and refused to invest. Conrad got all excited about the profits the bankers were promising. He tried to get his father to invest but the Ol'' Man stubbornly refused.

"When Conrad heard that there were several English investors buying in on the deal he couldn't resist making a lot of money and proving his pa wrong. Conrad stole one hundred and fifty thousand dollars from his dad's bank and bought stock in the mining venture. It didn't take long for Ol' Man Bates to find out what Conrad had done and he booted him out. He took everything Conrad owned, including an inheritance from his grandmother, and disowned him. The only thing Conrad had left was the stock in the mining company. He was desperate so he went to San Francisco to sell the stock and get his money back. He couldn't afford any more than accommodation class so it was a long hard train ride.

"In San Francisco, Conrad found out that the stock was worthless. The whole deal had been a giant swindle to sell stock in a diamond mine operation near Rawlins, Wyoming. When Conrad realized he was broke and disowned to boot, he went crazy. He was drunk for days, got in several fights and was thrown in jail until he sobered up. After getting out of jail, he robbed a man and bought a train ticket for Omaha. On the ride back, he decided to get off in Rawlins and check it out. After several days of being hooted out of every bar and saloon in town, he thought of asking the local jeweler about the diamond mine. The jeweler remembered a man who had come in with a small sack of gems to sell. A quick search of the records showed he had purchased two gems from a Mr. Newt Harvey.

"By the time he got home, Conrad had made up his mind that Newt was behind the whole scheme and was responsible for the stock being worthless."

Shaking his head Wilbur said, "I don't know how Dad could be such a hex on Bates, but he was."

"Conrad didn't think of it as a hex or bad luck. He believed Newt had deliberately set out to ruin him and his father. All Conrad could talk about was hunting Newt down and killing him.

"He talked me in to going along and I sure regret doing that. In '73 we looked for him in Wyoming and Montana with no success.

James interrupted, "That's when Dad was in San Francisco and Tonopah."

"We went back to St. Louis so Conrad could plead with his father to release some of his inheritance. He did get some money, but it didn't last long. That was when Loupe confessed and the police arrested Conrad. Old Man Bates got him released and Conrad decided to go west to avoid being sent to prison. By the time we got to Cheyenne it was early in '75 and we were nearly broke. Conrad figured it would be best if we outfitted ourselves to go north and slip into the Black Hills to look for gold."

Delaware came in the back room and stood nearby to listen as O'Toole continued.

"We tried panning for gold along the way but never got much. We had just started prospecting in the Black Hills when the Army caught us and escorted us out. After we promised to stay out of the hills, the Army let us go. We traveled for a day then camped in a dry river bottom. Conrad wanted to lay low a few days, then try to sneak back into the hills. One day while resting in camp we heard shots, then horses and Indians coming our way. We climbed up the bank until we could see two men coming right at us with about ten or twelve Blackfeet chasing them. They came at full speed, jumping their horses off the bank and riding right through our camp. When the Indians got to the bank they saw our camp and came after us instead. We managed to catch one of our horses and shoot our way out. All the way back to Cheyenne, Conrad was yelling and screaming about the two men who led the Indians to us. He was sure that one of the men was Newt. It was making him insane."

Wilbur laughed, "It was Dad all right."

"We stayed in Cheyenne for the winter. It was hard and lean times but I swear he was living off his hatred for Newt and with the idea of revenge. The summer of '76 was when we got into big trouble over his blind rage to kill Newt. Conrad shot a man in the back thinking he was Newt."

Delaware stirred and spoke.

"I know a little about that myself. Your dad was making his usual visit to Cheyenne. Newt took a day to look at some land north of town. When he came to an abandoned farmhouse he stopped to rest. The windmill was still working and there was water in the tank. Newt was hot and dusty so he got the idea to take a cool bath before going on. He tells that after getting into the water a man, who was hiding in the barn, came out with a gun pointed at him. The thief gathered up Newt's clothes and took his horse.

"Newt had a four-hour walk to town in his long johns. When he got there he went into the back door of the SarahLyn and told Caesar what happened. All Caesar did was laugh, which made Newt mad as hell. He kept telling Newt it was his lucky day. Later when he got the story of the killing he agreed it was his lucky day."

Turning to O'Toole, he said, "So you were in on the shooting?"

"Yeah. We were leaning at the horse rail when this tall man rides up across the street and hitches his horse to the rail in front of a saloon called the Bloody Dog. Conrad swore it was Newt and asked a man standing next to us if that was him. He said it was because he recognized his horse and the hat. We crossed the street and went into the saloon. The man with the hat was standing with his back to the door. Conrad drew and shot him in the back. We escaped in the confusion. Trying to get out of town we were caught before we got very far."

"What happened then?" James asked.

"We were arrested and thrown in jail for murdering a drifter. When Conrad found out he had killed some stranger instead of Newt he just slumped in the corner of our cell and fumed. In a couple of weeks a judge came to town and the jury found us guilty of murder. Conrad was sure it went harder on us because we shot the wrong man and Newt was well-liked in town. The Judge sentenced us to five years of hard labor at the territorial penitentiary in Laramie."

"Five years!" You were in prison for five years?" James asked.

"Yea, we got out three months ago. For five years Conrad sat in his cell and thought only of getting out and looking for Newt. He even had come up with how he was going to kill him by putting a bullet in each arm and leg and then one in the heart. After our release we went south into Colorado and robbed a bank. From there Conrad insisted on going to Cheyenne to look for Newt. There he learned that Newt might be in Rapid City so we boarded the Deadwood Stage.

In Rapid City we found The Sarah Saloon but did not find Newt. We found out your dad was thought to be prospecting near Livingston, Montana. We took a stage to Miles City and the train to Livingston, hoping he was still there. Sure enough, that night Conrad got a shot at Newt as he ran into a saloon. We went after him, which was a mistake. The bartender hit us with birdshot from his sawed off shotgun. It was a painful couple of weeks for both of us. Conrad was not giving up though and decided to come back here to wait for Newt. You two walked in here tonight and now it's all over."

Chapter Seventeen
Calamity Jane

After O'Toole passed out, the boys came out of the back room and took a table with Delaware and Josh. Wilbur, always the first to think about his stomach, asked if they could get something to eat. The two found the steak and potatoes pleasantly tender and tasty and not over-cooked or burned, the way food had been prepared over the past month. Over whiskey and cigars the boys were regaled with stories of Newt and his exploits.

"Delaware, he was always putting money in on some scheme or another. Does he still have investments with other men here?" James asked.

"None that I know of, 'cept a few grubstakes."

"Delaware, tell'm about that badlands oasis he was always talking about."

"I'll tell it, Josh, jest as soon as you buy us a round."

Josh signaled the bartender. While the whiskey was being poured Delaware continued. "Boys, we all thought the world of your pa but sometimes he would get the strangest ideas in his head and drive us all nuts talking about it. You probably don't know much about this area but Rapid City was established to take advantage of the freighters coming from the mines in the Hills and going to Minneapolis. This is the last town to get supplies before going into the badlands. Also it's the first stop for rest and water when coming out of the badlands from the east. The railroad has changed it some but there are lots of emigrants coming along that road, hauling their families and driving livestock. Newt's idea was to build a station thirty miles closer to the badlands. He was going to stock groceries, supplies, animals, and tools."

Josh broke in, "And the water, tell'em about the free water."

"I was just getting to that. If you'd hold your water a mite I'll tell'em about it. Newt's idea was that traveling through the badlands would parch the emigrants and livestock real bad and he was going to be the first to offer free water for them and the stock. He figured the free water would make them stay a day or two more. While they was there he would sell lots of other stuff and keep the saloon and gambling tables busy. One other gimmick he thought up was to go out into the badlands two or three days' travel and put up large signs telling people that there was free water ahead."

"Did he do it?" James asked.

"No, he got side tracked, but we always expected to hear that he was headed for the badlands to open up his drug and general store offering free water."

"And Delaware would've gone with him too." Josh spoke up.

"Damn right I would."

Josh winked at James, "Delaware, tell them about Newt saving your life."

The red faced Delaware glowered at his companion before speaking. "It was in '76 over in Deadwood. I hit a pocket of gold at my claim and was in town to celebrate. Calamity Jane attached herself to me and we was making the rounds. After two days I was wearing out. We came in the saloon announcing that we were get'n married. Newt took me aside and tried to explain that marrying Calamity was dangerous. Her last three husbands had died mysteriously within two weeks of marrying her. I was not going to be swayed and kept insisting we was get'n hitched.

We had a few hours of drinking while we were waiting for the preacher. When Calamity passed out on the table Newt decided to put a stop to the festivities. He hustled me to the back room and locked me in the pantry. When the preacher showed up he was sent packing. Calamity woke up later the next morning asking for me. Newt told her I was killed by Indians. She shrugged and looked around for someone to buy her another drink."

The professor sitting at the piano continued, "A week later she came in and saw Delaware at the bar. She said 'I heard you was killed by Indians.' Delaware kept looking straight ahead and said, 'I was.'"

The men had heard the story many times but still laughed and enjoyed it. James turned to the professor, "Have you been here long?"

"I've been playing this here piano ever since your dad opened for business. Get a bottle and maybe I'll tell you something that might help you locate him."

The men made a place at the table for the professor. Wilbur poured drinks. By the time he finished pouring, the three men had downed their shots and wanted more.

The professor waited for Wilbur to pour the second shot to the brim before beginning his story. "Every year, about this time, Newt would start planing a vacation trip to Helena. Pretty soon he'd be gone and return in three or four weeks. We learned he was taking the stage to Cheyenne instead of Helena. The talk about going to Helena was just to throw people off his track. When I asked about his going to Cheyenne, he would say that he was checking on his investments but refused to say more. The men learned that the attraction was a female, but we never learned who it was for sure. Boys, I think Cheyenne is the best place to look for Newt." The two men talked more about Newt, running out of stories just as the bottle went dry.

The next morning over breakfast Wilbur and James hashed over the shooting of Bates and the information they got from O'Toole and the professor. It was evident that they could spend the whole year wandering around the country and not find their father. They agreed to ask around Cheyenne again. If they didn't have a lead in two or three days they would go on to Fort Steele to see Kyle Cobb.

The stage to Fort Laramie from Deadwood carried two more people than there were seats. Fortunately one was only going ten miles to his mine and the other rode on top. It was a tight fit in the coach and everyone was too uncomfortable to make much conversation. James was wishing they had bought horses instead of taking the stage.

When they reached the overnight stop the boys were really sorry they had taken the stage. The stationmaster's wife cooked and served thin soup with one slice of bread. The boys couldn't identify the black specks in the bread and were afraid to eat it. Wilbur's inspection of the soup revealed mysterious bits of meat and gristle that prompted a desire to take a walk instead. Travelers were expected to sleep on the floor wherever they found space, with no privacy for the women. The stationmaster sat at the table most of the night drinking and telling disgusting stories.

When time came for the people to be awake, some were already up and demanding the driver get started, because no one wanted the breakfast they saw being prepared. Just before dusk they reached Fort Laramie, finding sparse accommodations but much better food than the night before. The next day, the coach left well before sunrise, arriving in Cheyenne after dark. In their room at the Frontier House, James and Wilbur learned what "falling into bed" really meant. Breakfast the next morning consisted of a slab of meat covered with dark congealed gravy to hide its identity. Leaving most of the meal on the plate, they walked outside to recover. They spent the day going from one saloon to another asking about Newt. In most places they got suspicious no's or hostile silence from the locals.

On the second day James spotted The SarahLyn Saloon and Gambling Parlor. Once inside they knew that Newt would find it to his liking. They bought a bottle and settled at a table next to the piano. For the next few hours they drank and watched men come and go. An old man wearing a white shirt and string tie sat down to the piano to play while men shouted out requests. Wilbur was puzzled that the player ignored the song requests and didn't react to the crude insults over his playing. After watching for a time he realized the old man was deaf. During his performance the professor kept eyeing their bottle, judging the amount left. When the level was just right, he stopped playing. With a well-practiced line he asked for a drink. Before James or Wilbur could answer he picked up the bottle, drained it, and returned to his playing. It was then Wilbur noticed a sign posted on the piano. "Watch out for the professor."

Disappointment and failure continued to follow the two brothers the next morning when they could not get anyone to admit even knowing Newt. James and Wilbur reluctantly walked back to the depot and inquired at the ticket window about going to Fort Steele.

The ticket clerk had bad news. "Only one train a week going each way and you missed this week's run from here."

Wilbur leaned into window, "We stopped there a month ago. Was that a regular stop?"

"You must've had soldiers on board. We stop to drop off and pick up Army supply cars. Best way now is to go to Rawlins and then catch the local coming from that direction."

"Okay, we'll take two tickets to Fort Steele by going to Rawlins."

Chapter Eighteen
A Bowl of Chili and Dynamite

The trip from Cheyenne the month previous had started after dark. This trip in full daylight provided the boys with a thrilling scenic ride over the Laramie Mountains. Their train wound back and forth up the grade, exposing vistas they never dreamed were there. James and Wilbur spent the entire time looking out the windows, bouncing from side to side yelling at each other to look at some sight or animal. The ride up was capped with a spectacular view atop Sherman Hill before the train started down the other side. At Laramie the boys stretched their legs by running to a café for a quick bowl of soup and stale bread. A dash back to the depot was necessary to get aboard as the whistle blew. They passed through Fort Steele and rolled on to Rawlins.

The Union Pacific had established towns across Wyoming as crew turnaround points. Cheyenne was the state capital, Laramie had the territorial prison, but Rawlins' depended solely on the railroad for its existence. Here the dirty wooden buildings clustered east and west along the tracks and spread north for several blocks. Saloons accounted for most of the businesses along the front street facing the tracks. The upper floors were rented by the ladies who plied their trade in the saloons.

The boys swung down from the car and made their way through the depot to the street. At that hour there was lots of activity in the saloons and in the streets.

The recommended hotel was a block north of the depot on the second floor above a saloon and corner drug store. The boys pushed open the doors marked Cutler Hotel and stepped from the boardwalk onto the landing. To the right was a swinging door into the saloon for the convenience of those staying upstairs at the hotel. They could hear music and laughter from the dark interior. Ahead was a flight of stairs, going straight up for what seemed like a mile. The top step brought them into a high-ceilinged, dimly lit lobby. A small writing desk and two chairs filled the wall straight ahead. To the right of the desk was a hallway leading to the rooms. Turning further to the right they approached the counter. It held a small table lamp, registration book, and night bell. Tacked to the wall was a handwritten list of rates and rules of the house.

The landlady answering the bell was a bit of a shock, wearing a bright multicolored housecoat and with her flaming red hair, piled high on top. As they signed the register the large friendly woman recited the rules of the house. "I don't allow you bringing a lady to your room and no throwing things out the window at passersby. If you drink too much in the room, don't try to walk down the stairs." All the while she was sizing them up, deciding they weren't troublemakers. When she looked at the register and saw their names she paused and gave them a long cold look before handing them the key. "George, would you show these men to Room 103?"

Her husband George was well over six feet tall, balding and the friendliest man they had met. His smile was a little comical due to his missing two upper front teeth. "The bar is safe for the likes of you two. Just don't get too rowdy. My wife don't tolerate drunks in her hotel so don't come in making noises and talking loud. She'll take after you with her broom and sweep you back down the stairs to the street. I've gotten the wrong end of that broom myself. The U.P. Café is the best place to eat. Don't look like much but the food's good. The railroad crews eat there."

"Thanks for the information," Wilbur took the key offered by their host.

Surprisingly, the high ceilinged room was clean and neat considering the amount of dust and cinders that settled on the town every day. James and Wilbur decided they were too tired to go anywhere that night and went to bed.

The local to Fort Steele didn't leave until 2:15 the next afternoon so James and Wilbur ate a late breakfast. The U.P. Café opposite the hotel was only slightly cleaner than the other places but the food was good as the man had promised. Later they stepped into the bar at the hotel and took a table. A few regulars looked at the two strangers, then continued their conversations. After the beers had been served, Wilbur said, "What are we going to do if Dad isn't in Fort Steele? After two months of traveling on rough seats and bouncing stages, I don't think I can take much more. Even that wouldn't be so bad if it wasn't for the terrible food."

"If we don't find Dad in Fort Steele, we're going to Denver and decide what to do."

"And it'll give you a chance to call on Sarah May." Wilbur answered.

Just before noon they climbed up the hotel stairs to get their bags from the room. Returning to the desk, they rang the bell. It was several minutes before the landlady appeared. James asked if she would help them. She nodded and ushered them into her living room. Their apartment was two hotel rooms converted into clean and cozy living quarters. James asked, "Do you know a man named Newt Harvey?"

Her manner quickly had an edge to it and her voice lost its warmth. "You registered here as James Harvey. Is that your real name?"

"Yes, it is. Newt Harvey is our father. We have been all the way to Montana and South Dakota looking for him. We learned he might be in Cheyenne so we went there and no one would talk to us about him. We know he has a partner in Fort Steele and we intend to go there today."

Wilbur spoke up, adding, "And the two other men who were after him were killed in Rapid City. If we don't find him in Fort Steele or get a lead there, we will have to go back home with out him."

"What makes you think he's in Fort Steele?"

James answered, "We have his journal that mentions Kyle Cobb and that he and my father are partners in the trading post at Fort Steele. We hope Mr. Cobb will be able to help us."

"You two look like Pinkerton men to me, or maybe Wells Fargo agents."

"No ma'am, we're not the law. We are his family and want to find him."

"You say you have his journal. May I see it?"

"Yes," James reached into his bag and brought out the journal.

After reading through a few pages of the journal and a making long hard glances at James, the woman picked up a calling card and handed it to him. "When you see Mr. Cobb be sure to give him this card and tell him you talked with me."

James took the card and looked at the one line printed on it: A. Cutler.

With nothing more to say, the boys left the hotel and walked to the depot. The ticket agent was curious about their buying tickets with a stopover at Fort Steele. "What business you got at the fort?"

James spoke, "We have dealings with the trading post there."

They sat in the waiting room to watch people come and go. After twenty minutes or so they had seen everything there was to see and spread out to get a nap. An hour later the conductor came through and announced they were ready for boarding. James and Wilbur stirred and walked out to the train. They found seats and began the task of getting comfortable on the wooden benches. Meanwhile the telegraph key at Fort Steele began to chatter.

They were still trying to get comfortable as they pulled into the station at Fort Steele. The conductor announced that the local had to wait until the Super Chief went past on the main line before they could proceed. If they missed the train it would be two days before the next train arrived going from Laramie to Rawlins. In the depot they scanned the small group of people in the station for Newt or the hat, but saw nothing to catch their interest.

It was a short walk to the trading post where a young boy was sweeping the porch under the watchful eye of a large black dog. James asked, "What's your name?"

"Lewis."

"That's a good name. This is Wilbur and I'm James. What's your dog's name?"

"Kramer" The boy did not look up and kept sweeping.

"Is that so. We know a man who calls his dog Kramer. Is Mr. Cobb inside?"

The boy said, "He's gone. Don't know when he'll be back."

"Would you tell Mr. Cobb we stopped to see him? Tell him we'll be over to the saloon."

The boy nodded and continued his sweeping.

James turned to Wilbur, "We might as well go over to the saloon and wait."

"James, that dog looks like the one that stole my sandwich the other night in my dream. I'll wager it's Dad's dog. Now I wonder if it was a dream or if it really happened. How are we going to get out of here if we miss the train? I don't like the idea of waiting for a week to go on to Cheyenne."

James said, "We'll have to get horses and ride back to Rawlins and then take a train to Cheyenne. Ugh, this search is getting tiresome."

The fort saloon was crowded with soldiers. They dropped their bags outside and squeezed in at the bar. After two rounds Wilbur asked the bartender if they could get something to eat. "Only thing we got now is chili," was the response.

A soldier standing next to them turned and said. "It's the best chili I've ever had and I was stationed in Texas before this. Raising his voice, he shouted, "Chugwater, there's two men out here that would try some of your chili, if you'd serve 'em some." The cook looked through the doorway and signaled it would be five minutes.

At that moment they were approached by the soldiers who had crashed into them on their first trip. One said, "We'd like to buy you boys a drink for the way we roughed you up the last time." The five men took a table and sat down to talk.

James started, "Maybe you can help us. Wilbur and I have been looking for a man by the name of Newt Harvey. We learned he could be here. Do any of you know him?"

One private spoke, "Don't know him for sure but I know some one who might. While you're eating your chili I'll go check on it."

As they were finishing their second bowl of chili the private returned, "I was told that the man you want is holed up in a small cabin on the west end of Benton. He says that if anyone wants him, they'll have to come to him. He's not running anymore."

"Where's Benton?" James asked.

"It's an abandoned town site about a mile west of here. Just stay on this side of the tracks, can't miss it.

Both men were on their feet. James asked, "Where can we get horses?"

"Pete at the livery will fix you up."

"Thank you. Our bags are outside on the porch. Would you watch them for us? We'll buy you a drink when we get back."

As James and Wilbur headed for the livery, they heard the conductor shout, "All aboard." Amid steam blasts and whistle blowing, the train took the first lurch forward. the Super Chief rumbled past the waiting train and continued east to Laramie.

"Well, we gotta find him now," James said. Wilbur did not look optimistic.

Wilbur and James dismounted at the edge of the abandoned town and tied up the horses. The cabin sat at the far end of the desolate town. Its construction consisted of salvaged material from other buildings. Wilbur nudged James when they saw a tall man walking from the corral toward the small cabin. He stopped and looked at them and quickly stepped inside. The boys quickened their pace toward the cabin. The man stepped out with a rifle, raised it and fired twice over their heads. The astonished boys ducked and made for what was left of a small building. From the cabin came a demanding voice, "Don't come any closer or the next shot will be aimed to kill. I've got dynamite. You're not going to take me alive. Go back to Omaha and leave me the hell alone."

Responding to the sound of gunfire, six soldiers rode up to the crouching boys. "Men, he's been drinking for three days straight and he's crazy drunk. You had better leave this …." Two shots rang from the cabin, one striking a can to their left. "Prepare to return fire! Aim high so's not to hit him. Maybe it'll sober him up."

The cabin door opened and the men could see a case of dynamite sitting on the table inside. James stood up, "Don't Shoot! We're ……." His words were drowned out in the return fire from the soldiers. The door banged closed and moments later more shots came from the cabin window. The soldiers trotted a few yards forward and began firing at the cabin.

A tremendous explosion rocked the ground. The boys were stunned and dismayed as they watched the cabin disintegrate in a cloud of smoke and dust. Roof and walls blew apart and scattered over a large area. The blast left nothing in one piece and blew the fence over. The boys stood and watched in silence as pieces of the cabin continued to fall from the sky, landing all around them. It took a moment for the lieutenant to control his horse. He wheeled around and galloped to the smoldering ruins, yelling for Newt. The boys knew they were too late.

Chapter Nineteen
Shocked

James and Wilbur sat in the Cobb kitchen stunned and unbelieving. After the explosion Lieutenant West and his men escorted them back to the trading post and explained the details of Newt's death to the distraught Kyle and Carrie.

Carrie stood at the coal-burning stove stirring a large pot of soup. She kept looking at James, puzzling over the strange feelings she was having about the young man. During the meal she watched and listened as James talked, finally she could stand it no longer, "Just who are you?"

Kyle was as shocked at the tone of her voice as James was, "Carrie, we have no right in asking their business. Gentlemen, excuse my wife, but Newt's death has upset her terribly."

"Ma'am, I'm James Harvey and this is Wilbur. My mother and father adopted him. We've traveled from Omaha to Cheyenne to Helena to Rapid City looking for our father. A lawyer in Denver gave us a journal Dad wrote, and we learned about him by reading it. Every place we've been, people thought we were Pinkertons or bounty hunters and wouldn't talk. Now we're too late."

Kyle glanced at Carrie then back to James with some confusion. Then with a little shakiness in his voice he asked, "Do you have the journal?"

"Yes, I'll get it."

Kyle leafed through the pages, reading some passages with interest. James said, "There's a part in there about you and Mrs. Cobb when you were at Fort Laramie. Something about how Dad got you to ask her to go to a dance while two soldiers were fighting outside the school."

James remembered something else, "I almost forgot, I'm supposed to give you this card from the lady at the Cutler Hotel in Rawlins."

Kyle's leap from his chair sloshed soup and milk on the table and set the oil lamp rocking. "You're not Pinkertons?"

James stammered. "N-n-no."

"You're not here to take Newt back to Omaha?"

"No! We're his sons."

"Boys, I've got something to show you and supper can wait. Carrie, set another place at the table and you'd better get out an extra bottle. You two follow me." Kyle grabbed the lantern off the back porch, lit it and holding it high he stepped quickly for the barn. The small light thrown by the rapidly moving lantern made it difficult for the boys to walk without stumbling into things.

With Kyle urging them to hurry, they saddled up and followed him back to the scene of the blast. At the cabin site, Wilbur was trying to get his wind back while puzzling over the insane events. Confused and out of breath James could only say a few words at a time. "What's ...all ...about? Why ... we out here?"

Kyle too was out of breath but managed to give instructions. "Clear the area.... move that...more...lift that plank. Okay, Wilbur grab that ring and pull up the door."

The lantern cast enough light into the black hole for them to see the hat, then a face raised out of the shadows into the light. Kyle spoke, "Newt, the men you're looking at are your sons, James and Wilbur. Boys, meet your father."

Chapter Twenty
Together Again

Newt, James and Wilbur sat around the table in the Cobb kitchen and related their stories and adventures. Carrie and Kyle had retired for the night but Kyle returned from time to time to listen in. Lewis and Kramer, happy to be together, were sleeping upstairs. James told Newt of the situation in Omaha. Newt was visibly shocked and saddened when he learned of Mr. Walters' death.

"Your grandfather was a good man. I had a lot of respect for him. He was generous to everyone and helped me all he could. When he couldn't get my charges dropped, he suggested your mother should try to live in Montana or Colorado. When she visited me in Helena I thought my luck had changed and we'd be a family at last. The trip was just too much and I feel responsible for her death. When your mother died, I died a little, too. It took time for me to get over her death."

The boys realized that he still missed their mother. "Dad, we know some of why you had to stay in the territories but why so long. Didn't you know the charges had been dropped?"

"Even after the charges were cleared up, I had Bates and O'Toole after me. I couldn't be sure that Old Man Bates wouldn't send another bounty hunter after me. I worried if I returned to Omaha I would be putting you two and your grandfather in danger. In trying to get me, they might hurt you. Staying out here was safer for everyone and it was easier for me to hide out. I wrote one time about you living with me but your grandfather suggested that it was better for you to live in the only home you had ever known. He was right of course and Irene saw to it that you got an education and proper upbringing." Newt smiled at his sons with a joy he had not known for many years. "What made you decide to start looking for me?"

"Grandfather," said James.

"And Irene and Stewart Prosser," Wilbur added.

James explained the stipulations in Mr. Walter's will and related their meeting with Luis Eaton in Omaha. By sunup Newt had heard all about their trip to Cheyenne while reading his journal. James told about the chance meeting of the two pretty ladies on board. In the morning, Carrie fixed a big breakfast and the boys took turns, one eating, the other talking about their search. While Carrie was cleaning up, they went outside to have a smoke. The boys finished their tale of tracking him to Helena, Rapid City and back to Fort Steel. Newt was please to get news of his old friends.

Later, over chili and beer at the fort saloon, Newt told them of his movements for the past few years.

When the discussion got to what to do next, Newt said they needed to go to Cheyenne for a few days. Then they could return to Omaha. As they left the saloon, Newt suggested they go to the station and send telegrams to Omaha and Denver to give everyone the good news.

The boys spent several minutes writing the telegram and finally settled on:

WE FOUND HIM! WE'LL BE AT FRONTIER HOUSE CHEYENNE WYOMING – THEN IN DENVER. James & Wilbur.

Back at the kitchen table that evening they talked as a family. They made plans and argued over whether to go to Denver after a few days in Cheyenne or to go back to Omaha. James, had the strongest argument. "Dad, we're not going to live back east. We want to visit Denver and talk about living there."

"And see a certain lady too, I bet," Wilbur teased James.

"Boys you don't know how glad I am to hear that, but, what about Omaha? Your home and the business?"

Wilbur answered, "We'll have to go back to take care of business. But we're coming back here to stay."

"That's good because I sure want for us to live out here instead of back east. But I would like to see Omaha one more time."

Kyle came into the kitchen and sat at the table. "I told Lieutenant West about you wanting to get to Cheyenne. He telegraphed Rawlins and got the dispatcher to arrange for the morning train to make an unscheduled stop. By eleven o'clock tomorrow you'll be on your way to Cheyenne."

The next morning Newt took Lewis and Kramer for a walk. While Kramer sniffed around, they talked. "Lewis, you know I have to be gone for a while and I want to talk to you about Kramer."

Lewis turned to Newt, "I sure will miss Kramer"

"He would miss you more than he'd miss me so that's why I think it would be best if Kramer stayed with you. He needs an open place to run and play and someone who can run with him. I want you to have Kramer, but you have to promise to take good care of him."

"I will! I will! Yahoo, Yaaahoo! Kramer! Hear that! You're staying with me! Yahoo!"

The trip to Cheyenne allowed the boys to get better acquainted with their father. They understood more of the hurt he felt over losing Martha, Molly, and Alex. Wilbur was glad to hear about his parents and their friendship with Newt. Newt also filled in some of the stories written in his journal, especially about his dealings with the Bates family. The stories of James Knox Polk Miller, Tom Doyle and Reverend Hightower kept the boy's attention. They scarcely noticed the trip over Sherman Hill to Cheyenne. They, in turn related the information they had received from O'Toole and the men at The Sarah in Rapid City.

A telegram for James and Wilbur was waiting at the Frontier House.
TROUBLE AT HOME, IRENE SEEING GHOSTS,
GEORGE WORRIED, SERVANTS LEAVING,
COME SOON
Stewart Prosser.

James handed it to Wilbur remarking, "It must be serious, Irene's a no nonsense woman."

"Boys, if we take the train in the morning, we can be in Omaha in a day and see what the fuss is about."

After registering at the Frontier House, they headed over to the SarahLyn Saloon. Newt introduced them to the bartender, "Boys, I'd like you to met Julius Caesar Brown. We call him Caesar. Runs the cleanest bar in town." At that moment a woman walked up to Newt and gave him a big hug, "Boys, I'd like you to also meet one of the owners. James, Wilbur, this is Katie Gilbert. Katie, these two lawmen are my sons James and Wilbur."

"Nice to meet you two, especially since you turn out to be Newt's boys. Everyone here was convinced that you were Pinkertons and not to be trusted. Take a table over there and I'll get Dotty."

Dotty walked up with a big smile and gave Newt a long hug before turning to James and Wilbur. "Well, looks as if you two were telling the truth after all. I'm sorry we didn't help you. But with those two men after Uncle Newt we wouldn't talk to people we didn't know."

The evening was spent with Newt and the boys telling the two women about their adventures. The next morning they boarded the U. P. Flyer to be whisked across Nebraska, arriving in Omaha twenty-four hours later.

Chapter Twenty One
Home

When the carriage rolled up the drive to the Walters' Estate, Newt studied the large home and the ornate stone work extending around the front of the building. Not much had changed except for the heavier growth of shrubs and trees. He could see the magical touch of George's hand in the flower beds that burst with blossoms of every color and hue. No one came out to greet them and the usual workmen around the place were missing. After trying the front door and finding it locked Wilbur mused, "It's too quiet around here. Maybe there is a ghost, and everyone has been scared off."

James looked at him, "Don't be silly. They're here somewhere. Let's see if George and Irene are home." All three men walked along the west side of the house which Newt remembered had contained the library and billiard room. Wilbur tried looking in the windows but did not see anyone. A winding walkway led to the cottage hidden behind a tall hedge.

George Lansing opened the door, a smile wiping away the worried expression on his face, "James, Wilbur! 'An' God be praised, it's Newt. Come In! Come In!" George stepped back, "Irene! Irene! See who's here. We've got fresh lemonade. Settle yourselves while I get it."

The house was cool and the furniture looked comfortable, but all three men stood uncomfortably quiet. Irene walked into the room and headed straight for James and Wilbur for a big hug. Turning to Newt she beamed, "I am so happy that the three of you are together at last. I was afraid it might not happen."

Newt and the boys had been searching her face and eyes for a clue to the reason for the telegram, but they saw nothing different about her. George poured the lemonade into tall heavy glasses, the ice making music as they hit the fine glass. By the time he handed a glass to Newt it was already gathering moisture on the outside.

James took a long drink and with a satisfied look remarked, "Just like when we were kids. We would go into the kitchen and stand in the way until we got a glass of lemonade and a cookie."

George stood behind Irene as she sat in the wing-backed chair, "I have the house all ready for you. We have Olga to cook and clean for you today. We'll have more servants here tomorrow. There's two men working in the barn and they'll see to your bags. We can have a light supper tonight and if you're not too tired, we would like to hear about your trip."

James stood, "That will be fine with us. What time is supper?"

"We plan to eat at six o'clock."

"Good. That will give us time to get a nap in. Come over to the house anytime for a drink. I'm sure Dad will be into the whiskey by then."

George stiffened and his face changed, "Oh no, we'll be eating here. Irene won't go back into that house." The room was quiet, all that could be heard was the ticking of the mantel clock. The men looked first at George and then at Irene. They could see a difference in her eyes and the slight tremor of her hands.

Wilbur recovered first, "We would like to help if we can. We will go over to the house to freshen up and rest. Then you can tell us what has happened when we come for supper"

The light supper consisted of fried chicken, potatoes, cream gravy, peas and carrots. For dessert, the men dove into large slices of cherry pie. Wilbur leaned back in his chair, "It's been a long time since we had anything as good as this. I'd tell you about some of the food we were served on the trip but it would ruin this meal."

Everyone got comfortable in the living room to hear about the strange events. George began, "About three weeks ago, Irene needed to do some shopping. I took her downtown on the way to the livery to have Blackie's harness repaired. When I came back to get her, she was standing in front of the Childers School for Girls. She was just standing there staring at an upper window. I called to her but she didn't hear me. She just stood there and looked. I got down from the carriage and touched her arm. She was shaking and acting strange. I got her in the carriage and took her home. Now Irene, you tell them what you saw."

Irene stirred in her chair then spoke, "I was coming out of the dress shop across from the girls school and I thought I saw Molly going in the door of the school. I told myself I was mistaken, that it was just someone who looked like her. I crossed the street to the drug store on the corner for my pain powder. I came out and walked up the street in front of the school. I glanced up and there she was again, in the first floor window. I could see her as plan as day. It was Molly. Long black hair hanging down her back just like she wore it. She was close to the window and we looked at each other and she smiled. It was then I noticed her deep blue eyes! This lady had Molly's eyes and skin color She smiled and tilted her head just like Molly did. I have been with this family before Molly and Martha were born and I know what she looks like."

Wilbur looked at George then, Irene, "Irene, I'm sure you saw a lady that looked like Mother. It's a coincidence and you shouldn't let it bother you."

George continued, "That's not all. A few days later, we were out for an evening drive along Maple street. We were passing the house that Mr. Walters built when we first got to Omaha. Irene gasped and pointed to the window of Molly's old room. The woman standing at the window looked like Molly.

"More than a week went by without incident. We decided it was our old eyes playing tricks on us. Sunday last, after services, we went for a ride before dinner. When we came back through town, we passed the Methodist Church just as they were getting out. I stopped at the corner to let the William's family cross when I heard Irene mummer, 'Not again.'

"George, let me tell them what I saw. While we were stopped, I glanced at the church and coming down the steps was Molly. I just knew it was her. She came straight for us with that sweet smile of hers and those flashing blue eyes. What really gave me a start was the pin on her jacket. It was the cameo pin that was made for Molly when she was ten. Hers was the one with the blue stone to match her eyes. She walked by and when I looked back she was gone."

"Irene, are you sure it was Mother and that she was wearing her cameo?" Wilbur asked.

"You boys know I won't stand for nonsense. Lord knows you two tried everything you could think of to vex me. But I saw what I saw. That woman was Molly and it was her cameo she was wearing. Newt, you said that Molly and Alex were killed by Indians and I believed you up to now. But I'm not so sure any more. I need to know who that person is or if it's a ghost."

"Irene, I saw the graves and heard the story of their death. I don't believe in ghosts so there must be some other explanation about this woman and the cameo pin. Why did you not want to eat at the house?"

"George, you tell them."

"Yes, dear. Late the very next afternoon I was trimming the hedge with Irene sitting close by. She started to say something but instead she made a strange noise. I turned around to see what was wrong. She was pointing to the main house and babbling. I helped her in here and got her quieted down. She said she had seen Molly at the window of her old room. I went over to the main house and talked to the maid, Olga. She doesn't speak English too good yet, but she said no one else was in the house. I made the mistake of telling her what Irene had seen and it seemed to spook her, too. So now Irene is afraid to leave the yard and refuses to go to the main house until all of this is explained. It has us both jumpy and looking over our shoulders, but I don't know what to make of it. We hope you can find out who this person is."

Newt leaned forward, "Tomorrow while the boys are checking on their business, I'll ask around. I suspect there is a young lady here in town who happens to look like Molly. I'll find out who it is and get an explanation."

The next afternoon Newt returned to the Lansing's cottage and knocked. A voice came from the side of the house, "We're over here." Newt turned and walked around the corner and followed a path to a clearing where George and Irene were having tea.

"Join us. The water is still hot for a cup of tea." Irene seemed a little apprehensive at Newt's visit

"Thanks, I'd like that," All the while wishing he had something else to drink.

Irene poured and George spoke, "Did you learn anything today?"

"Yes, that's why I'm here. Irene, you can put your mind at ease. You are not seeing ghosts. The lady you saw is not Molly. Your mysterious lady is eighteen years old and just finished at a teacher's college back east. A teacher here at the school became ill and she was asked to fill in. I talked with her and know all about her. She and I have an interesting story to tell you and the boys. You can have supper with us tonight at the main house with no worries. In fact it will be a most pleasant evening."

Later the group was settled in the central section of the library for a glass of sherry while waiting for the supper to be announced. Stewart had also been invited for the evening to allow the boys to catch up on business. Newt dispensed the wine and cocktails while the conversation picked up on the exploits of James and Wilbur in Wyoming and Montana. Newt was having his usual whiskey. At a break in the conversation, Irene spoke to Newt. "Newt, I have waited long enough. I want to hear about this lady that looks like Molly."

"That's right. It's time to fill you in on what I learned today. I invited the lady to be with us tonight. At this moment she is in the guestroom upstairs."

"Here?" Everyone looked at Newt.

"Yes, I want you to meet and talk with her before we go in for supper. You'll want to know her as I do. She has had an extraordinary life. James would you pour another round while I get her?"

In a moment Newt was back, standing in the open door, "May I have everyone's attention? You have no way of knowing how much joy and pleasure it gives me to present

Rebecca Ann McCall. She's known also by her Indian name of Sky."

All eyes were on the beautiful young woman as she entered the room, "Good evening, it's wonderful to finally meet my family."

Chapter Twenty Two
A Heart of Stone

With only one cook and one server, the meal was not like it would be under George's supervision but no one noticed the problems. They were too busy talking and listening.

Conversation at the dining table centered on the beautiful young lady seated next to Newt. "In my journal I wrote of the seven or eight year-old white girl I got from the Nez Perce." Newt poured a new drink and continued. "When the Sioux attacked the wagon train at Devil's Gate they set three wagons on fire, trapping Molly in the wagon. I don't know why Molly couldn't get out but she must have managed to pick up Rebecca and drop her outside to save her. As the Indians were retreating, one must have seen the bundle and took it. Of course, Mr. Anderson thought the baby had died with Molly. The Sioux traded her to the Nez Perce when she was about four. She was with them for three years until I came along. The last time I saw Sky was in the summer of '73. I grubstaked her guardian, Belle, to a restaurant in San Francisco and helped them move out there. I did not see Sky again until today. Over the years I have received letters from Belle and Sky, keeping me posted on their welfare but I never saw a picture as she grew up. When we met today at the girl's school, I didn't know who she was until she told me her name and that she was from San Francisco. She remembered me as the man with the spirit bag on his hat who took her to Belle and later helped them move to San Francisco.

"I was still trying to put the puzzle together when I remembered the cameo. I asked about it and that is when another piece fell into place. From her purse she took out a small beaded bag like mine. She opened it and pulled out the pin and handed it to me. I turned it over and there was *terre* inscribed on the back It was the same pin that Molly had shown to me in Denver, in '63. That's how I came to realize what must have happened during the Indian attack."

Rebecca spoke, "I am not sure how I happened to have the pin. Uncle Newt thinks it must have been pinned on the blanket I was wrapped in. The Sioux kept it and let me have it when I was older. When they traded me to the Nez Perce I had the pin in this bag hanging on my neck. One of the women took the bag from me. I tried to get it back but I was too small. She stole the only item that was truly mine. I tried several times to get my pin back. When I didn't get it, I rebelled by acting like a wild cat."

Newt continued, "That explains Sky's actions when she was about to leave with me. That pin was her only true possession and link to the past and she would not leave without it."

James said, "I have my mother's cameo that matches that one except it has a black stone and the word *lune* on the back."

Wilbur asked, "Where is Grandmother Walters' pin?"

Irene answered, "It's buried with Mrs. Walters."

James turned to Irene. "The artist put the word for gem on the back of Mother's pin didn't he?"

"Yes, that's what ... Now George, don't say what you were about to say."

All eyes turned to George, "Well, it won't do any harm now. As you remember, the artist lived here for several months and got to know us all pretty well. He had many arguments with Mrs. Walters over the price and the way the pins were done. It wasn't until years later when we were putting the pin on her for burial that I noticed the inscription on the cameo was the French word for stone, not gem. I remembered several times the Frenchman would say something under his breath when Mrs. Walters was around. I didn't understand what he was saying then but when I saw the inscription I knew he was saying *'coeur de pierre'* or heart of stone."

Irene had been quietly listening and looking at Rebecca Ann. Now she spoke, "What about the other places I saw you?

"I'm boarding at the home where you saw me and I happened to be staying in the very room that was my mother's. When I learned that today, I went back and sat for a long time trying to imagine something of her. You saw me at the Methodist Church wearing the cameo. And yes, I was in this house standing in the upstairs window. I was here to help Olga learn English. She was showing me around the house. I'm sorry if I scared you, I didn't know I was upsetting so many people."

Newt added, "It took a bit of pushing this afternoon, but I finally got Olga to admit that Sky had been here. George's questions about the stranger at the window made her afraid that she might get fired, so she said there had been no one else in the house."

Wilbur had been studying his new sister with much interest. "James, we have a sister."

In a quiet voice, Rebecca spoke, "And I have two brothers."

Newt stood, "George, help me pour a round and we'll have a toast."

When everyone had a glass he raised his hand, "Martha, Molly, and Alex I hope you can hear me. Here's a toast to you three and a toast to James, Wilbur, and Rebecca Ann. Now a toast to Mr. Walters. You made this all happen and we thank you for kicking these two out of Omaha and making them come to find me."

George stood and turned to Newt, "From what I hear, these three fine young people would not be here if it weren't for you and your affliction of looking for gold."

Chapter Twenty Three
Old Friends

A fancy carriage rolled down Seventeenth Avenue toward Lincoln Street. The homes in the fashionable neighborhood reflected the growth and splendor of Denver in 1884. The driver turned into the private entrance and followed the driveway around to the front of the large estate. The home faced Broadway, looking over Denver toward the majestic mountains. Newt got out, telling the driver to wait. Before going up the steps, he paused for a moment, looking west at the mountains he loved. Knocking, he stood and fidgeted with his unaccustomed new clothing.

Augusta Tabor opened the door a few inches and looked at the face for a time, recognizing her caller only after he spoke. "Hello Augusta. I stopped to see if there was any dried apple pie left."

"Newt! How good to see you, I didn't recognize you in those fine clothes and without your hat. I'm sure we can find some pie for you. I don't get many visitors these days. It's nice that you came to see me."

Over pie and coffee the two old friends talked of past adventures and the hard work and fun they had shared. Both remembered the lonely times spent in the mountains looking for gold in the summer and the long boring winters. Augusta said, "Newt, I heard from Luis about James and Wilbur looking for you and I'm happy you are all together now."

"Finding me has turned out to be only the beginning. With the boys and their sister Rebecca Ann, my life has been busy. The boys sold the family business in Omaha and divided the entire estate three ways. James and Wilbur recently moved here to Denver and are investing their money in business and real estate. Rebecca has gone back to San Francisco. From what I hear she is doing well. She must have inherited her grandfather's ability to run a business. I suppose I'll divide my time between here and San Francisco."

The conversation turned to the unhappy conditions that currently faced Augusta. "Augusta, Horace and I have been friends and partners for all these years but I don't understand his recent actions. The stories about him and his antics with that woman must be hurtful to you. It certainly is a puzzle to his friends. I've seen men change when sudden riches are heaped on them. Sad to say, most die broke or insane. I hope it doesn't happen to Horace. The money is coming in so fast he has to hire people to keep track of it and there are lots of people hanging around to help him spend it. He'll come to his senses no matter how crazy he's acting now. I was sorry to hear that he married that woman as soon as you granted him the divorce."

"Newt, I would not help him waste what we both worked so hard to get. I refused to have any part of his political schemes and I wouldn't attend his fancy parties. And most of all I deplored the fancy company he was keeping. It was my hard labor and sacrifice that kept us going when his claims played out year after year. I stayed with him and followed him from camp to camp to build a good life for us and Maxey. When all this began to happen I was sure he would soon tire of it. I decided to stay here and wait. I see Maxey most every day and I have a few close friends."

"Your are fortunate to have Maxey here. I was very lonely with Martha and the boys living in Omaha and after Martha died I did not care much whether I lived or died. Sometimes I even wished Bates would get me. Now, things are different. I have two fine sons and a beautiful lady who is like a daughter to me. They are filling my life but there is room for someone else. I worry about you when I hear a new outlandish story about Horace. What I'm leading up to is I would like you to know that I'm still your friend and ....."

"Newt, you have been a good and loyal friend and I appreciate your concern. I gave him his divorce but I intend to stay here alone waiting for him to come to his senses."

Reading the expression on her face he interrupted, "I have said too much. Thank you for the pie. It might taste better with fresh apples, but the dried apple kind will always bring back good memories to me."

A short time later, Newt stepped from the house as the door closed quietly behind him. He drew in the sweet mountain air of Denver, exhaled, and stepped into the carriage. "Jake, I'm feeling a little down right now. Take me to the Windsor, so's I can pick up my spirits."

Chapter Twenty Four
Time Changes Everything

As James and Wilbur approached the corner of eighteenth and Larimer they saw a small group of men gathered around two men standing on the steps of the Windsor hotel. Wilbur recognized them as Billie Bush and Maxey Tabor, operators of the hotel. The boys stood nearby and listened while Billie quieted the crowd down.

"Now men, we appreciate the years that you have been staying and eating at the Windsor."

"And all that liquor we drank too, I'll bet."

"Yes, Newt, that too. But things are changing. We have more visitors from the east now and we have more women staying and eating here. They are complaining about men smoking and spitting in the dining room while they are eating"

A man in front of James yelled, "That's the trouble. A lot of those women are coming out here making speeches about giving women the vote and they want us to quit smoking 'cept in one stuffy room?"

"When Horace built this hotel, a smoking room was established, the first in America I might add, and it has not been used except for private meetings. All we're asking is that you do your smoking in there or in the bar, instead of in the dining room."

The rumblings continued, as Newt spoke, "Billie, some of us have a small share in this hotel and you'll want us to invest in the new hotel you're planning to build. Be hanged if I'll put my money in your Brown Palace Hotel if you intend to ban smoking in the dining room."

From the back one man shouted, "Hey, Newt, I hear Navarre's looking for investors." I'll bet he and his ladies will let you smoke in their rooms." This brought general laughter from the men.

Billie responded, "Gentlemen, please hear us out. Every week we have people by the hundreds coming to Colorado to live. They'll work hard and invest in our future. Look around and you'll see the influence that this is having. I remember a time when you came in covered with mud and we would clean you up, feed you and have a place for you to sleep. Our bar poured drinks all night if that's what you wanted. We even let Newt in when he's wearing that God-awful hat of his. Times have changed. You have changed. None of you are sleeping on the floor. You sit on nice furniture. Look at the fancy clothing you are all wearing now. You've got fine horses to ride or pull a carriage. Some of you even got married. You worked hard for your money so that you could enjoy what it will bring. You have changed and will continue to change with the times."

"Billie, we know you're right, but it ain't easy to give up a satisfying cigar after eating."

"I know, but give it a try. Come on in and I'll buy a round."

Newt, troubled and lost in thought, followed the men into the famous establishment with its eighteen foot mahogany bar. Several rounds were consumed before James and Wilbur could get him to leave the bar and move to the dining room. While Wilbur got more drinks, James tackled his father about their business plans. "Dad, we'd like to make some changes in our business partnership. Wilbur and I see a good future in owning property here in Denver. Ever since we sold the Walters' Wholesale to Stewart and invested that money out here, we have done very well. We don't want to hurt your feelings but it looks like our income from Leadville will continue to drop and we feel it is time to sell out."

"You're right, it hurts. Not because you want to get out of Leadville, but because I realize things are changing and the old times have passed. The excitement is gone and it makes me sorry knowing it's come to an end. Today I went to see Augusta and I guess that made me a little sadder." Newt's voice trailed off. He sat quietly in thought for a moment as Wilbur returned with the drinks. "And I miss your mother very much."

The boys sat silent until he spoke again, "Yes. We should sell our holdings in Leadville and concentrate our investments here. I'll probably use my share for a new investment I have been thinking about. Splitting your grandfather's estate with Rebecca hasn't hurt you at all. You'll do very well in this town. And she is doing well in San Francisco."

James leaned back, "Rebecca has a natural talent for business. We got a letter inviting us to come to San Francisco and invest with her out there. She mentioned a few things she is doing and we think she is better than grandfather Walters at making good investments."

Wilbur raised his glass, "We just hope to do as well here as grandfather did when he came to Davenport with only the clothing on his back and all his possessions in a bag."

Newt began to chuckle at that remark, "Did either of you two ever ask him what was in that bag?'

"No. We didn't. Do YOU know what was in it?" James asked.

"Yes I do. When I was there in '66, he told me that story about arriving in Davenport with all his possessions in a bag. So I asked what was in the bag. He got the strangest look on his face and then busted out laughing. He said I was the first to ask. Boys, what he had in that bag was one hundred and fifty thousand dollars in securities."

The look on the boys' faces went from surprise to a little anger to laughter at their grandfather's prank. Wilbur expressed annoyance, "All those years of believing he started with nothing. He was fooling us the whole time."

After dinner the three men headed to the bar and had a few drinks. Newt stayed long after the boys were gone, working on a bottle, while working on his thoughts.

Chapter Twenty Five
Down Under

Luis heard a commotion in the outer room that he had heard before. Amidst giggling and laughter, his secretary, Elizabeth, opened the door. A voice boomed. "I want to see the best lawyer in Colorado and if he ain't in I'll see Mr. Eaton."

"Newt, come on in and sit, I got the papers..." Luis looked at Newt for a full minute before he could continue. "...papers you need to sign. What the hell are you doing in that outfit?"

Newt stood before him in prospector's clothing. He was wearing his gold fever hat. "I stopped by to sign those papers and when we get done with that I want you to join me and the boys for a send off. I am going to Helena to get Tom. Then we're going to a strike on the Skagit River in Washington territory. I heard that they were getting gold out of the streams with their bare hands. Then I'm coming back here and ask'n Elizabeth to marry me. You've mistreated her all these years and it's time I rescued her."

From the front office came Elizabeth's voice, "Newt, you'd just better be careful what you say. I might say yes."

In a short time Newt and Luis left the office and walked up the street. "We're to meet the boys at the Windsor but first I want to buy a drink just for the two of us." Newt and Luis stopped at their favorite bar. O'Riley's Pub attracted all levels of Denver society to its dark interior. All men were equal in this establishment, one of the few to cater to the drinking habits of its clientele and nothing else. The only requirements were that the men behave themselves and have the price of a drink. No gambling or food was offered and no ladies were allowed to disrupt the masculine atmosphere.

After one round and the second poured, Newt continued, "Luis, this past year, since the boys found me, has been the best time of my life. And Rebecca is the nugget in our lives. It's been fun just to watch those three operate. They're gonna take grandpa Walters' money and turn it into a mountain before they're done.

"So, what's bothering you? It must be big from the way you have been acting lately." Luis threw his shot down and wiped his mouth.

Newt finished his drink and signaled the bartender, "Look at me, I've got more money than I'll ever spend and just when I could start taking it easy, I catch the fever again. You'd think that at my age it would be dead cold, but it's hotter than ever. I don't want to leave them but I hear the gold fields calling again. James and Sarah May will be getting married soon and I'm happy about that. Wilbur is mum about his personal life but he has made several trips to Cheyenne to see Dotty. Things are under control with Rebecca in San Francisco. So I guess I want to make one last strike before I get planted. The problem is, what I have in mind will take a few summers to prove out. Let's have one or two more and then go meet the boys."

Luis leaned over to Newt, "I've been watching you and I know when you're plotting something big and it's not that malarkey about gold along the Skagit River. I've made considerable money going along with your wild schemes in the past. I'll throw in with you again if you need a partner."

James and Wilbur were seated at their favorite table in the Windsor Hotel restaurant. James looked out the window and spotted Luis and his father walking toward the hotel. He could tell from Newt's gesturing and yelling he was agitated about something. "Wilbur look! Dad's going on about something and he's really got a thorn in his paw this time." The boys could hear Newt from the lobby as he complained to everyone they passed. As he and Luis crossed to the dining room he quieted down.

"Luis, what's got him so riled this time?" James asked, winking at Wilbur.

"Wouldn't ask if I were you. It'll just get him started again. Here's the papers all signed and filed at the courthouse. Horace bought everything you had up there. The bank will make the necessary transfers in the morning."

Luis and the brothers had cocktails while Newt ordered his usual straight whiskey. Newt sat with drink in hand and a cold cigar in the corner of his mouth. He was still nursing that small spark of an idea he had been fanning for a month. It was bothering him that he was hesitating to act on the idea. Deep in thought and unaware of his surroundings he lit the cigar as he worked on his latest scheme. His thoughts were interrupted when he realized several people were talking to him and getting louder too.

"No smoking? What do you mean, no smoking? There's no one eating near us. You mean to tell me that Billie Bush says that there's no smoking in here AT ALL?" At that moment the little spark of an idea he had been working on burst into flames. Standing, his gold hunting hat pushed back, he growled, "That's it! They've pushed too far this time. A man can take only so much. First I can't smoke in here when eating. Now I can't smoke when I'm drinking. Boys, you know what made me so mad before we came in here? Well, I'll tell you. Luis and I were having a quiet drink at O'Riley's. In comes a gaggle of those temperance ladies banging on tambourines and drums. They were singing some song and disrupting the men. All we wanted was a little peace and quiet. Then a big 'Ol gal started swinging an ax. She cleared a path straight for the bar and the mirrors. You should have seen what she did to that beautiful cherry wood bar. She put big ugly gashes in the top and the leaner and then attacked the mirror and glassware. It was awful! Why'd she do that? No one in there was bothering her." The dining room had gone quiet at Newt's outburst. "Just yesterday we had some of our local women walking around carrying signs and chanting about women's rights. They were even saying they had a right to vote. They'd been up to Leadville making speeches and getting Tabor to kick in some money. I hear they think allowing bars to be open on Sunday is uncivilized behavior. Man can't walk down the street without he doesn't get yelled at! He can't even drink in peace! Now, if he wants to smoke after he eats, he has to go to a special little room and sit in there like some dummy in a store window.

"I know what started all this! We voted to become a state and now we're losing our freedoms for it. When this great land of ours became a state the politicians got hold of it and things have been going straight to Hell ever since. Well, I know what I am gonna do. I'm packing up, taking my money and pulling out of this country. I'm going to Australia!"

Chapter Twenty Six
The Newport

Rebecca, Belle, and Charlene stood at the pier. Seamen from the clipper ship *Newport* were loading bags and boxes from the carriage under the watchful eye of Newt. The *Newport* was designed for hauling freight with only a few cabins for passengers. It would be a long journey to Australia. Satisfied the men knew which bags went to the cabin and which went into the hold, Newt joined the ladies, "I hope everything is okay. I'd sure hate to lose my stuff."

Two men attempted to lift the largest box off the carriage and wisely decided to wait for more help. Rebecca asked, "Uncle Newt, what's in that wooden box?"

"Delicate supplies that need to be protected."

Belle had been watching with a knowing eye. "Newt Harvey, I know what you got in that box." Turning to the others she said, "He's got the stuff for making Tangle Leg in there."

"Weeell, Australia is a long ways off and I'm taking enough to get me there."

"Uncle Newt, that still seems to be a lot to be taking with you. This ship has been getting there in less than sixty days." Rebecca pointed at the other crates, "What's in the other boxes?"

"I got another box packed with whiskey and the small box has cigars and tobacco. I figure they'll fetch a good price once the ship has run low and there's no land in sight. I'm gonna get back some of the money it's costing for this trip. Which reminds me, the captain hasn't come to collect yet."

"We hope you make it there safe and without running into bad weather." Charlene said, "We hear all sorts of stories and it makes me nervous knowing you're going to be out there."

Belle gave Newt a big hug, "We're all nervous about this trip. You're going to be gone for a long time. Come spring I could use your help when we build our new restaurant. I'll sure miss you. Take care of yourself."

Activity on the dock increased as the men began the final stages before departure. Next, Newt got a hug from Charlene and then it was Rebecca's turn. She started to give him a hug, then stopped, and took his hands in hers, "Uncle Newt, there is something I have been meaning to ask you and now's the time. Thank you again for taking me away from the Indians and for bringing Belle into my life. Most of all thank you for supporting me and for treating me like a daughter. Would it be okay if I called you Dad like James and Wilbur do?"

"I would be proud to have you call me Dad. There goes the horn. They want me to get on board. Where's the man I'm supposed to pay?"

"That's okay, Newt, go ahead and got on before they raise the plank. You can't let the whiskey and cigars go without you." Belle shoved him to the gangway. Newt kept going, mumbling under his breath. He stopped halfway, turned and ran down to give Rebecca a big hug. He ran back up the gangway to the deck and leaned over the railing.

"Dad?"

"Yes?"

"Dad, don't worry about paying your fare. We paid it!"

"You paid for my passage? That's too much! You might need the money!"

"Newt, listen to me." Charlene put her arms around Belle and Rebecca. "The three of us are partners in a new investment to broaden our freighting business."

Rebecca shouted, "Dad, WE own the *Newport*!"